FRAI

Franklin Horton

License Notes

Grace Under Fire

Table of Contents

Chapter One

Damascus, VA

Leslie Brown, a widow, lived off a meager disability check she received each month after the death of her husband. The terror attack that brought the United States to its knees occurred several days before her latest check was due to arrive. This was the time of month when things always got lean around her house and they started to run out of the basics. The timing of the terror attacks couldn't have been any worse for her on a personal level. Her pantry was already empty.

The check that she received was barely enough for one person, but she stretched it for two. She had taken in her grandson to raise. Her daughter Debbie wasn't anything to brag about. She hadn't finished high school, had never held a job for very long, and found herself with a successive string of useless boyfriends. When Debbie and her current boyfriend were between places to stay it had torn at Leslie's heart to see her grandson Dylan dragged from place to place. She asked Debbie if she would let him stay with her until they got settled.

The invitation was meant for a couple of days, a couple of weeks at the most, but it had been over year and Dylan was still with her. Her daughter made no mention of taking him back to live with her. Leslie loved Dylan. In some ways perhaps, she loved him more than she'd ever loved her daughter. She was glad to have him, glad to be able to provide a stable home for him, but she did wish that the money would go a little further each month. While Leslie knew her daughter received food stamps and assistance for Dylan, she had no idea where it went because she never saw any of it.

Leslie lived inside the town limits of Damascus, which rarely experienced power outages in her neighborhood. She didn't keep much in the way of emergency supplies. The day before, the water had quit running. Leslie and her grandson went to the creek that passed through town and filled buckets, bringing them to the house for flushing toilets.

A neighbor told her that she could put eight drops of household bleach in a gallon of the water and make it drinkable. Leslie didn't know if that was dependable information or not, but it was from one of those outdoorsy kind of people. The neighbor looked like the kind of person who would know how much bleach to add to a gallon of water so she believed the advice. She hadn't tried it yet though. She and Dylan spent the last day drinking all the oddball drinks that were still in the pantry, like juice boxes that had fallen behind other things, expired cans of orange juice, and stray bottles of Kool-Aid. The odd assortment of food and drink was like a game to Dylan and he didn't complain.

When Robert Hardwick knocked at the door, Leslie took it as a positive sign. The man had to have better resources than she had and hopefully whatever he wanted would benefit her and her grandson in some way.

She pushed open the screen door and smiled. "Hello, Robert. I'm surprised to see people out visiting."

"I'm sorry, Mrs. Brown, but this isn't a social call," Robert said, a grim smile on his face. "I need something and I'm hoping you can help me out."

"I don't have much but I'll help if I can."

"You know my wife had surgery..."

"How's she getting along with that? Is she okay?"

Robert nodded distractedly. "Oh yeah, she's okay. The problem is Grace."

"Grace? Is *she* okay?"

Robert sighed. "I have no idea. I *think* she is. She's on the road coming back from Oxford in all this mess. I have her going to a friend's house along the way for safety but she's not there yet. I need to go meet her at the friend's house and help her get home."

Leslie considered this, her brow furrowing. "Is your wife able to care for herself and Blake?"

Robert shook his head. "She's not fully back on her feet yet. She'd probably be okay, but I'd feel much better if I had somebody there to help her out around the house."

"So you'd like me to come stay and keep an eye on her?"

"If it's no trouble," Robert said. "I hate to ask in all this...mess. I hate to ask you to leave your home in the middle of

6

this disaster, but it's an emergency. You could bring your grandson, of course. Do you think you can do it?"

Leslie's heart raced. It was the best news she'd heard in days. She had seen the inside of the Hardwicks' pantry. They had a lot more food than she did. She and Dylan were a few canned meals away from eating nine-year-old cans of sauerkraut.

"Of course I'll do it," Leslie said. "I'd be glad to."

"When can you come?"

"I'd probably have to go back with you right now. My car is out of gas and people say you can't get any more."

"You can't," Robert confirmed. "I happened to have a little in this vehicle here and drove it down. I was even a little nervous about doing that, with people starting to act a little crazy out there."

"Could you give me a few minutes then to get some stuff together for me and my grandson?"

Robert nodded. "Take your time. I'll be waiting in the car."

The screen door shut and Leslie backed into the dark house. She turned to Dylan, who had been listening from the couch, driving a toy car over the uneven terrain of the cushions.

"Dylan, we're going to go stay at the Hardwicks' house. It'll be fun. You can play with Blake all day long. Let's pack a couple of bags. Get any toys you need to take and set them by the door. Don't forget to get your blanket and your pillow."

Blake ran off and did as he was told. Leslie went to the spare bedroom, her daughter's old bedroom, and retrieved her two battered suitcases from the closet. She went to her room and tossed in what clean clothes she could find. She did the same in Dylan's room while he gathered toys, aware that he didn't have many clean clothes either.

When she received her check they were going to go to the laundromat in town and wash all of their clothes. If things didn't get better, she'd soon be down at the river beating them between rocks. As much as she hated to, she was forced to throw a few of his dirty shirts and shorts in the suitcase because she didn't have enough clean clothes for him.

She picked up her purse and made another quick pass through the house, wanting to take a few things with her just in case. She went to her closet and retrieved the black metal lockbox with her husband's .38 caliber pistol and box of shells. She took it, lockbox and all. There wasn't much else in the house worth taking.

Leslie helped her grandson gather his toys, blanket, and his pillow, cramming them into thin plastic shopping bags from the local grocery store. They carried everything out onto the porch and she locked the door behind them. Robert came to the porch to help them carry their load to the vehicle.

As they drove out of the neighborhood she noticed that the town was overrun with hikers who'd come into town for the annual Hiker Days Festival. It was a big thing in the town and there was usually a parade that culminated in a town-wide water fight. That was her grandson's favorite part and her least.

It took them thirty minutes on winding roads to reach Robert's mountaintop home in Whitetop, Virginia. The home was accessible only by a steep gravel road that was often impassable in bad weather. Robert and his family didn't care. They preferred the rugged terrain and difficult to reach property.

When he parked the vehicle by the back door, the first thing that Leslie noticed was the muffled hum of an engine. She looked at Robert. "Is that a generator?"

Robert nodded. "The home has multiple sources for power. Part of it is solar, but my solar won't run the heat pump, and since her surgery, sweating makes Mrs. Hardwick's incision itch. She's more comfortable when the house is cooler so I have the propane generator running."

"Is that something I have to take care of while you're gone? Changing the propane tanks?"

"No. The propane is connected to a one-thousand-gallon tank. It could run for weeks if we needed it to."

Leslie wasn't used to this level of preparation. It required more money than she and most of the people she knew had at their disposal. "Certainly it won't be *weeks* before things are back to normal, will it?"

Robert didn't want to get into his theories about *collapsing systems failure* and how long the grid could potentially be down. "Let's hope not," he said vaguely.

Blake came out the front door. "Dylan! Come play video games with me!"

Dylan looked at his grandmother for approval and Leslie nodded with a smile. When he ran off to join Blake on the porch she said, "Robert, if you have video games, I'll never get him to go back home."

"Video games and electronics don't draw much power. They run off the solar."

Leslie looked at the rustic cabin-style home with a new appreciation. "It's a lot better than we had at our house."

Robert cleared his throat. "Look, I appreciate what you're doing for me, Mrs. Brown," he said. "But please realize this is only a temporary arrangement. Neither you nor your grandson should get too comfortable with it. There will be a point when I have to take you back home. I'm sorry, but that's how it will have to be."

Leslie was a little taken aback by Robert's bluntness. She had known the man for years and had helped their family on numerous occasions with shopping, canning, spring cleaning, housesitting, and various other tasks. While she sometimes suspected that Robert did it more out of charity than need, she wasn't in any position to object. Often the money he gave her for whatever task she performed made the difference between her family *having* or *not having*.

Perhaps sensing that he may have offended her, Robert clarified, "Of course, I'll pay you for staying here with Teresa and Blake."

"I do appreciate that," she replied. "The food was starting to run out. I'm hoping I can use whatever money you give me to buy some food. I hear it's mostly gone though. They say those hikers have about cleaned out the grocery stores."

"I can pay you in food, Mrs. Brown. Understand, though, you can't tell anyone where you got it. People are acting all crazy. If they think you have food they may hurt you or your grandson to get it. If I give you food, I need your word that you won't tell anyone where it came from."

"You have my word," she said.

"And of course you can eat well while you're here too." It seemed an awkward thing to say but Robert wanted her to be clear about it.

"The food we eat while I'm here doesn't count against what you're giving me, does it?" she asked.

"No, Mrs. Brown. You help yourself to what you can eat while you're here. When I pick you up and take you home, I'll pay you with a month's worth of food."

"A *month's* worth?" she said in shock. "Really? You can do that?"

He nodded. "A month's worth for two people. I promise."

"Then we have a deal," she said. "And you have my word that I will not tell a soul where it came from."

Chapter Two

The Hardwick Farm

Leslie was sitting on the back porch enjoying the morning view and drinking a cup of coffee. It was her second morning waking up at the Hardwicks' house. The door opened behind her and Teresa Hardwick stepped out, a mug in her own hand.

Leslie smiled. "How are you feeling this morning?"

Teresa set her mug on a steel mesh end table and eased herself down into the padded outdoor chair. She smiled tiredly at Leslie. "Better now that I'm sitting. I'm pretty sore."

Leslie nodded in understanding. "I had that done about twenty years ago. Awful surgery."

"Yes, it completely sucks. I have no doubt that if men had to have this surgery they would have already developed an easier way to do it."

Leslie laughed. "No doubt."

Robert's wife, Teresa, had always been a relatively healthy woman, but one day before the terror attacks rocked the country, she had a hysterectomy. While it was a common enough procedure and not particularly dangerous, there was a recovery period required. The procedure was invasive and the incision large enough that the recovery could be painful. It also limited one's mobility. Teresa could shuffle around between the bedroom, kitchen, and bathroom, but that was the extent of her travels.

The women sipped their coffee. Inside, they could hear the two boys laughing. They were watching a show on DVD.

"I'm going to have a hard time prying him out of here when it's time to go home," Leslie said with a sigh.

Although it wasn't intended as an appeal for sympathy, Leslie was aware that it may sound that way. She simply saw it as the truth. After living with modern conveniences again— entertainment, running water—it was going to be hard to go back to her powerless house.

Teresa took a sip of her coffee and did not respond. She was fully aware of her husband's attitude about these matters. You could help people but you couldn't take everyone in. Additional mouths eventually brought additional mouths with them, then the supplies ran out twice as fast. It had been hard for Teresa to grasp at first, but she fully understood the truth of what Robert said now. His primary obligation, and hers too, was to their family. She could not take food from their mouths to feed others. At least not for an indefinite period.

"Have you heard from Robert?" Leslie asked, breaking the awkward silence.

Teresa set her mug down on the end table. "No, I haven't. He said he might try to radio in but none of that amateur radio stuff makes any sense to me."

"Yeah," Leslie chuckled. "I'm still figuring out cell phones."

Leslie could see that the introduction of Robert into the conversation had reminded Teresa that her husband was gone. Worry spread over her face.

"I'm sure he'll be okay," Leslie said. "He seems to be all prepared for anything that might happen. Was he a Boy Scout?"

"He's something like that."

Leslie looked confused. "Something like what? What do you mean?"

"Nothing really," Teresa said. "He's just, you know, always been interested in survival."

"That why he has all this? The solar and stuff?"

"Have you ever read any of his books or know what they're about?"

Leslie shook her head. "No. I know they're about survival and fighting. He said there were lots of guns in them."

"He's really interested in that kind of thing. Plus the weather gets bad up here. Our attitude is if the weather's too bad we'll stay home, so we like to have the supplies to do that. We don't want to be stuck up here with nothing."

"I do like to read," Leslie said. "Just not that kind of thing. I'm more of a Harlequin type. I like the spicy stuff. You know what I mean?" She gave Teresa a sly wink that made it clear what she meant.

Teresa burst out laughing.

Leslie laughed too, but she had the feeling that the Hardwicks weren't giving her the full story. There had been that show on TV about people that they called *preppers,* people who were getting ready for the end of the world. Leslie suspected that the Hardwicks might be people like that but she was afraid to ask. What if she said something and they had to kill her to keep her quiet? The show made some of the people seem kind of scary.

"Do you mind if I do some laundry?" Leslie asked, trying to change the subject.

"Not at all."

"My grandson and I were planning to go to the laundromat, then all this mess happened before we got to go. I'm not sure either of us brought enough clean clothes with us, and you know how kids go through them. Most of my clothes are still at the house."

"If you need more clothes you're welcome to borrow my car and go get them. It doesn't have a lot of gas but it probably has enough to get you to town and back. You can bring your clothes back here and wash them. At least you'll go back home with a basket of clean clothes when Robert comes back."

"I might do that. I appreciate the offer."

Their conversation was interrupted by the two boys crashing through the door and onto the porch.

"We're starving!" Dylan squealed, rubbing his belly.

Blake was nodding along. "Yeah. I'm hungry too."

Leslie loved feeding children and she appreciated being in a home where there was enough food to feed them. That brought her back around to the thought of returning to her house. The idea of returning home, even with a month's worth of food for the two of them, worried her. Would a month be enough? What would happen when the month ran out? Would the world be back to normal by then or could this go on longer?

Leslie rose from her seat, trying to break the negative spiral her thoughts were locked into. "I'll fix you something."

"Yeaaahhh!" the kids chorused.

"Thank you," Teresa said. "I want to finish my coffee and then I'm going to lay back down. I can't believe I still feel so weak."

"Don't worry about it, honey. It takes a while for that feeling to go away. All of your energy is going toward healing your body right now."

Leslie left Teresa on the porch and went into the kitchen. She opened the refrigerator, enjoying the small miracle of the light actually coming on when the door opened. Then there was the additional miracle of the cool, edible food inside. It was amazing how a few days without modern conveniences made her appreciate this convenience again.

"What do you boys want?" Leslie called from the fridge.

"Eggs," Blake said.

"Yeah, eggs," Dylan piped in.

Leslie shut the door and looked to the wire basket of eggs on the countertop. It was brimming, and she had not even checked the henhouse today. They had an overabundance of eggs. It made her wonder about her daughter. Was she getting enough to eat?

Leslie doubted it. Paul, the scumbag she lived with, would not have any provisions for feeding the two of them. It was likely they were more concerned with getting high than getting fed. Food had always been second to drugs with them, clearly demonstrated by their pallor and sallow cheeks.

Still, all of these eggs were surely going to go bad. No one would miss a dozen, would they?

She could check the chickens when she left to go pick up her laundry. Whatever she found in the henhouse, she could take with her and give to her daughter. She could also check the refrigerator and see if there were any other leftovers that were about to go bad. She could clean the refrigerator out and take the old food. Then at least they'd have something.

Leslie wasn't able to get away from the Hardwicks' house without Dylan wanting to go with her. She had expected that. He didn't like to leave her side anymore. In providing the comfort and sense of security that he was missing with his own parents, she and Dylan formed a bond that made them nearly inseparable. Blake had wanted to go with them too, but Leslie assured him he needed to stay with his own mother. While no one was looking Leslie gathered some of the old leftovers from the fridge and put them in plastic shopping bags. She put them in the back seat of Mrs. Hardwick's car, along with the morning's eggs.

She drove about twenty minutes toward the town of Damascus then took a left turn onto a road that headed in the direction of North Carolina and Tennessee. She spent twenty more minutes on that road, taking a few turns onto increasingly remote gravel roads. Before long, she found herself at the decrepit trailer were her daughter Debbie was staying with her boyfriend.

Most homes looked bad now, with overgrown yards and piles of garbage, but it was clear that this home had been miserable even before the terror attacks occurred. The yard was littered with old tires and the dead vehicles that had shed them. The front porch and steps were ill-fitting, obviously obtained from another trailer.

The mere sight of the trailer made Leslie's heart sink. It was all she could do not to turn the car around in the driveway as quickly as possible and flee from this place. She hated to expose her grandson to this, to the sight of his mother and what she'd become. It hurt Leslie that her daughter obviously thought so little of herself that she allowed herself to live in such squalor. Leslie had raised her better than that.

She eased the car into the neglected driveway. It had been a long time since it had seen gravel or any care at all. There were deep ruts in some spots that made the undercarriage of the car drag. Leslie parked and turned the ignition off. She sat in the car and watched the trailer.

"Is Mama home? Are we going in?"

"I don't know, baby," Leslie replied. She was watching for signs of life, trying to make up her mind. Despite wanting to turn around, she'd come this far and felt like she should see it through.

A scrawny, shirtless man burst through the door and glowered at them. Seeing who it was, he tossed his head in a dismissive gesture, turned around, and went back inside. The rude jerk was her daughter's boyfriend Paul. Leslie took his dismissive gesture as a sign that her daughter was home. Had she not been, he probably would have been even ruder.

Leslie opened her door and slid out, being careful to take the keys with her. If the car was stolen, she had no idea how she'd get back to the Hardwicks'. She opened the back door and let Dylan out of his child seat, picked up the bags of food, and the two of them headed toward the front porch.

Leslie leaned close to Dylan and whispered in his ear, "Be careful. These steps are rotten. I don't want you to fall."

"They need new steps, Granny. Don't they?"

"They do, sweetie."

Paul had left the front door open. There was no screen door. Without air conditioning, they left the door open most of the time with nothing to stop the bugs, snakes, and rodents from wandering inside. The idea of her grandson sleeping in there disgusted her. In fact, the idea of *anyone* sleeping there was disgusting.

Stopping at the opening, she looked into the dark maw of the trailer. She could see very little, each window covered with a towel or sheet serving as a curtain. Her nose told her way more than her sight did. The place smelled of mildew and rot.

Leslie knew that soon enough many places would smell like this, without the benefit of modern heating and air-conditioning. This place smelled as if it always been this way. It smelled like the body odor of people who lived in the dark recesses of humanity, scared of the light of day. It smelled like abuse, crime, and neglect. It smelled like drug use and alcoholism. Like apathy and early death and the unloved.

Leslie rapped on the aluminum door frame and faked a cheery voice. "Hello! Anybody home?"

A high-pitched and agitated voice responded from the darkness. "Dammit, woman, you know we're home. You done seen my ass on the front porch."

That was Paul in all his glory.

Leslie ignored him, unfortunately used to his demeanor. She did not raise her daughter to be such a person but it had become increasingly apparent that her daughter saw *herself* as this kind of person. Leslie had tried for years to encourage her to make something of herself but had given up when Dylan came along. He was now Leslie's priority. Her life was about making him more than his mother.

"I brought some food," Leslie announced. She went inside and set the bags on the coffee table. In the muted light coming through the door she could see that the glass tabletop was littered with powder residue. There were various lengths of drinking straws and a couple of rusty razor blades. Meth heads were like the U.S. Postal Service—come rain, snow, hell or high water, terror attack, or the apocalypse, a junkie was going to junk. Leslie felt vomit rise in her throat.

"There's some eggs. There's also some leftovers."

Releasing the bags, she stepped back from the coffee table. This would have been the point in the conversation where a guest might normally be asked to take a seat, but Leslie did not feel comfortable sitting in this house. It wasn't like Paul was likely to extend an invite anyway.

The idea of stray razor blades and needles was concerning, but she found herself more worried about the intangible residue of seeing such things. She worried about Dylan's memories of sitting in this house. She wanted to turn and run, to take her grandson and go anywhere but here. She wanted to tell him that the woman on the couch in front of them was not his mother but some stranger.

Leslie noticed Paul staring at her with his usual look of disgust on his face.

"Now what the hell are we supposed to do with that shit?" he asked.

Leslie shrugged, unable to ignore his lack of gratitude. "I reckon if you're hungry enough you'll eat it."

Paul leaned forward, flipped open the tops of the bags, then flipped them back shut dismissively. "What the hell good is that? You got some way to cook it?"

Leslie met Paul's eye. "I'm sorry. I thought you might be hungry and I wanted to bring some food by."

Leslie glanced over at her daughter, who hadn't even said a word. Her gaze flitted around the room taking in Leslie, her son, and whatever else she was seeing there in the darkness. Her perception seemed impaired by whatever drug they'd managed to scrounge up. At some point, she finally processed that Dylan was there and that he was her son.

She raised her arms in an open gesture, flipping her limp hands at him as if beckoning. "Baby, you come over here to your mama and let her love on you."

Despite the intention, it was not an altogether heartwarming gesture and Dylan hesitated. Leslie could tell he was scared. She put her hand on his shoulder and patted it, while at the same time pulling him tight against her. "It's okay," she assured him. "You can go over there."

Dylan's lack of response to his mother's request angered Paul. His eyes narrowed and his face reddened. "Boy, you get over here to your mama. *Now!*"

His tone of voice shot icy daggers through Leslie. It confirmed what she had always suspected, what she feared that Dylan went through when he was with Debbie and Paul. Paul was a bully and Debbie would not stand up to him to protect her son.

Behind her back, Leslie hooked a thumb in the back pocket of her jeans. It brushed the reassuring grip of her .38 revolver. Despite being a hiker town, Damascus sometimes had a hard undercurrent. There were drugs, rough men, and violence. Leslie knew how to shoot and she was never one to be intimidated by men. If she had to, she would blow Paul's brains all over the cheap paneling of this trailer.

"Go ahead, Dylan, give your mother a hug," Leslie encouraged.

Dylan looked up at Leslie for reassurance and then did as she asked. Leslie locked her eyes on the scumbag's, showing him that she was not afraid of him and at the same time daring him to say another word to the child. Dylan went to his mother and she pulled him into her lap hugging him tightly, nuzzling against him in the way that a child might snuggle against a stuffed animal. It was not a natural and genuine type of affection, but the overly-dramatic reassurance sought by the intoxicated.

It made Dylan uncomfortable. He looked at Leslie, his eyes asking for rescue. He was not used to this kind of attention from his mother. Debbie was whispering in his ear but Leslie could not hear what she was saying.

The boyfriend swept his open hand toward the shopping bags on the coffee table. "That all you brung?"

"All things considered, I would have expected a little more gratitude toward someone that brought you food. It's more than you deserve. When's the last time you got out and earned a meal?"

He ignored the remark. "Where did you get this shit, anyway? We was down to your house the other day and the cabinets was damn near empty."

Leslie raised an eyebrow at him. "What were you doing in my house without me there?"

"It was a social call," he replied. "Debbie here wanted to see her baby."

It was on the tip of Leslie's tongue to respond that if Debbie was *that* interested in her child they would be living together. She didn't want to plant that seed in Debbie's head though. Dylan was with her now and she fully intended that it would stay that way. She had already steeled herself that there might one day be a confrontation. If it came to that, she intended to threaten them with everything she had, from physical violence to reporting them for food stamp fraud.

From the corner of her eye, Leslie could see the Debbie was tickling her son and making him giggle, whispering in his ear, and getting him to whisper back in hers. Leslie returned her attention back to the boyfriend.

"So your social call involved you going through my cabinets?"

"We was a little hungry. Surely you wouldn't begrudge family having a bite to eat?"

She didn't respond to that but made some noise in her throat that she intended to be noncommittal. She didn't acknowledge him as family.

Not taking her eyes off Paul's, she said to her grandson, "Dylan, honey, we better be going. I'm sure these two have stuff to do." She knew they didn't have anything to do unless it involved stealing or getting high.

"Next time, bring something that don't need cooked," the boyfriend spat.

"I ain't the Piggly Wiggly," Leslie replied. "There ain't likely to be a next time."

"If you happen to luck up on some food the way you lucked up on this, I expect you to keep us in mind. Else I'm sure you'd go all brokenhearted if Dylan was to have to come live with us," Paul said, a jagged smile breaking his scruffy face.

Leslie shrugged. "We'll see about that."

Franklin Horton

This apparently wasn't the fear reaction Paul was shooting for. "Damn right we'll see. A boy should be with his mother. You know the law would agree with that."

Leslie couldn't hold back a laugh. "The law? You of all people are going to be throwing the law at me? You think I don't know the shit you do? You think I don't know how a low-down, lazy piece of shit like you, who doesn't hold a job, pays for his drugs?"

Paul's eyes ignited like a furnace flaring to life. When he rose to his feet and started making his way around the coffee table, Leslie knew she'd pushed him too far. She was in danger now.

She pulled the .38 from her pocket and thumbed back the hammer, just like she'd practiced when imagining this very moment. "Dylan, get in the car."

Debbie latched on to Dylan and he started squealing in terror. Paul kept inching toward her. Leslie flipped the gun a hair to the right and fired a hole in the paneling. It silenced the entire room and stopped everyone in their tracks.

"Dylan, get in the car," Leslie repeated, her tone firm but urgent.

"Bitch, you shot a hole in my wall!" Paul spat through clenched teeth.

She pointed the gun at him. "Next one will be somewhere you can't patch."

Paul flexed his scrawny arms like he was itching to choke Leslie to death.

She was not impressed. "I'll do it in a heartbeat. Try me."

"You'd shoot the man your daughter loves? Right in front of her? You think she wouldn't turn your ass in?"

Dylan came to Leslie's side and she steered him toward the door. "Honey, go get in the car *now*."

"Bye baby, mommy loves you," Debbie slurred.

When Leslie heard the car door shut, she looked back at Paul with venom. "You need to understand that if I have to kill you, I've already accepted that I'll probably have to kill Debbie too. Now, you may be wondering what kind of mother would shoot her own daughter. It's the kind who doesn't want her grandson to be raised within reach of a piece of crap like you. I see people like you two on the news all the time. The boyfriend who beats a child to death while

20

the child's mother sits there and does nothing. It's people just like you. If killing the two of you is all I have to do to keep Dylan safe forever, I'll do it and I'll still sleep at night. I love that little boy more than I've ever loved anything in the world and I won't let anything hurt him."

From the corner of her eye, Leslie could see that her daughter was crying. That hurt a little but in some ways Leslie hoped it might be a wake-up call. Maybe her daughter would realize how far down the ladder she'd slid. Leslie backed up until she was framed in the trailer door, staring into the dark recess of the living room.

"I don't want to see either of you again for a long, long time. Don't come to my house again."

Leslie backed across the porch, went down the steps, and traced her path back across the trash strewn yard. When she reached the car, she turned back toward the trailer again, looking to see if anyone had followed her. No one had. She had no idea what they were doing in there right now and she didn't care. All she cared about anymore sat in the car waiting on her and she got in to join him.

Chapter Three

The Hardwick Farm

It had been a mistake to go to Debbie and Paul's. It had been a mistake to expose Dylan to the conditions that his mother had chosen to live in, that she had chosen *over* him. Leslie decided instead to focus on doing the best she could for the Hardwicks. When Robert returned and they had to move on, she would come up with another plan. She would find a way for them to survive. She always had.

The Hardwicks' home had a natural gas water heater. Leslie drew a shallow bath and helped Teresa into it. While Teresa couldn't submerge her incision, Leslie knew from her own experience that simply being clean would make her feel better.

After Teresa's bath, Leslie kept the children entertained. She tried to keep them from making too much noise when Teresa was trying to sleep. She kept the house clean and kept everyone fed, including the goats and chickens. One evening she even built a small campfire and allowed Dylan and Blake to roast marshmallows just to do something different.

Every day she walked past the Radio Room, as the family called it. Inside, she could see flashing lights and digital displays, an array of equipment she didn't understand, with buttons, dials, headphones, and microphones. All of it was silent. There had been no word from Grace, no word from Robert.

As much as she felt bad about the missing family members, Leslie sometimes found herself wondering what it would be like if they never came back. She didn't know how much food the family had but it seemed like they had enough that they could live comfortably without Robert and Grace. God forbid something happen to them, but if it did, she thought Teresa may need her help around the house more than ever.

After dinner that evening, Blake and Dylan settled down to watch a movie while Leslie washed the dishes. Teresa had eaten with them at the dinner table that afternoon, which Leslie took as a sign that she was feeling a little better. After Leslie had her chores done, she went to the porch with a cup of coffee. It had been her ritual at her own home, to have a nice quiet cup after the dinner dishes were done. While she had access to coffee, power, and a nice back porch she would continue to enjoy the practice.

Teresa had gone to her room to rest. Leslie sat on the back porch and enjoyed the view of the dense green forest, soaking in the quiet of the mountains. She thought she heard an engine at one point, which struck her as unusual since there weren't many vehicles moving. Still, there must be some. The Hardwicks had running cars and she assumed there would be others around too. It was a farming community and many of the people stored fuel at home for tractors, mowers, and ATVs. The way sound traveled in the mountains, unable to find a clear path of travel, made it difficult to pinpoint where sound originated from.

She assumed it was somebody passing on the road, on a four-wheeler, dirt bike, or maybe even a lawnmower. People had been seen riding all manner of vehicles on the road as the fuel supply dried up. A gallon of gas took you a lot farther in an ATV than in a car. Eventually, it became clear that the sound was getting louder. Whatever it was indeed getting closer. She stood and went to the porch railing, watching the gravel road that came toward the house.

She felt a pang of fear, of concern for the safety of the children and Teresa. She assumed the responsibility for this home as a favor but these were also people she cared about. She patted her back pocket and felt the reassuring heft of the revolver. She was afraid to leave it in the house anywhere, afraid that one of the children might get it, so it was safest to carry it in her pocket.

Soon a motorcycle came into view. It was a brightly-colored dirt bike with two riders, a man and woman, neither wearing a helmet. She reached for a pair of binoculars that sat in a window ledge. Raising them to her eyes, she let out a curse. It was her daughter on the back of the motorcycle driven by none other than that lowlife Paul.

Had they followed her? How had they figured out where she was? And what were they doing here? Nothing good could come of this.

Leslie pushed her way through the back door and into the living room. She turned off the movie the children were watching and they made sounds of protest.

"I need you two to go to Blake's room," Leslie said urgently. "I need you to play back there until I come get you."

"Why?" Dylan asked. "We were watching something."

"I said now," she snapped.

Scared by her tone, the children ran to Blake's room. Leslie wanted this over with before Teresa heard anything. The Hardwicks had promised her food and she didn't want to blow that. She had promised them discretion and it was a promise she intended to keep. She stomped through the kitchen and out the back door. She stopped on the porch and watched the motorcycle park in the gravel driveway.

Her eyes landed on Paul and he grinned at her.

"So you *are* here," he said. "I didn't think the kid knew what he was talking about."

Dylan, Leslie thought. All that whispering on the couch. His mother had plied him for the information. The thought made Leslie sick, that Debbie would use her son like that. She shouldn't be surprised though. Debbie had failed to meet Leslie's expectations over and over again. When had she ever exceeded them? When had she ever even met them? Yet another failure should not have been a surprise.

"You all can't stay here. You've got to go. Now."

Debbie wouldn't meet her mother's eye but Paul continued to smile at her.

"Now, that's not a very hospitable attitude. You come around waving Debbie's son in front of her and it made her miss him. She only wanted to stop in for a little visit with her boy. You can't begrudge that."

Leslie lost her temper and stomped off the porch. She approached the motorcycle and shoved the disgusting man. "Get out of here now!"

Paul lashed out with his fist before Leslie even had time to know it was coming. She had not expected the scrawny little druggie to have the strength or speed to get the jump on her. She had assumed that if he tried anything she could step back, draw her pistol, and finish things.

She couldn't have been more wrong.

She fell to the ground, stunned and reeling. She tried to push herself into an upright position, tried to get back to her feet. Paul wasn't having that. He jumped off the bike. It turned over behind him, taking Debbie down with it.

Paul lashed out with a kick and caught Leslie in the side of the head. She cried out, trying to block her face. Paul's boot met her face, her ribs, and her stomach. He stomped her head and she lost consciousness. The last thing she saw was the dispassionate gaze of her daughter, not crying, not protesting, not intervening.

Chapter Four

Arthur Bridges' Compound - Mountains of North Georgia

Grace jolted awake with a start, her hand fumbling for the reassurance of her Glock 19. So used to sleeping in her clothes and being at the ready, her hand first dropped to her hip, expecting to find the weapon in its holster. When she didn't find it there, she patted the bed around her and sat bolt upright. Seeing where she was, that she was safe, she took a deep breath and took in the room around her.

"It's okay," she whispered. "It's okay."

It was a strange room but Grace knew where she was. She was at Arthur Bridges' compound. She was under the same roof as her dad for the first time in months. It was the best night of sleep she'd had since the world fell apart around her.

After reorienting herself she saw her familiar Glock sitting on the nightstand. With Arthur's extensive security measures and his full complement of guards, she had felt comfortable enough to sleep without her pistol on her side, although she kept it within reach. She wiped the sleep from her eyes and memories flooded back to her. All the things she had gone through—the terror attack, having to flee Oxford, and all the experiences on the road. A good night's sleep could only push the world back so far. It would inevitably come crashing down on her like a truck load of bricks.

She'd never have made it this far without her dad and the measures he took. The storage locker he had left her, the supplies he provided, had made things easier, but the most valuable tools she had had were inside her. It was the things he had taught her from the moment she was a little girl. How to survive, how to be resourceful, and how to figure things out. Most importantly, how to be brave when you were scared inside.

On second thought, maybe she could have made it without the gear he left her, but she was glad she hadn't been forced to find out.

She threw back the covers and got out of the bed sheets fully clothed. Her dad had brought her clean clothes but she'd been too tired to put them on. After dinner last night, after relaxing for the first time in a week, a wave of exhaustion swept over her and she'd been unable to stay awake any longer.

Across the room was the bag her dad brought her with the clean clothes and fresh gear. There was another bag beside it, one she hadn't opened. It was fresh clothes for her friend Zoe. The sight of that bag made Grace sick. Zoe hadn't made it. A man they'd encountered at Sonyea Brady's farm had killed her, and they had buried her on the farm. At some point, Grace expected she'd be relaying that news to Zoe's parents. It would be the hardest thing she'd ever had to do in her life.

She put on her belt, slipped the paddle holster with the Glock into the waistband of her cargo pants, put on her ankle holster with the North American Arms .22 caliber mini revolver, then strapped on her knives. Armed up, she gathered all her gear and set it on the bed, making sure she had everything. She caught sight of a mirror and stopped to look at herself.

She was not the same girl that had undertaken this journey a week ago. All of the things that had happened to her, all of the things she experienced, she now wore like a cloak. Her experiences sat on her skin like a layer of dust that could not be shaken off, like tattoos that told a story. The deaths, the killing, the horrors she had seen. A week ago she'd been going into class like any other student. Today, she stood here dressed like she was going into battle.

A week ago, her day was rigidly structured around a schedule of classes and work. Today there was no structure at all. She may have to fight, she may have to kill, she may even be killed or injured herself. She didn't know what she would face, but she was ready.

Whatever was coming her way, she was ready.

An unfamiliar sound drew her attention, heard and felt at the same time; a low rumble that became an enormous *thwapping* sound she recognized as chopper blades. Her heart clenched with fear. It was hard not to react to the unknown with a slight degree of paranoia after the thing she'd experienced. She shouldered her pack, gathered her other gear, and left the room.

She didn't see anybody in the house so she walked straight through to the front porch where she found her father and Arthur Bridges watching a chopper set down in the main yard of the compound. Grace had never seen anything like it before close up. It was some type of military-looking helicopter, black with no insignia and no markings.

"Friend of yours?" Robert asked, looking at Arthur.

Arthur didn't take his eyes off the chopper landing on his property. "A stockholder," he replied.

Grace knew from her father that Arthur operated his survival compound as a corporation. On the books it was a survival school with hundreds of mountaintop acres of deep forest. Arthur allowed various people who met his specialized criteria to maintain a presence on the property. They did so by buying stock in the company. By purchasing a certain amount of stock one might buy the privilege of placing a shipping container of survival gear on the property. For a larger stock purchase, a person could build a cabin or a small house on the property.

Everyone had been vetted by Arthur to assure they were of a like mindset. Arthur maintained majority stock ownership and control. He also reminded everyone that this was not a democracy. You were welcome to own stock and you were welcome at the compound based on your level of ownership, however, the final decision on any matter rested in Arthur's hands. He was the dictator here. His party, his rules.

"His name is Kevin Cole," Arthur said.

"Kevin Cole?" Robert repeated. "Doesn't ring a bell."

"He's a Beltway guy," Arthur said. "Former Special Ops. Runs a top-end security firm in DC now. They do a little of everything—executive protection, executive security training, family security training for Foreign Service families that are preparing to be sent overseas, stuff like that. He even does executive recovery if you have a kidnapped businessperson in a foreign country."

Robert nodded. "That's an interesting resume."

"He's an interesting guy," Arthur said. "We met at a trade show years ago. We know a few people in common. He heard about my *school* here and wanted in."

Arthur often referred to the compound as a school because it sounded less threatening to anyone unfamiliar with the place. Prior to moving to this compound, Arthur had also done a lot of work within the DC Beltway. Generally, to identify someone in the DC area as a private contractor implied that they were paid by the government to so some particular kind of work, either on or off the books.

Arthur really had been a contractor though – a building contractor. His specialty was building secure residential vaults. Whether your vault was intended to be a safe room for your family, for gun storage, or for secure document storage, Arthur was the guy. He made a lot of money in the paranoid DC community as a contractor for the person with a very specific set of needs and requiring the utmost discretion.

He worked for the ultra-rich and the ultra-paranoid, for people with top-level security clearances. Because a lot of these folks maintained secure documents in their home for work, construction of the vault was often paid for by the government. Those contracts were extremely lucrative.

"He still lived in the DC area?" Robert asked.

Arthur nodded. "Yes, but this was always his bug out plan. He has a cabin here. He's an old country boy from Tennessee originally."

"And he obviously has the resources to procure special helicopters for private jaunts," Robert quipped.

"Obviously."

After the helicopter had settled onto the ground, the pilot cut the engine. Arthur pulled a radio from his belt and thumbed the mic switch. "Joe, can you bring an ATV and a trailer to the landing pad, please? We have an arrival." Arthur released the mic button but kept the radio raised, listening for response

"Roger that," came the reply.

The engines wound down and the rotors slowed. A door popped open and a man emerged. He wore a battered ball cap and aviator shades, tan cargo pants and a white T-shirt, over top of which he had a load-bearing vest covered in magazine pouches and other gear. He wore a drop-leg holster with a pistol, an AK-47 hanging casually at his side. He scanned his surroundings, and when he spotted the group on the porch he recognized Arthur and threw up a hand in greeting.

Arthur waved back. "Let's go meet the new guest."

Chapter Five

Arthur Bridges' Compound

There were plenty of hands available to help offload the chopper. In about twenty minutes they had a stack of hard plastic Pelican cases, military duffel bags, soft-sided canvas luggage, and various hard storage totes. Grace recognized several of the Pelican cases as being rifle cases or multi-pistol cases, but others were unfamiliar to her. They could have contained anything from a high-end thermal scope to spare underwear.

Arthur had introduced Grace and Robert to Kevin Cole as *friends of ours*. Arthur employed a trick of the Mafia in his introduction, a technique familiar to all in his circle. If you introduced someone as a *friend of mine*, it implied that they were not part of the circle. If you introduced someone as a *friend of ours*, it meant they were in the circle. Robert and Grace were introduced as friends of ours. To be part of that particular circle meant they had a preparedness mindset. They were *switched on* as the expression went.

When Kevin asked if they lived at the property, Robert told him they were only visiting.

After two trips in a side-by-side ATV with a trailer, all of Kevin's gear was stashed at his cabin. Arthur invited him to join Robert, Grace, and himself on the porch for a cup of coffee and a debriefing. Arthur wanted to hear about his trip and Robert was anxious to hear any news from the rest of the country. He assumed that anyone coming from the DC area certainly had more information on the state of the nation than folks isolated in the recesses of the Appalachian Mountains.

Soon they were gathered on Arthur's porch sitting in plastic chairs. The pilot joined them on the porch also. He was dressed similar to Kevin in tactical clothing. He was also wearing a tactical vest with a pistol mounted in a cross-draw holster.

"This is Chuck," Kevin said, introducing the pilot. His slight hesitation at the name led Grace to believe that it was not the pilot's real name.

She understood why real names might not be used. A trip like the one Kevin had just undertaken could not possibly be a sanctioned use of such an expensive helicopter. It had to be an off-the-books trip, a plugged-in individual taking advantage of his connections.

Chuck nodded a greeting to everyone. Arthur pointed him and Kevin in the direction of the kitchen. They went and grabbed a bite of cold breakfast, both men returning with ham and sausage biscuits. It was the kind of food a lot of people might have turned their nose up at a month ago, but now a cold biscuit was a hell of a lot better than no biscuit.

"Do you mind me asking what's going on in DC?" Robert asked.

"Pure craziness," Kevin said. "People are going absolutely bonkers. Everyone is even more paranoid than they were a month ago, and that's saying a lot. Top government officials have been dispatched to command bunkers. That's left all the middle echelon people fighting over what's left. There are a lot of turf issues going on as you can imagine. It's hard to get answers to questions with the command chain so broken. People are doing what they want, despite whose toes they might be stepping on."

Arthur was shaking his head. "I can only imagine," he said. "Like a bunch of damn vipers crawling all over each other."

"We're not hearing anything down this way," Robert said. "Nothing. Everything we get is second or third hand, most of it coming from ham operators passing on gossip or rumors."

"The Beltway is like Beirut right now," Kevin said. "The infrastructure has fallen there just as it has in other places. The majority of folks don't have any resources, so they're beginning to turn on each other. You don't have a lot of prepper-types up there, and what preppers you do have are afraid to go out of the house now. A lot of them feel like they stayed on too long and now it's not even safe to leave the city. Those with any work connection to the military or inner circles of the government have moved into their offices. Any place that can offer any security, and that might have a few cases of water and MREs."

"That's awful," Grace said.

Kevin nodded. "It *is* awful. There are some people, like me, who had a plan and had the resources to put their plan into action.

31

That's why I'm here. I know I'm not the only one bugging out, either—choppers are shuttling in and out of the city like Uber cars when the bars close."

"That leaves a lot of folks trapped in the city," Arthur said, shaking his head. "That's an awful way to die."

"It's part of the deal in working inside the Beltway," Kevin said. "It's like selling your soul. If you work in that city you understand that the emergency planning is only for the upper echelon. If you truly understand the risk of living and working there, then you better have your own safety plan and it better be a darn good one."

"Hearing news like that leads me to believe it may be a long while before things straighten out," Robert said. "It'll take a long time to replace all those people who disappear. It won't be so simple as flicking a switch to get the lights back on and the government up and running."

"Then there's the looting," Arthur said. "If a lot of public buildings are damaged, it will take a long time to get the secondary governmental operations back into play. You may have a working congress but not a working VA or IRS."

Robert glanced at the pilot. "Not to be nosy, Chuck, but what are your plans?" Are you returning to the snake pit? The way Kevin describes it, I'd be pretty hesitant to go back there."

Chuck laughed. "No, I've got to get back. I'm still on the clock. This was a little side jaunt. I need to get back before somebody notices that bird missing."

"You're on the clock? People are still working in DC?" Arthur asked.

"Oh yeah, people are working," Kevin said. "The pay makes private contractor pay in the Middle East look paltry too."

"So people are still getting paid?" Robert asked. "I assumed the banks were probably shut down like everything else."

Chuck and Kevin exchanged a look. "In our line of work getting paid has never been as simple as a direct deposit into your banking account. Sometimes it goes into foreign accounts and makes a few hops before it finally lands in a place you can spend it," Chuck explained. "Other times payment is in hard goods rather than money."

"Right now there's such a shortage of security professionals that you can pretty much name your currency," Kevin said. "People are being paid in MREs, ammunition, weapons, and even fuel. Others are using crypto currencies like Bitcoin or even gold coins."

Chuck nodded. "We can name our own price if we're willing to stay."

"I hope you stuck it to Kevin here pretty good," Arthur laughed.

"No, Kevin and I go way back," Chuck said. "We've worked together on a lot of jobs. This was a charity run."

"It's a shame my daughter and I have all these vehicles and gear," Robert said. "Sure would be nice to have you drop us off when you fly over home."

Kevin shrugged and looked at the pilot. "Yeah, we can't do anything with truckloads of gear," he said. "Dropping you off wouldn't be any trouble at all though, as long as it's not too far out of the way."

"We have horses too," Grace said. "I'm not sure how they'd feel about flying."

"Pretty sure that horses and choppers don't mix unless the horses are highly sedated," Chuck said.

Robert was still working the idea around in his head. "You know, I'm not sure Sonyea is even well enough to travel. She's still healing and we could be here another couple of days. What do you think of the idea of you and Tom going ahead of us, Grace? Chuck could drop you off close to home if he's agreeable to that."

"Is that possible?" Grace asked. She looked at Chuck. "You could do that?"

"If you've got a decent landing zone it's no trouble at all."

"Tom uses a standup track chair," Grace said. "Can you transport that?"

"Not a problem," Chuck said. "That's a UH-60. It can handle it."

"The chopper is equipped with a rescue hoist," Kevin said. "He can hoist the chair in and out."

"I guess we need to ask Tom if he's willing to leave his mother in my hands," Robert asked.

"Not necessarily. I could go on alone," Grace said. "I can take care of myself."

"I know you can," Robert said. "But I'd feel more comfortable if you had some backup. No use doing anything alone if you don't have to."

"When are you leaving, Chuck?" Grace asked.

Chuck looked at his watch. "Probably in about thirty minutes. There are some things I need to do."

Grace looked at her dad. "I guess I need to get on the ball then. I'll go talk to Tom and see where his head is on this. Then I need to get my gear together."

"Chuck, I appreciate you doing this," Robert said. "My wife is recovering from surgery. I left her with a friend looking in on her, but she's not back on her feet yet. I was pretty worried about leaving her alone."

"No worries," Chuck said. "Somebody meet me at the chopper in thirty minutes and let me know the game plan."

Chapter Six

Arthur Bridges' Compound

Tom had no initial reaction when presented with the idea. He received the information in the stoic manner of someone used to receiving serious news. While Grace tended toward thinking and processing things out loud, Tom liked to weigh consequences internally before reacting.

Grace was beginning to understand the man a little. When she looked in his eyes she could tell he was torn between his duty to his mother and his concern for her. She wasn't intentionally trying to put him in a situation where he had to choose one of them over the other. The situation was what it was and he would have to figure out what he was doing to do. She couldn't make that decision for him.

Robert accompanied Grace to speak to Tom, wanting to offer his assurance that his mother would be in good hands.

"I know you'll take good care of her," Tom said. "I like the idea of her being able to remain under a doctor's care for a few more days. Are you sure you can manage to get all this gear back to your place? I'm not sure if my mom will be up to driving."

"She'll be fine. If she's up to it, I'll let her drive my Jeep. I'll drive Grace's truck and pull the trailer with your horses and gear. If she's not feeling up to it, I'll leave the jeep here to pick up later. No worries."

Tom nodded, processing the information, struggling to make the right call. "It's funny how this would've been no big deal two weeks ago. We could have called each other. Now, with no communication, everything is a bigger deal. Decisions have to be something you can live with because you can't change your plan midstream."

"That's the way the world has been for most of its existence. It's only recently we got spoiled with technology," Robert said. "But if you all take the chopper, you'll probably have access to my ham setup a couple of hours after you leave. The frequency for reaching this compound is written down on a notepad. You'll be able to call back and let me know you guys are safe."

"That doesn't help us if *you* run into trouble on the road," Tom said. "How are you going to call for help?"

"Trust me, I know that. That's exactly what I've been going through with Grace on the road. You just have to trust that people make good decisions."

While Tom mulled it over, Grace began to process the situation from her parents' point of view. She understood what it must have been like for them to not know where she was or what she was doing. Sure, they got an update on Facebook from Chin's place, and there also been a few updates from Sonyea's ham operator neighbor. But the *voids*—the gaps when they weren't getting any information– must have been agonizing.

"I still think it's the best plan," Robert said. "We make sure your mom gets a couple more days of professional medical care just in case there's any complications and you guys get expedited travel. Then my wife is going to be in better hands that much sooner and that's one less thing I have to worry about. The only thing this leaves hanging out there is your mom and I on the road. I'm prepared for that."

Tom nodded. "I'll go."

With his agreement, the morning kicked into turbo. The laid-back pace of waking in the secure compound came to an end and Grace and Tom began the hurried process of packing gear for the chopper ride out. Grace did a quick check to make sure her Go Bag was fully stocked. She replaced all of the items that she'd used or taken out over the last week from the spares her dad brought.

He'd brought a zippered duffel bag with the spare gear in it and she used that to carry all her gear. She crammed her Go Bag into the cavernous duffel, along with some extra clothes, spare magazines for her weapons, and some extra boxes of ammo. When she had her gear packed she dumped it by the chopper and went to help Tom.

Before they left Sonyea's farm, Tom threw together a Go Bag for himself. He did the same thing Grace had done, making a brief run through of the bag to make sure he had everything he might need due to the change in plans. While they expected to be safe at Grace's home in a couple of hours, they knew they couldn't depend on that. They needed the gear to live out of their Go Bags for a couple of days if it came to that. Plans were constantly changing, expectations constantly shifting.

Tom packed as much extra ammo and weaponry as he could fit in his bag. Robert and Grace helped him carry his gear to the LZ. Besides his Go Bag, he had thick black *something* rolled under his arm.

"What's that?" Robert asked.

"Flexible solar panel," Tom replied. "The track chair is capable of ten miles, depending on the terrain. I can squeeze a little more range out of it if I can charge the batteries on the go."

When they had a small pile of gear beside the chopper, Grace and Tom went to say goodbye to Sonyea. Even though they expected to see her again in a couple of days, no goodbye in this new world was inconsequential. You never knew when the next reunion would be, or even if it would occur at all. There were simply too many ways to die. Too many things that could go wrong.

"Mom, I'll see you in a few days," Tom said.

"I know," Sonyea replied. "Everything will be fine."

It was apparent that neither Tom nor Sonyea was the type for long, drawn out goodbyes. They exchanged a few more words and Tom gave his mother a hug and a kiss on the cheek.

"Sonyea, I'll check back in on you in a little bit," Robert said, and followed Tom and Grace from the room out to the helicopter, where Chuck was already pitching their gear on board.

"Should we keep weapons handy or do you want them stowed?" Grace asked. "Did you run into any trouble on the way down here?"

Robert was impressed Grace asked this question. It was yet another reminder that his daughter was a capable and forward-thinking young lady.

"No hostiles," the pilot said. "I'm fine with you keeping your weapons handy, just make sure you don't shoot a hole in my chopper. This is an expensive bird."

Grace slid into the back of the chopper and her dad handed in the last of the gear. Grace placed the bags where the pilot directed her. When Tom positioned his chair beneath the hoist, preparing to enter the helicopter, Robert went to help him.

"No, Dad," Grace said. "He's got it."

Robert backed away. "Sorry, Tom. I should've asked. It was reflex."

"No big deal," Tom said.

Tom finished maneuvering the chair, deftly swinging himself into the chopper. Initially, Grace had behaved just as Robert had, thinking Tom needed her help. Tom needed no one's help though. Sonyea had raised an independent son and he was still independent.

Chuck hoisted the track chair into the helicopter. "If everyone's ready to boogie, we'll get the hell out of here."

Grace went to her dad one last time and wrapped her arms around him. She squeezed him tightly.

"I love you, Grace," Robert said.

"I love you too, Dad."

"I'm so proud of you. Be careful. Be safe. Look after your mom, and I'll be there as soon as I can."

Grace started to say more, but she felt herself tearing up. She'd done well on her own but it didn't mean that she didn't feel like she needed her dad. He seemed so much better at these things. He seemed always to have the answer, to always know what to do in the worst situation. She wiped the tears away and nodded. She released her dad and the pilot pointed her to a chair. She sat down and began strapping in.

Robert extended a hand to Tom. "Take care of my little girl," he said, a little choked up himself.

"I'm not sure who took care of whom," Tom said. "You raised a tough girl."

Robert couldn't respond. He nodded teary-eyed at Tom, finished the handshake, and moved to the pilot, who was strapping himself into his seat.

"Chuck, I can't thank you enough for this."

"Glad I could help," Chuck replied. "May need a favor from you one day too."

"You got it. Safe travels," Robert said. He backed away from the chopper, giving a parting wave.

The pilot closed the door and gestured to headsets hanging near their seats, and Tom and Grace each slipped a pair onto their head. Grace struggled to catch a glimpse of her dad as the sound of the powerful engines increased. She could feel the vibration throughout her entire body.

The rotor speed increased and shortly she felt the tenuous grip of the Earth let loose and the helicopter began to rise. She craned her neck and saw her dad below, shielding his eyes with one hand and waving with the other. She raised a hand to him, although she knew he couldn't see her. She looked back to Tom and found him watching her.

Despite the fact that she was prepared for this trip, despite knowing this was what she needed to do, she felt a moment of vulnerability. Tom sensed it and extended a hand to her and she took it. In her acceptance of his outstretched hand she felt a change. Nothing in her world would ever be the same again. Not her, not her relationship with her parents, not her future, and not her relationship with Tom.

Chapter Seven

En Route to Damascus, VA

"That's the Great Smoky Mountains we're passing over," Chuck said.

Grace had been to the Smokies several times. While she had hiked there with her mom and dad and little brother, she'd never seen them from this perspective. From the sky they appeared so organic—multicolored, rippled, and convoluted, with pockets of mist lingering in dark recesses.

"They're beautiful," Grace said. The word seemed so inconsequential, a poor attempt to describe the beauty she was seeing.

With the speed of the chopper, they were out of the area quickly and over the lesser, but still beautiful mountains of western North Carolina.

The rest of the trip over North Carolina was not quite so dramatic as the majesty of the Smokies. Still, it was a beautiful state. The mountains were only slightly less magnificent than what they had just seen, densely forested and green. Grace's family lived so close to North Carolina that they been there often. The state line was only fifteen minutes from their home. Her parents had told her to the point of nausea how they honeymooned in nearby Asheville.

"We're approaching the Virginia state line," Chuck said over the comms. "It should only be a few more minutes."

"Find Damascus first," Grace said. "From there I can use the road to guide you to a landing spot."

"Your dad said there was a place in town we could land."

"There should be several options right there in town," Grace said.

"That Damascus?" Chuck asked, gesturing ahead and to the right.

Grace strained against her seatbelt to see where he was pointing. Ahead, the small town was barely visible. Few things protruded above the thick trees. Had they been moving faster, or even just been a few miles off course, the town would have been completely swallowed by the mountains.

"Can you slow down a little so I can orient myself?" Grace asked.

"Sure."

The pilot guided the chopper to what appeared to be the largest structure in the densely wooded community. Though he didn't know the town, it seemed obvious that this would give Grace the best chance of figuring out where she was. As they neared the towering church steeple, they overflew the town park.

"Shit, what's going on down there? That's the biggest cluster of people I've seen outside of a FEMA camp," Chuck said.

Grace and Tom struggled to see beneath them to the big grassy field where the town hosted festivals and events. It was where kids came to swing and old people came to walk their dogs. It also served as a launching point for those making day trips on the Virginia Creeper Trail or heading out for hikes on the Appalachian Trail.

Now the field was packed with small tents and outstretched tarps. Smoke rose from numerous campfires. There were clusters of people sitting on the ground, stretched out in the sun, or standing in circles. It indeed looked like a refugee camp.

"They look like hikers," Grace said. "The Appalachian Trail passes right by here."

"Maybe with all the shit going on they decided to get off the trail," Tom said.

Grace nodded. "Could be. They look like through-hikers. Most of those are solo tents."

When Grace leaned to get a glimpse out the window she caught a flash of light from the ground. Almost immediately she heard the pinging sound beneath her feet.

"What the…?" Chuck said.

"Incoming! Incoming! We're taking fire!" Tom barked.

The pilot reacted instantly, banking the aircraft sharply. Grace felt herself being pulled against the straps of her seatbelt. The G-forces were so intense that she was glad she was buckled in. Had she not been, she would be bouncing around the interior of the chopper like a pinball. There were more flashes from the ground but they were out of range.

"Shit, I didn't expect that," Chuck said. "I was expecting a bunch of hippies playing hacky sack and smoking weed."

"These hippies had guns," Tom pointed out. "We're going to need to find a new place to land."

Chuck was silent, studying his display panel intently.

"Chuck?" Grace asked. "What is it?"

"It will have to be close," he said. "My fuel calculations are tight up against the range of this chopper. I don't have any planned refueling stops along the way. What I've got is what I've got. I can't burn up fuel cruising around looking for a new landing zone. I'm not trying to be a jerk, but it is what it is. We need to be on the ground in about sixty seconds or I'm screwed."

"I understand," Grace said. She looked at Tom, anxiety straining her face.

"It'll be okay," Tom assured her.

"Any sports fields?" Chuck asked.

Grace thought a minute. "The high school football field!"

"Which way?"

"West. A couple of miles."

The chopper veered left. Her stomach lurched but she wasn't sure if it was from the movement of the helicopter or from the impending unknown of landing in her hometown. She wasn't sure what was going on down there but it seemed like they were under occupation by ill-intentioned hikers.

Tom eased his hand over onto hers, squeezing it. "We can do this."

"That it?" Chuck asked, pointing at a two-story brick building in the middle of a once-manicured field.

Grace jockeyed her head around to verify that he was pointing at the correct building. It was a small town and there weren't that many brick buildings. "Yes, that's it!"

Chuck veered in that direction. In seconds they were dropping down to the ground in what seemed certain to be a devastating impact. Thankfully, Chuck was a skilled pilot, and eased the chopper down at the last second.

"Hot landing," Chuck said. "Grace, pitch out your gear and take cover."

Grace didn't like the urgency of the situation. It made her feel like she was back in the danger zone of traveling the highways alone. She hadn't expected to feel that upon reaching her own hometown.

"Grace!" Chuck repeated. "You gotta move."

She snapped into action, removing the headset and hanging it in front of her. She opened the door and slid their gear to the edge. She jumped out, pulling the duffels from the chopper, and dragging them clear. She ran back to see if Tom needed any assistance.

He had maneuvered himself to the door and used the hoist to lower his track chair to the ground. He disengaged the rigging while Chuck retracted the hoist line. Shortly, he was in the chair and strapped in.

Grace scanned the chopper to make sure they hadn't left anything.

"Good luck!" Chuck yelled.

Grace gave him a thumbs up. "Thank you for this!" she yelled over the noise of the chopper. "I appreciate it very much."

"I wish I could've done more! Sorry about the turn and burn!"

Grace shrugged, unable to make out what he was saying any longer. She slid back out the door of the chopper and crouched over her gear, using a hand to cover her eyes.

Tom, unable to duck down while strapped into his chair, reversed the chair and backed clear of the rotor wash. There was a whine of acceleration and Grace was pummeled by the increasing downblast, then it was over and the sound of the chopper retreated into the distance.

Grace opened her eyes and looked at Tom. He was smiling at her and she started to smile back. For a second the world was peaceful again, then she caught movement in the distance behind him.

"Shit, we have company!" she said.

In the distance they could see several folks, maybe a dozen, running toward the field. Tom spun his chair to catch sight of them, the tiny drive motors whirring to life and spinning the rubber tracks.

"You have to run!" Tom said urgently.

43

Grace racked a round into her AR pistol and turned on the optic. "I am not leaving you. I've got this."

"You have no choice. We can't outrun them. The track chair is not that fast."

"We can fight our way out of this. I can take out those guys before they even get close. I've shot drills like this my whole life."

Tom's mouth tightened and his voice rose in urgency. "We're in the middle of the football field! There's no cover, Grace. This is not the place for a gunfight."

The approaching men spilled through the gate at the end of the field. They spread out and were running full-tilt. They could start shooting at any time and the fight would be on. Grace wanted to take the fight to them.

"I can do it," Grace pleaded. "Let me do it."

"Go! Get the hell out of here! Your family needs you. I can take care of myself. You getting captured too serves no purpose."

Grace screamed in frustration. Her mind raced. She had to be practical. She hated to admit it, but he was right. Free, she could try to help. She could try to break Tom loose. Captured, she would be useless.

But what if they weren't going to capture him? What if they were coming to rob and kill him? Thoughts came so fast she couldn't process them, couldn't think.

She realized she had to leave. She had no idea what these people wanted but they had guns and they, or people like them, had fired on the chopper. She grabbed her gear bag and threw it over her shoulder. It was heavy and would slow her down but she needed it. She had to have her Go Bag, her weapons, and ammo.

She stood and ran, then turned back to Tom. She opened her mouth as if to say something but she wasn't sure what. She stood there with her mouth open, staring at him, and he looked back at her. They'd been through so much. Was this the end of it all?

"I know. I know," he said, feeling the same thing.

Grace stood there frozen.

Tom stared at her. "Would you get going?" he said, his voice gentler this time. "Please?"

Grace closed the distance between her and Tom, throwing her arms around him, and kissing him on the cheek. She pulled back and stared into his eyes.

"Take these and get going," he said. He extended a small backpack toward her. "It's my AK pistols."

She took the bag and slung it over the other shoulder. Voices were getting closer now. She ran as fast as she could, fully understanding now why her dad had insisted running be a regular part of her training. Not just any running, but running with packs, running with cinderblocks, running with sandbags, and even running with only one shoe. Saving your life would not always take place under ideal circumstances. It may be inconvenient and uncomfortable, and that's exactly what it was now with the two large bags of gear banging against her.

Grace ran without looking back, trying to put as much distance between her and the approaching horde as she could. She'd gone to this high school. She'd been on this field many times and she was familiar the terrain around it. Still, she didn't know who was chasing her, and didn't know if they knew the area as well.

Tom watched her go, more concerned about her fate than his own. She flew through an opening in the fence and disappeared. He toggled the joystick and moved his chair to face the oncoming force. They had guns and yelled at him. He raised his hands over his head to present the least possible threat. His mind went back to his military training—what to do, what to say if you were captured.

In seconds the group was surrounding him. Some stayed at his side, the rest were directed by the apparent leader to take off after Grace. For a moment Tom wished he had held onto his weapons and taken the whole group out. It wouldn't have served any purpose though. He wasn't on a suicide mission. He couldn't outrun these men and engaging them in a firefight would have only gotten him killed. He would have to take his chances as a prisoner and hope Grace had some tricks up her sleeve.

One of the group approached Tom with a pump action Mossberg 500. He kept the weapon trained on Tom while looking him up and down, examining the standing track chair. "What are you supposed to be? Some kind of transformer?"

Tom had heard stuff like that before. He was unfazed. "My name is Tom Brady."

One of the other men in the group, red haired with a bushy beard and a bandana around his head guffawed. "Tom Brady? Like the football player?"

Tom smiled. "Better."

Chapter Eight

Damascus, VA

Grace was running full-tilt when she cleared the fence around the football field and bounded over a steep embankment, dropping into the parking lot where the football players parked during practice. The parking lot was completely empty of cars, with only a rusty green trash dumpster in a far corner. She briefly considered diving into it and closing the lid behind her but it seemed too obvious. It would be the first potential hiding spot her pursuers would come upon and surely they would look in there.

She paused for a second. She could go left onto the gravel road that connected the small parking lot with a larger main parking lot or she could take to the woods. There was a trail there, a path students used when they were ditching school to smoke weed. This time of year the trail would be overgrown and perhaps even completely invisible if the people pursuing her didn't know to look for it. She would go that way, into the concealment of the forest.

The two bags were getting heavy and she had to adjust them when she started running again, the straps sawing into her shoulders. Had she known she was going to have to carry both bags for such a long distance she would have packed more carefully. She could do nothing about that now. She gritted her teeth, trying to keep the rattling bags as quiet as possible. She ran as if her life depended on it, since it quite possibly did.

When she entered the woods, she cast a backward glance over her shoulder, looking for pursuers, and the move cost her. Her toe caught the gnarled roots of a poplar that rose up from the trail. Grace went flying, the bags tumbling, and she landed hard on her shoulder.

Yet there was no time for falling, and no time for assessing damage. She stood mechanically, shouldered both bags, and took off running again. She could hear shouting in the parking lot behind her. Whoever the men were, they'd come that far. She had to assume that they would keep coming. She was not safe yet.

Grace barreled down the trail, the heavy bags snagging on tree branches and causing her to bounce from side to side as if the forest itself was playing pinball with her. Since her fall, the difficulty of the trail was getting to her. She was sucking air, and being tired and winded would affect her judgment. If she didn't calm down, she also wouldn't be able to shoot worth a crap if the fight went that way. She had to hole up, even if it was only for a few minutes.

Ahead, the mountain laurel began to thicken at the sides of the trail. The gnarled stalks of the tree wove itself in dense and nearly impenetrable clusters. It became difficult to see very far in any direction. It was exactly what she wanted. This was the spot she needed. She charged into the dense cluster of trees.

Her first attempt at getting through the laurels was an illustration of the type of bad decisions people made when tired and frustrated. She tried to bully her way through, practically throwing her body against the limbs. It didn't work. She rebounded with scratches on her forearms and stomach before stopping and taking a deep breath.

You've got to slow down, she told herself. *You've got to think.*

She pitched the bags ahead of her through an opening in the laurel, then climbed in after them. It was like she was working her way through a tangled spider web, the branches jumbled together in a haphazard and illogical manner. When she made a little progress she planned her next move, looking for a clear opening in the maze.

When she could no longer see the trail and no longer hear the voices of her pursuers, she dropped the bags and backed up against the base of a tree. She worked to calm her breathing and slow her racing heart. Her mind kept going to Tom and what was going on with him. Was he safe? Had he been injured? What were they going to do with him?

She allowed herself to wonder for a moment if he was already dead put she pushed the thought from her mind. She couldn't let herself think that way.

Grace shouldered the AR pistol and confirmed that the optic was ready to go. She checked the chamber and confirmed there was a round in the pipe. She pushed all thoughts out of her head except for processing the information her senses were feeding her. The pounding in her chest slowed as her breathing came under control. She listened.

The disturbance she'd created coming into the woods had silenced the birds and squirrels. Every animal in this section of the forest had gone on alert, disturbed by her chaotic passage through the woods. In a moment, she picked up the distant sound of yelling. People were searching, looking for her. They shouted back and forth, looking for clues, trying to find where she had gone, but they could not. She could tell from listening to them that they were disorganized and were not trained in doing what they were trying to do. They didn't know the signs to look for.

She wanted to position herself to see them but was concerned about making any movement. If someone was standing out there listening as intently as she was, any sound might give her away. She had to be content to crouch in this cluster of laurel and try to be invisible. She didn't know how long they would wait on her but logic told her it wouldn't be long. With all that was going on in the world, why would they spend that much time looking for one girl whom they knew nothing about? It wasn't like she was somebody valuable.

Had they known she had a bag of weapons or that she could potentially lead them to her dad's cache of survival resources, they may have pursued her further, but they had no way of knowing any of that. Surely they would give up the search and go away. To be certain, she would wait for at least an hour before she disentangled herself from the thicket. If she heard nothing then, she would make her move and get out of there.

She knew exactly where she was and how to get home. There was no reason to rush. No reason to do anything stupid.

Chapter Nine

Damascus, VA

The men who'd taken Tom were not responsive to his questions. Whenever he asked them anything about who they were, who they worked for, or where they were going he was met with silence and stares.

"That thing better make it to the park," one of the men said. "Because I'm not carrying you. If you can't make it, we'll tie you to a truck and drag your ass."

"I should be able to go ten miles," Tom said.

"That'll get you there," the other man said. "We're not going far."

As he been trained to do in the military, Tom tried to observe as much as he could about the men who'd captured him. He guessed that none of them had a military background based on the way they handled their weapons. Even hunters would have been more familiar with weapon-handling than these men appeared to be. There was also nothing about them that gave any indication they were locals.

With no other clues, he looked at their clothing. Both were wearing low-top hiking shoes that looked like Solomons or Merrells. What tags he could see indicated that most of their clothing was by companies like Kuhl, The North Face, and Mountain Hardwear. Even with the scraggly beards, the body odor, and the nasty T-shirts, these were people wearing expensive, high quality clothing that marked them as hikers. Grace said her hometown was on the Appalachian Trail, and that Damascus was known as the friendliest town on the trail.

Tom's captors led him off the football field and into the nearby parking lot. He spotted two Jeep Wranglers with the tops removed. That explained how the men got to the football field so quickly from the town park.

"You're gonna have to drive yourself, dude," one of the captors said.

Tom shrugged. "That's fine. You guys can all take Jeeps as far as I'm concerned. Just tell me where to show up and I'll meet you there in a little bit."

"Not a chance, asshole," the man who appeared to be in charge said. "I'm putting two guys with you. Try any funny stuff and it won't go well for you."

"What if he can outrun us on that thing?" a man named Mike asked.

The leader looked at Tom and raised an eyebrow.

"It only goes at walking speed," Tom said

"He could be lying," Mike insisted.

"I'm not lying about that," Tom said "No matter how fast it goes, it clearly can't outrun a bullet, right? If I tried to run off, wouldn't you just shoot me?"

"He's got a point," the leader said. He swung himself into the driver's seat of the nearest Wrangler. "The rest of you guys load up."

The men clambered aboard the open vehicles. The two men that the leader designated to walk with Tom stood nearby with sour expressions. They were not excited about having to play escort to Tom. They frowned as the Jeeps roared off.

"So where are we headed?" Tom asked.

A man named Jeremy gestured with his gun and the trio began walking. With no traffic visible in any direction, they stayed to the center of the main road, a divided two-lane state highway. They passed several houses and businesses. There were rental cabins and bicycle shops, a couple of factories. Unlike many of the places Tom had passed in his travels over the past few weeks, this area appeared abandoned. There were no people sitting on the porches of the dark houses, no armed men guarding their businesses.

"Where is everyone?" Tom asked. "This is the quietest spot I've seen in days."

Mike shrugged "Everyone left."

"Watch with the mouth," Jeremy spat. "No one said you could be giving away information."

Mike gestured around him. "What?" he asked. "That some kind of state secret? I'm stating the obvious."

"You know how they are," Jeremy said. "They're funny about things."

"I'm funny about things too," Mike said. "I'm funny about being told what to do. I'm funny about being made to walk when other people are riding. I didn't sign up to be on the second string of somebody's team. I didn't sign up to do all the shit work in some dinky town where I don't want to be."

Tom listened eagerly. Anytime there was dissent in the ranks there was an opportunity to pick up information. Those dissatisfied with the status quo were always inclined to share a little more information than they were supposed to. It was a way of getting back at the people in charge, a way of getting a little satisfaction to soothe their own personal aggravation.

"I'd just be careful what I said."

"You going to rat me out?"

Jeremy didn't answer.

"So why did everyone leave?" Tom asked.

"It's a small town," Mike said. "There weren't many people living in town to begin with. Most of the people around here live outside of town. The town itself only had a couple of hundred people."

"So why did they all leave?" Tom asked again. "It's not a good time to be traveling the roads. Most people I've seen are sticking close to home. Even without food and power, they're going to be a little more comfortable there than they are out on the road."

"This is a hiking town," Jeremy said. "All this bad stuff happening—the power going out, the fuel shortage— just happened to coincide with a festival the town has every year. It's a little appreciation thing they do for the hikers spending money in the local economy. There's all kinds of free stuff, and it's also a way for hikers to get to know each other and have a rest break. By the time they get here, the hikers are already several hundred miles into the Appalachian Trail."

"That's what you all are doing here?" Tom asked.

"Yes," Mike said.

The second man nodded in agreement. "We came for the festival and got stuck."

"How many hikers show up for this festival?"

Jeremy shrugged. "Hundreds? Thousands, maybe?" Mike nodded. "Yeah, probably thousands."

"So you outnumbered the townspeople?" Tom asked, a picture beginning to form in his head. He could see a town outnumbered by an occupying force. He could see the nervousness, the unrest. He could imagine that being the recipe for a confrontation or even a disaster.

"The festival never happened," Jeremy said.

"All the hikers were already here for the most part," Mike said. "But the power went off before the festival could even get started."

"A lot of the festival vendors still had gas," Jeremy said. "So they all left. The rest of us were afraid to leave. We didn't know what was going on and none of us wanted to go out there on the trail where you couldn't get any information."

"What was the town's response?" Tom asked.

"Most of us only had enough food to get here," Mike said. "Everyone comes into town to resupply. There were a couple of days where there was plenty of food to go around. The restaurants were trying to use up their refrigerated and frozen food so everyone was eating well. It was like a big free party. Then the locals began to get a little concerned because the grocery store started running low."

"What happened then?" Tom asked.

"They asked us to leave," Mike said.

"Who did?"

"The sheriff. He had some other people with him. A couple of guys with guns."

"Let me guess, you overpowered them?"

Jeremy nodded. "We had to. What else were we supposed to do?"

Tom had no answer.

"He walked into a big mob of people and started yelling. He was barking orders and waving his gun around and kind of being a dick," Mike said.

"How did it go down?"

"Someone threw a rock. It hit the sheriff and he fired in that direction. A few people fell and it drove the mob into a frenzy. Before most of us even knew what was happening, the sheriff and those men were on the ground being beaten. Their guns got taken. Then there was a gunshot and somebody, I don't know who, killed the sheriff."

"What about the other men who were with him?"

"We weren't sure what to do at first. If we let them go home, they might come back with more men and more guns and we wouldn't have a chance."

"You killed them?"

"No," Jeremy said. "We took the sheriff's keys and we took over his office. We took the guns, the emergency supplies, and we hit every business in town using those guns to get what we wanted. We turned on the town before the town could turn on us."

Chapter Ten

Damascus, VA

After she'd heard no sound for a long time Grace slipped from her hiding place and cast a wary eye to the trail. She saw no one, no movement, no indication anyone was lurking around. She slipped back into her hide, knowing there was no way she could make any progress without consolidating her gear into a load she could manage.

She unzipped the large duffel and pulled her Go Bag from it. The remaining items in the duffel were some fresh clothes that her dad had brought her, some spare ammo, and some spare magazines. She was tempted to lighten the load in her Go Bag by dumping out a few items but that was strictly against the rules. Her dad had trained her to never do that. She *always* wanted her Go Bag to be ready. That was the rule. She might be close enough to home that she could probably get there today, but what if things didn't go as planned? She could be stuck somewhere for the night and the things in the Go Bag would help her survive.

She took as many of the spare loaded mags for her weapons as she could and found space for them in her Go Bag. She would have to leave Tom's gear, his AK pistols, and all of his spare ammo behind. She just couldn't carry it all.

She dug into her Go Bag and removed a contractor-grade garbage bag. Her dad had impressed upon her the importance of carrying these long ago. They weighed very little and could be slit open for an emergency shelter or be worn as a raincoat. In this case, they could also help assure that the cache of weapons and supplies she was going to leave behind would remain dry.

A nearby poplar had turned over in the wind, the roots of the tree pulling up and taking a large chunk of earth with it. The divot of earth where the roots had been was at least six feet across and about two feet deep. It would make a perfect place to stash the gear. She slid Tom's duffel into the garbage bag and placed her own in there with it. Knotting the top, she found a broken limb about four feet long and used it to rake loose dirt and leaves over the bag. Soon it was completely hidden.

Grace removed a bottle of water from a side pouch on her Go Bag and took a drink. Knowing she might not stop for a drink again soon, she forced herself to slow down and take another. She replaced the bottle in its pouch and shouldered the bag. She slung the AR pistol's single-point sling around her neck and her right arm, but held the weapon across her chest, at the ready. She couldn't run with it bouncing around in front of her.

Finally squared away, she took off at a jog. After negotiating this path with the two large duffels of gear, she practically felt weightless now. With her physical conditioning she could do this all day.

Grace tore her way back up the trail, returning to the parking lot. This trail would not take her in the direction she needed to go so she needed to get off it and change directions. She cautiously worked her way toward the football field, making sure no one was waiting on her. Seeing Tom gone from the field hit her like a punch in the gut. This was where she'd been forced to leave him. At the same time, it was better than finding him lying there dead.

His absence only turned up the heat on her resolve. She had to help him. If the people who had taken him were part of the same large group that was camped out in the park in the middle of town, she had no idea how she'd save him. There were too many of them. She was only one girl. Yet admittedly, she was one highly-trained and relatively dangerous girl. She knew how to shoot, how to fight, and how to survive.

She skirted the perimeter of the football field property, staying close to the weeds behind the bleachers where some concealment was offered. When she reached the edge of the sports field the property opened up into a huge meadow that ran all the way to the highway.

She was close to the road but she did not want to travel on it. There was, however, an old railroad bed that ran parallel to the road

56

and had been converted into a bicycle trail. That would take her in the direction she needed to go. As an outdoor and hiking destination, the town had dozens of trails extending out from it. Some were spur trails that accessed the Appalachian Trail. Others were part of the Virginia Creeper Trail, the Daniel Boone Heritage Trail, or the Virginia Birding and Wildlife Trail.

She understood that she could easily run into a trap on the bike trail. She was fully aware that there could be people on ATVs or jeeps traveling the trail. If she ran headlong into them, she might not have time to hide. There could be people on bicycles. There could even be people waiting for someone just like her to come running along that they could rob.

Still, she had to make time and cover distance if she was going to accomplish anything. Seeing no movement anywhere she felt safe enough to crouch low and run hard across the open meadow, a distance of perhaps two hundred yards. At the far side, she dropped down in high weeds. She spun around, her weapon raised, scanning where she'd come from for any sign of pursuit or movement. There was nothing. One hurdle down. Thousands left to go.

She took a moment to let her breathing and heart rate steady from the sprint, then she was off again. Parallel to the road, she worked her way through tall weeds into the forest, using the trees to maintain a visual barrier between herself and the road, something that would give her that extra moment to react if someone came along. If she could do this for another mile or so she would come across the bike trail and then she could make up for lost time.

When she reached the bike trail Grace accelerated. She covered the two miles into town without so much as a break. She couldn't stop her mind from wandering through the fact that she'd been on this bike trail hundreds of times. Then her mind wandered to the recollection that she met her friend Zoe—her *late* friend Zoe—on this same trail. Her mind went to a dark place and she had to pull it back. She couldn't let herself go there right now. There was work to do.

As she neared town, the distance between the highway and the trail varied. Sometimes she would be exposed and in the open. Other times, the trail wandered a little further away from the road and dense vegetation concealed her from the road. When she hit those concealed sections, she ran harder, less concerned about drawing attention. When she came upon the more exposed sections, she slowed and made sure the coast was clear before venturing out of the woods.

Coming upon one of the last exposed sections before town, she slowed again. Sure enough, she caught movement and ducked into the vegetation to determine her course of action. When she got a clearer look she at the road she realized it was Tom and two armed escorts. Her heart raced.

She threw her AR pistol up to her shoulder, firing up the optic. The red dot sight provided no magnification, only a variable-sized red dot that represented the bullet's point of impact. She lay the dot between the shoulder blades of one of Tom's captors. She could hit him at this distance. She hit targets and steel plates at this distance with this very weapon on a regular basis. She slipped the safety to the FIRE position.

It would be exactly like a shooting drill she'd run with her dad on multiple targets—hit one, engage the second target, and drop him too. She paused. Her trigger finger was extended beyond the trigger guard but she curled it inward, resting it on the curved steel trigger. She could feel its smoothness beneath her finger, knew that only the application of heavier pressure was required to make the shot. Everything in her wanted to pull the trigger. Everything in her wanted to put these men down and get her friend back.

What would happen after she pulled the trigger?

Her dad had always told her she had to think several steps ahead. It would take nothing to kill these men, but what would happen next? She would have to make sure they were out of the fight and then she would have to get to Tom.

Then what?

They would have to get away. *Could* they get away?

The experience on the football field earlier replayed in her head. This close to town, to the crowded park, people would come running, and some of those people would have guns. She and Tom would not have time to make an escape. They would not even have time to find a place to hide. By the time she got to Tom's side, a crowd would be on them and he could not outrun them. There was no guarantee she'd be able to outrun them, either. Running was not a viable escape plan in this instance.

She removed her finger from the trigger and made the weapon safe. She sagged and tears welled in her eyes. She let the weapon settle back to her chest. Having to leave Tom to his captors once had been bad enough, but having to do so a second time was devastating.

She made the decision then that, since she had eyes on Tom, she'd follow the men and see where they took him. She wasn't about to go walking into the camp, but if she could watch from a safe position she might gather intelligence that would help her recover him later. She pulled the monocular out of her pocket, settled into a more comfortable position, and watched.

People were everywhere. She had never seen her small town with this many people except during the Hiker Days festival. Because she'd planned on staying in Oxford that summer with her friend Zoe she'd kind of forgotten about the festival. She and her family had attended for as long as she could remember. She recalled that Hiker Days took place around this time every year. It would certainly explain why all the people were here. Had they come for the festival and then gotten stuck just like the people she'd encountered along the interstate, huddled in overpasses and trying to survive?

Chapter Eleven

Arthur Bridges' Compound

Robert, Arthur, and Kevin Cole were having lunch on the porch of Arthur's home when a chirping sound erupted. The men looked at each other curiously then Kevin realized it was coming from the cargo pocket on his pants. He fished a satellite phone out of his pocket and checked the display.

"It's Chuck."

Robert exchanged a look with Arthur. He couldn't help but feel panic, an unreasonable rush of fear that something was wrong. It was the reaction of a parent concerned about his child.

Arthur held his hands up. "Don't worry yet, Dad," he said. "Remember that girl got herself here to my place. She's incredibly capable. You raised her right."

"Trying not to worry is easier said than done," Robert said. "It's an involuntary reaction."

Robert tried not to eavesdrop but at the same time he was concerned about the conversation taking place. He had worried about sending Grace on ahead but she had been insistent about getting herself home to her mother. She had earned the right to make a few of her own decisions. He understood that and wanted to give her that freedom. Still, if it had been a bad call, if something happened to her, he couldn't ever forgive himself.

"Thanks for the heads-up," Kevin said into the phone. "We appreciate it. I'll talk to you again soon." He clicked off his phone and shoved it back in his pocket.

"Everything okay?" Robert asked.

"Chuck just wanted to report back. He said the situation in the town was a little hinky. There was a mass of people camped out in a park in the center of town."

Robert slapped his head in frustration. "I forgot about that. I didn't come through town on my way down here so I didn't realize those hikers were still there. They've been rolling into town for about two weeks now for this annual local festival. I guess some of them are stuck there now. They're a pretty harmless bunch though."

"Chuck said they took fire," Kevin said, his expression serious.

Robert looked shocked. "He has to be mistaken. There's a lot of hunters in the town. It must have been one of them."

"He said there were armed men visible in the camp," Kevin told him. "They saw the flashes before they pulled off. He said he left your daughter and Tom in the high school football field and they were safe when he left. He just wanted to make you aware of the situation."

Robert sat back in his chair and let the news sink in. He abruptly stood and looked at Arthur. "I appreciate your hospitality but this changes things. I can't sit here while my daughter is back in the shit again. This doesn't feel right."

Arthur nodded. "I understand. I would probably do the same thing."

"Thank you again." Robert stood. "I need to go tell Sonyea I'm leaving."

Arthur nodded toward the door. "I think she knows already."

Robert and Kevin turned to find Sonyea standing in the door with the doctor. The doctor did not look pleased.

"I'm ready to go," she said. She was already dressed and wearing a sidearm.

"I told her I'd like to hang on to her for a few more days," the doctor said.

"And I told you that people in Hell want ice water," she replied, reaching over and placing a hand on the doctor's shoulder. "I appreciate everything you've done. Without your care, I'd probably be planted in the pasture right now."

The doctor patted Sonyea on the back. "Just please be careful," he said. "You're still weak and have some stitches. Don't overdo it. You're only patched up, not repaired."

The doctor looked at Robert. "I gave her a couple of pain meds and five days of antibiotics. Hopefully that will get you home. After that, you're on your own."

Robert nodded. "I hope to be home this evening."

"I hope you are too," Arthur said. "Though there are no guarantees out there. You know that as well as I do. There's an unknown around every corner. Even with the fuel to get you home, you can't be certain there will even be a road there. Everything is coming apart at the seams."

Robert nodded at Sonyea. "Looks like I'll have a tailgunner."

*

It didn't take Robert and Sonyea long to get their gear together. In less than thirty minutes, Robert had transferred his personal gear over from his Jeep to Grace's truck. They could have taken his Jeep and traveled light, but everything that Tom and Sonyea brought with them was in that trailer. It was stuff they would need for settling into a new environment.

Some of the men from the compound helped them gather the horses and load them onto the trailer.

"Are you sure you want to fool with those horses and that trailer?" Arthur asked. "They are no trouble. You can leave them and come back another time. That trailer means you can't go off road and it limits your maneuverability. Plus, you won't have any acceleration."

"I've thought about all that," Robert said. "It's like you said though. You don't know what's around the next corner. There's no guarantee we'll be able to get back anytime soon."

Arthur stood there with his hands in his pockets. He was a quiet man and he was a good man. It seemed a contrast that he operated such a militarized compound deep in this rugged country.

They fueled the truck from the cans in Robert's Jeep. There were extra cans still in the trailer that Grace and Tom brought from Sonyea's farm. They checked the truck out and everything seemed solid for the short trip.

Robert and Sonyea armed up and settled into their positions in the truck. Robert placed a chest-mounted magazine carrier in the floor near his feet. Laying against his thigh and pointing into the floor was his truck gun. It was a short AR pistol identical to the one he made for Grace. He'd machined the receiver himself from a kit. There were no markings and no serial number. Just as he'd told

Grace, if one of them had to dump their weapon on the run it could never be traced back to them.

He set Sonyea up with his backup truck gun, a Kel-Tec KSG. It was twenty-six inches long, a 12 gauge shotgun with twin tube magazines. He could load each magazine with a different type of load, such as six buckshot rounds in one and six slugs in the other. A switch let you choose which magazine fed the chamber. On the dash in front of Sonyea lay an olive drab bandolier with elastic loops full of shotgun shells. After all, you never knew what was around the next corner.

They waved good-bye and Robert made a wide turn in the compound's dusty parking area. He eased down the road, passing a guard tower and various armed members of the inner perimeter security. Further down the gravel road, camouflaged sentries opened gates for their passage. When he finally pulled out of the last gate and onto the main road, he didn't see the men that allowed him to exit but he could feel them watching him.

"You ever think about moving your family in with these folks?" Sonyea asked. "They've got one hell of a setup."

"I considered it, and I maintain a good relationship with them in case I ever need to take them up on their offer, although it's not the kind of environment where I want to raise my children. I want them to be able to experience a life that is a little less...*militarized*."

Robert and Sonyea were elated to begin their journey home. The hospitality provided by Arthur Bridges had been about the best anyone could expect under these circumstances and they were appreciative. However, they missed their families. It was an ache that would only be satisfied by a reunion.

They were relaxed despite the circumstances. They suspected there would be obstacles along the way. They knew there would be more populated areas where they would have to be on guard and where they might encounter trouble. They expected their first rough spot to be in North Carolina. In the western hills there were a lot of tourist destinations. There would be people trapped there by circumstance who had no resources and would be desperate for anything they could get their hands on. Those places should be the worst they encountered. What Robert and Sonyea did not expect was trouble within the first hundred yards of their journey.

When he heard the blast of the rifle, Robert was more confused than startled. He assumed that the firing was probably coming from Arthur's compound. Perhaps someone was training or even hunting. Then there was the devastating impact of the heavy .50 caliber round slamming into the engine of the truck. There was eruption of metal fragments and steam as coolant sprayed onto the hot exhaust manifold. Sonyea screamed and Robert cursed, slamming on the brakes. The vehicle lurched to a stop. Only then did Robert think about the horses in the back and that he probably should have stopped gentler. He yanked Sonyea's head down, ducking beside her.

"Are you okay?"

"No! You're tearing my incision open."

Robert released her but she stayed down. "Are you hurt?"

"No. I don't think so."

Robert waited on a follow-up shot but none came. Maybe the only intention was to disable the vehicle. Then a second round pierced the windshield flying just over their ducked heads, spraying them with shards of glass. Sonyea screamed again, Robert flinched.

"We've got to get outta here," he said. "We're sitting ducks. Can you run?"

"If someone's firing at me? Uh, probably!"

"Grab your bag and your weapon. I'll cover you. Run like hell."

"I think that last part goes without saying."

Robert threw open his door, leaned out, and fired three quick rounds through the gap between the door and the vehicle. Sonyea took this as her cue to bolt from the cab of the truck. She snatched up her shotgun and her pack and slid out the door. She kept her head down and ran as close to the truck and trailer as she could. Robert fired three more shots then grabbed his own Go Bag and took off running. He expected to see Sonyea in front of him, booking for the tree line. Instead, he found her fighting with the door to the horse trailer.

"Get out of here!" Robert yelled.

"Not without my horses!" Sonyea said firmly. In seconds she had the doors to the livestock trailer open.

"They're already saddled?" Robert asked in surprise.

64

"Yeah, because things like this can happen."

Robert shrugged. She had a point.

Sonyea sprang onto the back of one of the horses and took up the reins. "Can you ride?"

Robert mounted the other horse awkwardly. "If someone's shooting at me? Yeah, I think so."

Sonyea kicked her horse and it shot off down the road. Robert followed suit and was close behind her. Shots rang out behind, gouging troughs in the dirt road. Robert assumed he was dealing with trained shooters who would have no trouble gauging the lead on a rider. He tried to make his horse weave but nearly fell off in the process. Fortunately for them, it didn't take long to close the distance to Arthur's gate.

As they approached Arthur's gate someone slung it open and they rode through without slowing. Camouflaged men in tactical gear spilled by them on both sides. They ran the horses along Arthur's road though there was no one to open the gates for them further in. Robert assumed that all the men who'd been manning these gates earlier were now engaged at the perimeter of the property. The pair didn't slow until they reached the main compound, where they found Arthur, Kevin, and the doctor waiting on them. All were wearing plate carriers and carrying rifles.

The doctor slung his rifle over his shoulder and ran forward to help Sonyea off her horse. "You're bleeding," he said.

Sonyea nodded in Robert's direction. "He about pulled my arm off."

"Trying to save your life," Robert said.

"What the hell happened?" Arthur asked.

"It sounded like a .50 cal," Robert said. "Someone center-punched the truck. Then I guess we didn't get out fast enough. They popped a round through the center of the windshield."

"The guys at the gate said it sounded like a .50 too," Arthur said.

"You think you've been compromised?" Robert asked.

Arthur shrugged, a frown on his face. "That's always possible. I try to run a pretty low-key operation though."

"There's nothing low-key about Blackhawks swooping in and dropping off folks," Robert pointed out.

Kevin looked harshly at Robert. "If I led folks here, they wouldn't have had time to deploy yet. There's no way to know who that is out there. I don't care how low key you try to be when you're building something like this, people are going to notice. Hell, there's probably satellite footage of this property being cleared. There's probably thermal footage of the occupants. People notice stuff like this."

"We knew that was a risk," Arthur said.

"I'm sorry your security has been compromised, Arthur," Robert said. "What most concerns me personally is getting back to my family. Especially with what Chuck said."

"We still have your Jeep," Sonyea reminded him. "We could try again in that."

"I wouldn't go anywhere until I knew what was out there," Kevin argued. "If there is another ambush waiting out there, next time you may not get away."

Chapter Twelve

Arthur Bridges' Compound

Random gunfire continued throughout the morning, keeping the residents of the compound on edge. Arthur had a pre-staged command bunker in the basement of his home. Sonyea and Robert were seated at a table there, still looking a little shaken from their experience. The doctor had patched up Sonyea's torn stitches and was hanging around listening to the radio chatter. Kevin and Arthur were there, as well as several other men from the compound.

Arthur put down his radio and took a sip of coffee. "The men on the perimeter say that whoever is firing on them is dug-in. They can't seem to peel up an edge. They're also well-equipped. We sent two snipers out in Ghillie suits and they took fire before they got too far. They barely made it back alive."

"Thermal," Kevin said. "They've got someone monitoring the woods with thermal."

"Hell, who knows?" Arthur said. "They could have satellite support."

Sonyea shook her head. "We're screwed."

"We don't think like that around here, ma'am," said one of the men Robert didn't know. He had the bearing of a lifelong soldier. He wasn't being harsh with her, only making sure she knew the score.

"This is probably a rogue operation," Kevin said. "I've met people over the years who joked that their bugout plan was just to swoop in and take someone else's setup. That's what this feels like."

"There was this woman I used to work with who told me I was wasting my time buying bullets," Robert said. "She told me I should can food like she did, that she canned hundreds of jars every year. I told her that my system was to buy ammo and keep a list of people who canned. It was a joke in my case, but it's the same principle."

"Exactly," Kevin said. "There are people at all levels of government who have the ability to track groups like yours, Arthur. This may well be someone simply carrying out their own personal bugout plan."

"They're not getting a damn thing from me," Arthur said. His mouth was set firmly and his statement was not merely bravado. He appeared to be ready to go down with his ship.

"Although I appreciate everything you've done for us," Robert said, "I'm not ready to make my last stand here, Arthur. I've got a family to get to."

"Same here," Sonyea said.

"I understand," Arthur said. "I don't hold that against you."

"Do you think we could take the horses?" Sonyea asked.

Robert looked at her. "I've barely ever ridden a horse."

"I thought you were all about flexibility? About adapting to conditions?" she said. "Isn't that what you preach in your books?"

Robert frowned. Nothing worse than having your own words thrown back at you. "I'd be willing to try the horses, but it means giving up on all the gear. We'd have to cut down to the bare minimum."

"We'll hold on to your gear," Arthur said. "Once we run off whoever is peeing on our parade, that is."

"Can you live out of your Go Bag?" Robert asked.

Sonyea nodded. "I've done it. Have you?"

"I have. It's barebones and it sucks. It's not comfort."

"Embrace the suck," Kevin said.

"It concerns me that this could take weeks," Robert said. "That's weeks our family won't know what's going on. That's weeks we won't know if Grace and Tom made it home. Those will be long weeks."

Sonyea considered this.

Kevin cleared his throat. "I might be able to help there. I may know a guy."

Arthur raised an eyebrow at him. "A guy I don't know?"

"A guy *nobody* knows," Kevin said. "Or I guess I should say a guy few people know."

"He lives close to Damascus?" Robert asked.

"I think so. I know he lives in the coalfields close to where Virginia, Kentucky, and West Virginia meet."

"That's my general territory," Robert said. "It should be close."

"Who is this guy? A prepper? A survivalist? Retired military?" Arthur asked. "It kind of surprises me to hear of new like-minded people. After you've been at this a while, you think you've met everybody."

"He's none of the above," Kevin stated. "This doesn't leave this room. Are we all clear about that?"

He looked around the room and caught every eye. They all nodded their assent.

"I'm serious about this," he said. "This is stuff no one talks about."

"You have my word," Robert said.

"Mine too," Sonyea said.

Apparently, Kevin had reason to trust the other men in the room without confirmation since he didn't ask them. "This guy is a specialist," he said. "A world-class tinkerer. He designs and fabricates specialized low-tech gear for operators."

"What, like James Bond stuff?" Robert asked.

Kevin shook his head. "Nothing like that. This guy is old school. He's a machinist and a welder. If you needed a pool cue that could double as a sniper rifle, this is your guy. If you needed explosives hidden in the lug nuts of a car so that the wheels will blow off at a certain speed, this would be your guy. If you need throwaway suppressors, this is your guy. He does all kinds of crazy gear—special stuff that people ask for or things he comes up with from his own twisted mind."

"You know him personally?" Arthur asked.

"I've worked with him for years," Kevin said.

"Where did you meet him?" Arthur asked.

"It's complicated," Kevin said, choosing his words carefully. "Let me just say that he committed an act that made some people in government aware of his talents. They made him an offer he couldn't refuse. He's been working for the alphabet agencies as a freelancer ever since. They call him The Mad Mick."

"You think The Mad Mick could check in on my family?" Robert asked. "I don't want to send him out into danger if he's some kind of shop rat."

"He's not really a mad scientist," Kevin said. "He's about your age. He's a little out there but he's fully operational. He's the rare guy who cannot only build the weapon but use it too. He has no reservations about pulling the trigger on someone."

"Do you think he'd do this favor?" Arthur asked.

Kevin nodded. "He owes me, but that's not why he'll do it. He's a family man with a daughter of his own. He'll do it because of that."

"How can you get in contact with him?" Arthur asked. "Is he a ham?"

"Better," Kevin said. He fumbled in his pocket and pulled out his satellite phone. "He has one of these."

"I'm already in your debt," Robert said.

Kevin looked Robert in the eye. "I suspect that by the time this whole mess is over, all of us will be owing a few favors. Just give me a credit on my tab."

Chapter Thirteen

Jewell Ridge, VA

The man known as The Mad Mick seemed like anything but a madman as he sat rocking in an antique porch glider. The glider was making the slightest of squeaking noises as it moved on its old mechanism. Rather than being annoying, The Mick found the noise to be comforting and somewhat nostalgic.

The glider sat on what looked like an old country porch. It was around eight feet deep and twenty feet wide with an overhanging roof of rusty tin. The porch looked like it could have belonged on a country house anywhere in rural America. On the side of the hanger-sized steel building, however, it seemed a little out of place. The Mick had never once lived in a house without a porch and he wasn't about to start now. For some people, the heart of a home was the kitchen. For The Mick, it was the porch.

The Mick drank coffee from a ceramic mug that said Coffee Makes Me Poop. While he enjoyed his first cup of the morning he watched the whorls of mountain fog begin to dissipate in the rising heat. His goats and chickens plundered and foraged in the massive parking lot that was slowly being overtaken by weeds. The parking lot was surrounded by eight-foot high chain link fencing with three rows of barbed wire at the top installed by the company that had built, then abandoned, this facility. Had it not been for this fencing the pervasive coyotes would have already decimated his small homestead.

The facility had once been the home of a successful coal company. The property was over three hundred acres and had several mines onsite. There was a single-story brick office building, several shop structures, and open steel sheds for heavy equipment. There was even a helipad. Documents the company left behind indicated that they had spent over six million dollars developing the facility. When they mined out the property, they declared bankruptcy, picked up, and left. The property sat empty for eight years before the Mick was able to purchase it for about two hundred thousand dollars. Actually, it was purchased *for* him by his employers, but that was just a technicality. It was his.

The problem with selling the place had been the location. It was on a remote mountaintop in coal-mining country. There were no other business around that needed a facility like it. No one locally had the money to buy it for just the land. It was over an hour to the nearest town by winding, poorly-built roads. The Mick thought it was damn near perfect. Besides living here, he operated a machine shop that did welding, fabrication, and other small industrial jobs. It was the perfect cover.

To his right, The Mick heard the sound of a girl's voice. The massive industrial shop building that The Mick had chosen for his home had heavy steel doors but he had installed old-fashioned wooden screen doors on some of the openings to allow ventilation. Of course, he had to have one opening out onto his country porch. It was part of creating the atmosphere, after all. His daughter Barb came pushing through the screen door. She was his only other employee, a welder and jack-of-all-trades like himself.

"Your satellite phone is going off," she said. "It's disturbing the peace."

"I'm busy with my coffee. You can take a message."

She raised an eyebrow at him, a mannerism she'd clearly inherited from her late mother. "You might also get up off your lazy ass and answer your own calls. I'm a lot of things around here but secretary is not one of them."

"I knew there was a reason we named you Barb," he said, winking at his daughter. "Always a sharp comment."

"If we're earning our names, then *you'd* be Barb," she replied. "You've always been the prick of the family."

Resigning himself to the fact that he was losing this battle, he rose from his seat and headed for the screen door. He brushed by his daughter, pausing long enough for her to give him a kiss on the cheek, then headed off toward his office. This was not the office that handled the business of the machine shop, where he invoiced local mining and gas companies for the small jobs he did for them. This was the office from which The Mick ran his real life.

He picked up the satellite phone and studied the caller ID with interest, understanding that what was displayed may be totally unrelated to who was actually on the phone. When it rang again in his hand, he clicked a button and spoke. "The Machine Shop, can I help you?"

"You're still open?" replied the voice. *"Can't keep a crazy Irishman down, can you?"*

"Well, a suit-wearing, pencil-pushing bastard like you wouldn't know anything about real work," The Mick replied. "The working man can't take a day off just because the world goes to shit. Those kinds of holidays are only for you white collar folks."

"I'm glad to hear that your work ethic hasn't suffered," Kevin replied.

"So what's up? You trapped in Washington and needing me to come rescue you?" The Mick teased Kevin relentlessly about living and working inside the Beltway.

"I'm safe," Kevin said. He did not go into detail. His bug out plan was not something he talked about. *"I do need to ask a favor, but you're certainly free to say no. This is not work, it's personal."*

"Ask," The Mick said.

"Damascus, Virginia," Kevin said. *"How far away are you from there?"*

The Mick consulted a map on the wall. A red pushpin indicated his facility. He traced a road with a fingertip. "Maybe seventy miles or so. Maybe a little more."

"Do you have a way to travel there other than walking? If you have to walk, I'm not asking. That would take so long as to make my request pointless."

"I have multiple options for travel," The Mick replied, not going into detail.

"I choppered in to the place I'm staying. When the chopper left, he took a friend's daughter and a veteran friend of hers, dropped them off near her home in Damascus. Her dad is going to

try to make it there by road but we're not sure how long that's going to take with things being what they are. The pilot called back just a little bit ago and he was concerned. He said the town appeared to be occupied by armed folks and the group took fire during their flyover."

"He wants me to make sure his baby got home safely?"

"Basically."

"I'll do it."

"You're free to say no or take more time to think about it," Kevin said. *"I know it's a lot to ask."*

"I'm a dad. I'd be glad to check in on her."

"Are you sure it's okay? I hate to put you to any trouble."

"Nah, you don't give a shit about my trouble. You've put me to trouble more times than I can count. Besides, there are some things worth a man's trouble and this is one of them."

"I owe you."

"Indeed you do. I can tell you where the repayment starts."

"With what?"

"I'm only The Mick for business. If it's personal, call me Conor. That's me real name."

There was a pause for a moment. *"Understood, Conor. Be safe, my friend."*

The Mick clicked the phone off, picked up his coffee, and went back to the porch. Barb was sitting on the glider now doing the same as he had been doing earlier, watching the chickens and goats forage the crumbling parking lot. She looked at her father with a question on the tip of her tongue. She wanted to ask what he had gotten himself into. It was clearly something because she saw it written all over his face.

"What is it this time?" she asked. "For some reason, I mistakenly assumed that with the world falling apart you might have a few days off."

"Someone asked me to check in on somebody. It's a favor. A *personal* favor."

"I thought the whole point of having this secure bug out location was so we could hole up here and wait out the problems of the world." Barb sighed. "What's the point if you're just going go running around out in the chaos and get yourself killed?"

Conor shrugged. Guilty as charged.

"So you have anything to say for yourself?" she asked.

"I've been wanting to try out the electric motor that I just installed on one of my bikes. A mountain bike with motorized assist. This would be a perfect opportunity."

Barb threw a hand up in exasperation. "You've got acres of parking lot here to try it out on. Instead you're going to take a chance on getting yourself killed."

"I'm not going to get myself killed. I'm just checking in on someone. A friend of a friend. Actually, a friend of a friend's daughter."

"Well, just go ahead. You're gonna do what you're gonna do anyway. Trying to talk sense into you is like trying to talk to one of the goats. Actually it's worse. The goat halfway listens because he thinks you might feed him. Talking to you is more like talking to a rock."

"It's been said before."

She paused a second and let her frustration pass. "I reckon I can keep an eye on things. We know who really runs things around here anyway."

He knew she could. The girl was tough as nails. She was a generation removed from Ireland but still had the grit, the determination, and the backbone of an Irish woman. She could do anything she set her mind to.

As their Irish heritage made her determined and strong, it also made him loyal. Despite his loose connection with a girl named Grace, for which there was no connection at all, he could not sit there in comfort and peace if there were something he could do to help the child. He had to make an effort. If it were his daughter on the other end, he would hope someone would go to this same trouble.

"So when you leaving?"

"Reckon I'll pack today and leave tonight," he said.

"How far is it?"

"I suspect about seventy or eighty miles."

"How long a trip on that contraption of yours?" she asked.

"It should make 25 to 30 mph if I'm on relatively flat road," he replied. "I don't know yet what it will do on hills or off-road."

"Is there anything I can do to help you get ready?" she asked.

"You might throw together a couple of days' worth of food while I get my gear ready."

Not one to put off work, Barb rose to get to it. As she went by, she stopped and asked, "This girl…what's her name?"

"Grace."

She nodded, considering the name. "Grace."

Chapter Fourteen

Damascus, VA

Grace moved a short distance off trail. She didn't want to take any chance on someone coming along and wondering what she was doing. She found a spot where she was reasonably concealed by dense vegetation but could still see through the bushes to the park.

She dug out her monocular. It was a cheap Chinese thing her dad bought for about fifteen dollars but it did the trick. It wasn't the kind of optic you would take on a Montana elk hunt but it would do for looking across a parking lot or a short distance through the woods. She trained the monocular on the crowd.

Having grown up in a town that saw hikers year-round, she could tell that's exactly who these people were. There was no other explanation for them being here other than that they had come for the hiker festival and gotten trapped by circumstance. What didn't make sense was that most of hikers she had known over the course of her life were friendly and generally easygoing folks. In fact, she and her parents had often extended hospitality, known as "trail magic", to hikers. They opened their home to some on occasion such as when unseasonably bad weather stranded an unprepared hiker in town or when someone just needed a break from the rigors of the trail to get their head back in the game.

Most of the hikers Grace could see were unarmed and appeared to be occupying themselves in conversation, playing hacky sack, or even playing musical instruments. Those were the kind of hikers she was used to seeing. Others had guns and were stationed at the perimeter of the crowd. Those concerned her.

There were open fires with food cooking in large pots. These were not the kind of pots that hikers would carry around. These were more like commercial pots from restaurant kitchens and she wondered where they had got them. She also wondered where they got the food they were cooking. The small police force in the town would probably not allow these hikers to be running around with guns. Something had to have happened. It was yet another concerning thing that she didn't have answers for.

Up until this point she had maintained some fantasy that she would reach town and break Tom free, then the two of them would continue on happily down the road to her parents' house. Seeing this crowd, their guns, there was no way she was walking in there and taking him. While his track chair gave him mobility, it did not give him speed. She would have to wait. She would have to go on to her parents' house first. As much as she hated the idea, she may even have a wait for her dad and Sonyea to show up and help her recover Tom. The thought crushed her but she had to be practical.

She put the monocular in the pocket of her cargo pants. After some deliberation she decided to stash her AR pistol in her pack, also. One of the reasons she carried this particular pack and this particular gun was that it afforded her optimal accuracy in a weapon that would just fit inside her pack. She hated to put the weapon in a place it would be harder to reach but if she ran into people the weapon would draw attention. The pack by itself wouldn't among this crowd. This was a town used to seeing people with packs. She still had the pistol within reach, she just hoped she didn't need it. A gunshot in proximity of this crowd would certainly bring people running.

She slung her pack on her back and started moving again. This was where she was closest to town, where she was more likely to encounter other people. People in this town used the trail as a back road and informal route through town. Many people would bicycle into town in the evening to eat dinner, have a few drinks, and ride back home unconcerned about being pulled over for drunk driving.

Grace continued on at a walking pace, afraid that running might draw attention. She wanted to get closer to the mob but not pass through it. In a group this size, she might blend in, but it was also possible she would be called out as someone who didn't belong. One side of the park was bordered by a street lined with small houses. Her best bet would be to try to get behind that neighborhood and weave her way in to a decent vantage point.

She left the trail to cross the main street through town. She saw no one close enough to worry about, so she went straight across the road and through the yard of the nearest house. When she was behind it, she took to an overgrown gravel alley and followed it for several blocks, trying to maintain an awkward balance between vigilant and nonchalant.

As she got close to the park, she began looking for a place where she might observe it, and hopefully Tom, from concealment. One of the houses situated right alongside the park had an enormous RV in the driveway covered with a stretchy tan cover that fell all the way to the bottom of the tires. She worked her way to the house, concerned with the increase in the noise level she could hear from the park. She was getting too close for comfort.

Working her way in behind the hedges to the side of the house, she crawled along in the gap between them and the house. It was a prickly crawl, the ground covered in sharp needles from whatever kind of bushes these were. The needles poked through her clothing and gouged her skin as she crawled. She kept her eyes open for snakes. The area was home to copperheads and timber rattlers, as well as all the non-venomous snakes native to the region. None were pleasant to crawl up on in tight quarters.

When she reached the front steps, she was within twelve feet of the back of the RV. She studied it for a moment, noting the shape of a ladder beneath the cover. That ladder would lead her to the top of the RV, and perhaps the best vantage point she would find. When she was certain no one would see her, she shot across the gap between the hedges and the RV, ducking beneath the cover. She wasted no time crawling up the ladder as quickly and quietly as she could.

Fortunately, when she reached the top, she found that the cover was lifted above the RV's top by the air conditioning unit and several other things she didn't recognize, creating a kind of tent about eighteen inches tall so the cover was not lying flat on her. She also discovered that it was incredibly hot and stuffy under the cover.

To the rear of the RV, and hopefully more hidden from the park, she slid her pack off. On her belly, she then crawled as far forward as the tented section of the cover allowed. She removed her Esee knife from her belt and slipped it through the fabric of the cover, making a slit in it. With her fingers, she pried the slit open enough that she could see through it. It also allowed the entry of air that was just slightly cooler and more breathable than the air trapped inside with her.

It didn't take her long to spot Tom moving through the crowd for several reasons. For one, the track chair made him stand about a foot taller than everyone else, also propelling him at a smoother pace than that of people walking. Then there was the fact that the sight of the tall man in the track chair brought activity to a halt and caused the crowd to part for him.

Taking her eyes from him for a moment, Grace looked around to make sure that she had not drawn any attention while getting on top of the RV. She saw no one even close to her position. As long as she didn't move too much she thought she would be safe there.

Tom was still being escorted by the two armed men. She wondered if they'd even searched him. While he'd given her his two primary weapons, the AK pistols, he carried backup weapons in the form of a .38 revolver and a discreet knife. Both would likely be useless to him in this situation. The odds were against him.

In the center of the park there were a couple of picnic shelters and a stage for outdoor concerts. The picnic shelters had been walled off with blue tarps and black plastic, turning them into more weatherproof structures. Grace noted that there were more men with guns clustered around these shelters.

From her vantage point on the RV roof, Grace watched Tom being led into one of the picnic shelters. The tarps prevented her from seeing inside. Her heart raced, wondering if he was in danger. Part of her could just not reconcile the fact that these hikers and backpackers, a group of people she'd seen her entire life, were carrying guns and pointing them at people. It was simply not characteristic behavior.

She kept her monocular trained on the entrance to the picnic shelter, trying to see through the gap at the entrance. She could see nothing. After several futile moments of trying to make out what might be happening in there, she gave up and began moving the monocular around the area, trying to pick up any intelligence on the group.

She examined the cluster of shelters and the stage area, paying the most attention to the men with guns. Without fail, all appeared to be hikers and not local men. Their clothes gave them away. While some carried tactical weapons, others held hunting rifles, an assortment of bolt-action rifles and lever-action rifles.

Grace noted an odd thing about the weapons. Many of them had the same square emblem on the butt stock. At first she took this as a sign that the men were part of a group, that there was some type of logo or symbol unifying them. Then it hit her that she'd seen that sticker before. It took a moment to remember where, until she recognized it as the familiar price sticker of the local gun store. These guns were stolen.

Whatever had happened here had led this group of hikers to break into the gun store and clear out the inventory. She didn't know how she felt about that. Somehow it was comforting that this was not an occupying force, a gang who showed up with weapons to take over her town. On a tactical level, it also made her aware that the majority of these people would not be trained shooters and may not even be familiar with the operation of firearms. Were there to be some type of engagement or firefight that could be an advantage. Just from this preliminary intelligence gathering, if she had to take on a pair of guards, she would single out a pair with slower cycling weapons.

Having garnered that piece of information Grace scanned the crowd. She wanted to determine why the unarmed people remained there. Was it that they had no place to go? Were they being held prisoner? Were they being protected from some other force?

She could pick up little bits from what she saw. Since many backpackers carried them now, there was an array of solar chargers laid out charging phones. She could even see people attempting to text or call with them, the futility and frustration evident on their faces as their attempts were not successful.

Her experience of the last week told her that the communication infrastructure was spotty and intermittent. Sometimes you could get signal and get a text out but calls were very difficult. The center of town here only had limited service in the best of times, but if the generator providing power to the local cell tower had run out of fuel then they probably wouldn't be getting any signal at all.

She could see small clusters of intense discussion. Sometimes there would be one or more people in the cluster crying. They looked frustrated, desperate, and depressed. They looked like people who wanted to go home and were just trying to find a way to do so. Grace couldn't help but think if she were that desperate she would get up and do something about it. She wouldn't just lay there and cry about it.

Everything she saw made her think that perhaps these people were not prisoners but being guarded against an outside force. She wondered if that outside force may be the townspeople themselves. The relationship between the town and the hikers was complicated. There were times that the town could be clannish, redneck, and backwoodsy. Tourism was increasingly becoming their bread and butter. Although being welcoming to the tourists was smart business, it was easy to imagine that the welcoming attitude might wear thin when resources dwindled.

Catching movement at the picnic shelter, Grace retrained her monocular in that direction. Two men held the tent flap out of the way and Tom motored out the door in his track chair. Just outside the door he stopped and glanced around, perhaps looking for Grace in the woods and shadows on the fringe of the park. Part of her wanted to stand up and wave, telling him that she was there. Part of her worried that such an action might get her killed.

There was an intense discussion rising between Tom and his captors. He and one of the men he was talking to were becoming more animated. The gestures did not appear threatening but it was difficult to tell from a distance. It seemed to her that Tom might be asking questions. She was becoming more familiar with his gestures and that's what they seemed to indicate.

The men he was speaking to were pointing in a particular direction. It seemed clear to her now he was asking directions and they were providing them. The whole thing did not make any sense to her. If these people were not dangerous, why had they fired on the chopper? Why had they taken Tom prisoner? It just didn't make sense.

Tom extended a hand, shook with two of the men, then abruptly spun his track chair and began motoring off. Part of her wanted to slide down the ladder and take off running after him. Still, she could not forget what had taken place. She did not trust these people. She would not let them see her and she would not let them know she was armed.

Tom moved through the crowd toward the bridge. Once he crossed that bridge he would pick up the same bicycling trail that she had used to get to town. He would not be returning in the direction of the high school, but headed out of town, in the direction of her home.

She slid backwards on her belly, retreating from her observation post. Halfway across the RV roof she snagged her Go Bag and dragged it along with her. When she reached the ladder, she awkwardly felt around with her toe until she oriented herself and climbed down. At the bottom, she slung the pack on her back and used her shirttail to wipe the sweat from her face. It must have been 120° under that cover.

She retreated back through the yards and rejoined the alley, then took off running as hard as she could to the south. She knew what she was doing now. She had a plan. If she could follow this alley to the end, she would swing east and cross the river. There was a railroad bridge there from an active line but she doubted the trains were running anymore. Once across the bridge she could weave her way through more backyards and rejoin the trail. Hopefully soon after that, she could catch up with Tom.

Taking advantage of her familiarity with the town, Grace wove her way through back streets and intercepted Tom before he had gone too far. She approached him cautiously, calling out well before she was close to him. She didn't want to startle him because she knew something that the people back at the park didn't know, which was that Tom had a backup pistol hidden on his body. It was small caliber and low capacity, but in a pinch, he could have taken some people out. Grace didn't want to be the one that startled him and accidentally got taken out.

When he saw it was her, his face lit up. "Grace!"

She ran to him and threw her arms around him. Getting ridiculously emotional wasn't the plan but she couldn't seem to stop herself.

"So how come they let you go?" Grace asked.

"The whole situation wasn't what we thought. They believed we were here to take them out."

"Take them out?" Grace echoed.

Tom nodded. "As in arrest or kill them. There was some kind of altercation. The grocery store was nearly empty and the townspeople were blaming the hikers who'd come in for this festival. The sheriff tried to run them out of town and things got ugly."

Grace frowned. "I just can't picture that. I have a hard time not seeing hikers as hippies. I always think of them as anti-gun people."

"Not all hikers are hippies," Tom said. "I know several guys who came back from the Middle East and hiked long trails to clear their head. The guy who seems to be running the show back in the park there, he's one of those guys."

"A veteran?"

"A *combat* veteran. It was before your time, but there was a movie called *First Blood*, about this guy named Rambo, based on a

David Morrell book. Rambo was a Vietnam veteran who been pushed too far and snapped. This was the same kind of deal. You take a guy who has been in combat, who has spent a lot of time in the shit, and he can only be pushed so far."

"I can understand that but did they really think we were here to kill them?"

"Apparently they killed the sheriff and some folks who came with him. The hikers thought we were state police or something, like a SWAT team, come to kick ass and take names. That's why they fired on us, and why they rushed the football field."

"You were able to convince this guy we weren't a threat?"

"I didn't know the guy, but we knew the same places. We both spoke Army. I told him the deal and he could tell I was on the level. I said I was here to help you find your family."

"So do they even have a plan? What are they gonna do, just wait for rescue?"

"They don't know what they're doing. Haven't figured it out yet. It's a day-by-day thing. In my opinion, they're probably too big and diverse a group to come up with a single plan. They'll never agree on anything."

"I'm glad they let you go. I didn't have a plan either."

"I figured you left," he said. "I just asked directions to Whitetop Mountain and I was headed in that direction. I was going to find you."

"I never left you. After I came out of the woods, I followed you. I had to know what was going on. Even if I couldn't get to you, I had to know what was going on."

He'd been so distracted by their intense conversation that he just now noticed she didn't have all the gear he'd handed her on the football field earlier. "Did you have to cache the gear?"

She nodded. "I couldn't make any time carrying all that stuff. But now that we're a team again, I could be back with it in an hour."

"I hate to ask you to do that. I feel naked without my guns though. Besides, I'll probably need that solar charger for my track chair tomorrow, if not today."

"I don't mind doing it. It's a small price to pay to have you back on my team."

Tom scanned around them, taking in the neighborhood. "I just need a place to hide out and lay low until you get back."

Her brow furrowed in thought, then her face lit up. "I think I know a place. The lady who is staying with my mom lives right here in town. I know where her house is. I even know where her spare key is."

"Great. Let's take a look."

In less than ten minutes, Grace stopped in a gravel alley near the house. "You stay here," she said. "I'll check it out."

She detoured down another gravel alley and moved among an erratic cluster of houses. She took a concealed position between overflowing garbage cans and a nearby lilac bush, dropped to a knee, and observed the house.

She immediately noticed Mrs. Brown's car was gone. Grace took that as a good sign, hoping it meant that Mrs. Brown was with her mother and Dylan, just as she was supposed to be. There was an abundance of trash in the yard, which was the way that people had taken to disposing of their waste since most public services, including trash collection, were no longer available. The refuse did indicate to her that someone had maintained residence in the home after the collapse had occurred.

Grace really, really hoped that Mrs. Brown and her grandson were at her parents' house. If that was the case then the trash could belong to Mrs. Brown's daughter and her useless boyfriend. Grace had heard all about those two from Mrs. Brown and they sounded like real quality people.

Grace hoped the daughter and her boyfriend were not in the house now, but she was going to check it out anyway. She wanted the house as a place for Tom to hide out but she also wanted to make sure that Mrs. Brown hadn't given up on caring for her mom and just come home.

She was razor focused, what her dad would call *mission mind*. She accepted that checking the house was a step that had to be completed before she could go on to the next one so she just had to do it. She had always been taught not to allow obstacles to delay her any longer than practical. Once she knew what had to be done, she just had to do it. Acknowledge the obstacle, then plow through it.

She jogged to the back door, crouched down on the porch, and looked around behind her. Hearing nothing new, nothing concerning, she raised her hand and tapped lightly on the half glass door. Nothing. No footsteps, no voices, and of particular importance, no racking of a shotgun slide.

She tapped again. She wanted to give the occupants plenty of time to come to the door and lessen the chance of her being shot as an intruder. When no one came, she raised her hand and twisted the door handle. Just as she expected, it was locked. Grace duck-walked to the side and flipped over the welcome mat. Beneath it lay a shiny Kwikset key. She smiled.

Just where she remembered it being.

She slid the key into the door, unlocked it, and turned the handle. She pushed it open a couple of inches, positioning her body off to the side, hoping the wall would shield her if someone started firing. No shot came.

She leaned toward the opening and called, "Hello!"

No response.

"Hello!" she said louder.

Still nothing.

She shoved the door all the way open and it banged lightly against an interior wall. She pulled her body away from the opening, thinking that if there was going to be a shot this would be when it came.

"Hello?"

She made a quick check behind her again then eased inside the door. Her muscles were exerted from the run and had stiffened while she crouched. They protested as she stood fully but she didn't have time for discomfort. She flipped the safety off on her AR pistol and shouldered it.

While she was not exactly a one-woman SWAT team, Grace had trained for this. Although it would seem crazy to some families, she had the childhood memory of a snowy day in mid-winter when the family had been trapped in the house all day long. Using Nerf guns her dad made a game out of learning how to clear a house. She learned how to enter a room, how to turn a corner, and how to hold her weapon.

Her dad's method worked because the lessons stuck. As she got older, her dad had paid for them to have better training. She enjoyed shooting, and Grace had been a natural at the tactical training because she thrived on the physicality of it.

The first thing that hit her inside the house was that the kitchen was in a state Mrs. Brown would never have left it. Empty food packages were scattered around the kitchen and dirty dishes were piled up in the sink. Flies hovered around the sink and maggots writhed on crusty dishes.

The refrigerator door hung open, a rank odor reaching Grace's nose even from across the room. The garbage can overflowed into the floor. A can of beans on the top of the pile was alive with more maggots. Had there been more food in Grace's stomach, it would have joined the overflowing garbage. She gagged and fought the urge to throw up.

She tried to shut down the sensory overload. There was too much information here to take in and remain sharp. Unfortunately much of that sensory information was in the form of smells. Very unpleasant ones. She worked her way through the house, room to room, and found it empty. The rest of the house was as every bit as bad as the kitchen. The worst had been the bathroom. Whoever had been staying there had continued to use the toilet even when it could no longer be flushed. The waste was piled higher than seat level. If Grace were to try and shut the lid, she'd have to force it down.

She backed out of the disgusting bathroom, shutting the door behind her. She leaned back against the wall and fought to clear the nauseating odor from her nose but it pervaded this whole part of the house. She staggered back toward the kitchen trying to hold her breath, not allowing the rank odor into her nose and mouth. When she got to the kitchen she finally breathed again. Even sucking in air that reeked of rotting garbage was an improvement over that of human waste.

It wasn't until she got outside that she was certain the desire to vomit had passed. When she found Tom, he asked her what was wrong, but it was nothing she could describe. She just shook her head in disgust. He'd find out soon enough.

Mrs. Brown's backyard was sheltered by hedges and a tall fence. Rather than go back inside, the two sat down against the fence and had a snack. It was late in the day and they had not eaten since breakfast. In her Go Bag, Grace found some beef sticks, some Skittles, and some small plastic tubs of single serve peanut butter. It wasn't a gourmet meal but it pushed the hunger back.

When they finished, Grace handed her AR pistol over to Tom.

"Take that with you," he said, trying to give it back to her. "You might need it."

"I'm going to run. It will only slow me down. I've got my Glock and I'll be fine. I already know what's back there and how to avoid it. Besides, I'll have your guns when I come back."

Tom shrugged. He wasn't happy with the idea but Grace was not irrational. He had to trust that she'd thought things out and knew what she was doing. Still, things were never so simple as she described.

"What's our plan when you get back?"

Grace looked at her watch. "There'll still be a couple hours of light. How about when I get back we throw up that solar charger and put a little more juice into the batteries on your track chair? Maybe we even take a nap and recharge our own batteries. Head out of town in the dark."

"That'll work," Tom replied.

"The bike trail is pretty wide and smooth. It'll be easy going and may not be too hard on your batteries. If there's a decent moon we can probably see the trail without night vision. If it's too dark, we can use my night vision monocular and you can follow me. I've got some mini red chemlights. I can put one on my back. You just follow the red light."

"Sounds good. You get on the road then and you be very, *very* careful."

Grace stood and slipped on her Go Bag. Even though she wasn't taking the AR pistol she would not go anywhere without the Go Bag. It could do way more for her than the weapon ever could. She started out of the yard and then came back, leaned over, and kissed Tom, surprising both of them. Before he could get a word out, she bolted.

Chapter Fifteen

The Hardwick Farm

Dylan and Blake were playing in Blake's room. They were not excited about their movie being interrupted but, in the manner of children, they had already forgotten about it and gone on to other things. They were going through a box of Hot Wheels cars, arranging them and driving them around the floor. They didn't hear any of what was going on out in the yard. In fact, distracted by the cars, they had no idea Leslie Brown was unconscious in the yard.

Immersed in their play, they were startled when the bedroom door opened. They looked up, expecting to see Mrs. Brown telling them they could come back to their movie. Instead, Debbie's face peered at them through the crack. Dylan was startled, not expecting to see his mother. Blake was also startled because he did not recognize the woman and immediately wondered why she was in his house.

"Mommy?" Dylan said. "What are you doing here?" It was not excitement in his voice; it was fear.

"That's your mommy?" Blake asked.

Dylan nodded.

"How did she get to my house?" Blake asked.

Dylan shrugged. He didn't have any more idea how she got there than Blake did.

Debbie eased into the room and sat down on the floor. She took Dylan in her arms and hugged him. "I'm proud of you, baby. You did good. You helped Mommy."

Dylan stiffened. When he was with Paul and Debbie he never quite knew what to expect. Hugs were not always signs of affection. They could be precursors to something else. It was confusing and scary.

"Is Paul here?" Dylan asked anxiously.

Debbie nodded. "Yes, baby, of course Paul is with me. We came to see about that food you were telling us about. It's better than we imagined. I can't believe they have the power on here."

Blake shot Dylan an angry look. "You told them!"

Franklin Horton

Dylan look scared. "I'm sorry. She kept asking me things and I told her where I was and what I was doing. I told them you had food and power. I didn't mean to."

"You're not my friend anymore," Blake pouted.

Debbie shot Blake a look that scared him. "Don't you fuss at my baby, you little bastard. Family is supposed to stick together. He was just looking out for his mommy."

Blake kept his mouth shut but he was fuming inside. He could see why Dylan was scared of this woman. Even if she was Dylan's mother she did not seem like most of the other mothers he knew. There was nothing nice in this woman. She did not seem like the kind of mommy you could go to for a snack or a Band-Aid. She seemed like the kind of woman that hit children and talked mean to them.

A crash in the kitchen startled Blake. He sprang to his feet and started out of the room. Debbie's arm flashed out and snagged him around the waist.

"Now where do you think you're going? You just sit down."

"It's my house," Blake said. "I need to go check. I'm in charge while my Mommy is sick. I need to help Mrs. Brown."

Debbie let out a sigh and did not release her grip on him. "Mrs. Brown isn't feeling good. Mrs. Brown is *my* mommy, and if anybody checks on her, it will be me. Everything will be okay if you just do what you're told."

"This is my house," Blake insisted. "Let me go!" He struggled against Debbie, trying to get loose.

Without warning, Debbie lost her temper and slung Blake hard. He fell down on the hardwood floor and slid several feet. Hot Wheels cars went flying in all directions. Blake landed on his back, one of the cars gouging into him, and it hurt. His eyes watered and he fought back tears. He would not let this woman see him cry.

Debbie was suddenly on her feet and waving a finger in his direction. "You sit your ass down! You're not going anywhere. You listen to me or I'll give you a whipping you won't ever forget!"

Blake looked at her defiantly, still trying not to cry. He did not want to give her the satisfaction. Grown-ups weren't supposed to act like that. He'd never been around people like her. His back hurt so badly.

There was another crash in the kitchen and Debbie looked in that direction. It didn't sound like something spilled. It sounded like someone was raking things out of the cabinets. Debbie went back to the bedroom door and opened it, looking down the hall. She turned back to the children. "I'm going to go check on what's going on in the kitchen. I'm going to make sure Mrs. Brown is okay. If either of you comes out of this door you'll be sorry."

She looked hard at Blake, making sure he understood the warning. Blake glanced at Dylan and could see that he was terrified. Blake could tell he'd been talked to this way before. Maybe Dylan was telling the truth. Maybe she *had* tricked it out of him. When he looked back at the door, it was shut and Debbie was gone.

"Your mommy is mean," Blake said.

Dylan only nodded, his eyes wide with fear. "Paul is worse. He hits me."

"Your mommy talks like she'd hit you too. She said she'd hit us if we left the room."

"She might slap you in the face or spank you really, really hard. Paul hits you like a grown-up though."

Blake got up from the floor and went to his dresser. He opened the top drawer and dug around for a moment, coming out with a short fixed-blade knife in a plastic sheath. The knife was thin and had a skeletonized handle. There was a clip on the sheath and Blake clipped the knife inside his shorts, hiding the handle with his t-shirt.

Dylan watched curiously. "Are you going to kill my mommy?"

Blake looked at him seriously. "If she tries to hurt me or my family I'll kill her. That's what my daddy said to do."

Dylan thought for a moment. "I hope you kill Paul. He's a son-of-a-bitch."

Blake's mind raced. He wondered what had happened to Mrs. Brown. There was more going on, he could feel it. He thought about his mother and wondered if she was okay. He wanted to go check on her but he was afraid to leave the room, afraid Debbie or Paul would catch him and hurt him. Even with the knife, he was not sure he was big enough to fight them.

His parents talked to him about how to fight off bad people but the last thing they always said was run away and scream for help if you could. Here, at the remote cabin, that wouldn't help. There was nowhere to run and there was no one to hear him if he screamed.

Chapter Sixteen

The Hardwick Farm

Leslie didn't exactly regain consciousness as much as awareness seeped into her aching body like rain through a cheap raincoat. When she woke up, she realized that she had never hurt so badly in her entire life. Not after childbirth, not after her hysterectomy, not even with the death of her husband.

Neither eye would open, making it hard for her to tell whether she was really awake or just imagining the entire experience. She gingerly felt her face and immediately realized why her eyes wouldn't open. Her face was a distorted mass of swollen and scabby flesh. Between the swelling and the unexpected textures, the face she'd touched her entire life was nearly unrecognizable to her.

She put two fingers against what she thought was her eyelid and attempted to pry it open. A mix of blood and discharge had glued the lids together. As she forced them apart, she could feel eyelashes being torn out by the roots. When the lids of one eye were open, the light coming through the tiny slit made her head explode in pain. When she took her fingers away, the swelling forced it closed again. The only way she could keep it open enough to see was to keep her fingers in place, manually holding her eyelids open.

The pain in her head, in her eyes, and throughout the rest of her battered body led to her regain consciousness quickly. It was then that she became aware that her legs were cold and damp. She started to move a hand to her thighs and cried out from the pain in her arm. She knew this pain. She'd experienced it before, as a child. Her arm was fractured.

She tentatively moved the other arm and found it was still operational. She moved it to her thighs and realized she had lost bladder control while she was being kicked.

"That bastard," she hissed.

She tried to push herself up and found that she could not. The pain in her arm was too much and there was a new pain in her chest that she suspected may be broken ribs. She was lucky none had punctured a lung. She wouldn't have survived that. She wasn't certain that she'd even survive what had already been done to her.

With her good arm she felt for her back pocket, thinking of revenge. One thing that may conquer her pain and get her to her feet was the desire to go put a bullet in Paul's brain. The pistol was gone

Paul had probably remembered it from when she pulled it on him in the trailer and shot into the wall. There was no way he was going to leave a pistol on her. When she rolled over onto her stomach she experienced a broad spectrum of pain. Besides her broken ribs, her back hurt in a way that took her breath. She could feel things inside her, organs and such, that were swollen and displaced from their normal location. She accepted the fact she was probably going to die. She could only hope that she lived long enough to see Paul go first.

Using her good arm, she eventually worked her way into a kneeling position. From there, with several more minutes of excruciating effort, she was able to rise to her knees, and then stand. When she made it to her feet, her head spun and she saw white bursts of light behind her eyelids. She felt like she was going to faint.

Leslie threw her hands up to her face, trying to rub away the dizziness, and the movement of her broken arm was immediately sobering. She straightened, pried her eye apart, and looked around. She was in the yard and it was still daylight. Those were the only things of which she was sure. She could hear nothing from the house and see nothing of any consequence.

She could not go in there now. She was in no position to take Paul on. If he got a hold of her again he would kill her. She feared for her grandson but she would have to hope that somehow Debbie's maternal instinct would make her protect him until she could get herself together. Leslie did not know what else to do. She did not have any keys to the vehicles and knew of no other means of escape or getting help.

She spotted the barn and knew it would be open. The family didn't keep it locked. With her good arm, she kept her eyelids pinched open, holding her broken arm against her chest. In that manner she gimped on to the barn. It seemed to take forever and at one point she became concerned that someone might be following her. Had they been, there was nothing she could have done.

Once at the barn, she had to let go of her eye to slide the rolling barn door open. Pushing on the heavy door put a lot of stress on her torso and everything inside her screamed out in pain. She bit it down, literally biting her tongue to keep from screaming. When she had the door open just enough to get through, she slipped inside and pushed the door back closed.

She pried open her eyelid again and scanned the dark interior of the barn. There was enough light coming in around the cracks of the door that she could see well enough. This was where the family kept their tractor, animal feed, and livestock bedding. In one corner she saw several bales of hay. She went over and used her good arm to drag two hay bales side-by-side. There was an empty feed sack at her feet and she spread it out on the hay bales. As gently as she could, she eased her aching body onto on the hay bales and lay down. In a matter of minutes she was unconscious again.

Chapter Seventeen

Arthur Bridges' Compound

Robert and Sonyea again headed out of Arthur's compound, this time by means of an old logging road. Arthur made them a crude map showing the relationship between the logging road, the compound, and the surrounding public roads. While both of them were painfully aware that plans could change instantly, they had a general idea of what they wanted to do. They were going to follow the logging road to the cleared right-of-way beneath the high tension power lines and then follow it. It would be rough going but it would get them to the next stage of their journey.

Robert had ridden a horse before but not enough to brag about. He was not accustomed to their ways. Sonyea led and he followed behind, impressed at her grace and ease in the saddle. Not only was he uncomfortable in the saddle but he was distrusting of horses in general. He expected that any moment the horse would dump him to the ground out of spite and take off running. Sonyea had laughed at him when he mounted the horse and giggled every time she turned around and looked at him.

"Relax," she said. "You have a long ride ahead of you. You might as well make friends with the animal."

"I'm more comfortable with things with motors."

"The horse can be your best friend if you let it. This is an experience you and the horse are sharing together."

"We'll see. Not sure about that whole friendship thing."

Arthur's compound was bordered by national forest. Having bought property in such a location increased the amount of empty forest around him. When Robert and Sonyea neared the property boundary they began to encounter signs placed by Arthur warning stray hikers that they were entering a Live-Fire Training Range and were at risk of death if they continued.

The signs were accompanied by a simple infographic that showed a skull being penetrated with a bullet and a few drops of blood spraying in the air. The message was clear: Keep out or die. Arthur found the signs to be more effective than simple No Trespassing signs.

Just beyond the signs they encountered marker trees. Some had three yellow rings painted on them, others had two white rings. They were painted that way by surveyors to mark the boundaries of the property. Shortly past the painted trees something zipped past Robert's head. His first thought was that it had been a hummingbird or some type of insect. When he turned his head toward it, he saw a chunk splinter out of a tree.

It was a gunshot.

His mind raced. *Bullets flying. No report, must be suppressed.*

Get down.

We need to get down.

He kicked his horse and it lunged forward. Sonyea was confused. He gripped her reins and slid off his own horse. Just as his leg cleared the saddle, suppressed gunfire stitched its side. The animal reared and dropped with an unnerving scream.

Robert grabbed Sonyea around the waist and dragged her from the back of her horse. She fell to the ground and he threw himself on top of her. His horse kicked and cried out. Sonyea's horse was terrified by the noise of the dying animal and bolted, taking off deep into the woods.

Robert drew his pistol and began firing over top of the injured horse. He couldn't see what he was firing at and didn't even know where to aim. He blasted away blindly, trying to keep the shooter from having such an easy job of it. Robert rolled away from the horse and stood up behind a broad poplar tree. He started to shoot around it but gunfire shredded the bark in front of his face, spraying him with splinters. He ducked back.

"Are you okay?" he called to Sonyea.

She was stroking the now-still horse and crying. She didn't respond.

"Are you okay?" he repeated.

Yes," she moaned. "I think so."

"We have to get outta here."

"How?"

She continued to stroke the horse and speak softly to it. It shuddered and stopped breathing. Sonyea began sobbing.

Robert's AR pistol was dangling around his neck on a single-point sling. He brought up the weapon and flipped the safety off. He fired two rounds blindly around the corner of the tree, following up with a quick glance to see if he could spot the shooter.

The forest was dense, the trees still leafed-out. The sun shining through the leaves created a carpet of dappled light that made it difficult to spot anything in the forest. There were so many chaotic patterns going on here naturally that even someone wearing street clothes would be difficult to spot. If the shooter had on camo, Robert didn't have a chance in hell of finding him.

"Were going to have to back out of here and get back to the compound. We'll retreat one tree at a time and try to cover each other. Do you still have a weapon?"

Sonyea reached to her hip and felt for her pistol. It was locked in the holster right where she expected it to be. She had lost the shotgun. She'd wrapped the sling around her saddle horn and it was probably still dangling there. She couldn't see the horse anywhere. It was probably long gone.

"I've got my pistol. That's it."

"It'll have to do. Get ready. I'm going to shoot. When I do, you go back to the next closest tree that will cover you. Zigzag, make yourself a hard target."

She nodded but Robert was focused on the woods. He didn't see her gesture.

"Did you hear me?"

"Yes," she replied shakily.

Robert fired a blind shot around the corner, then he drew the weapon to his shoulder and fired around the corner. At his first shot, Sonyea was on her feet and sprinting for the nearest tree. Robert heard the spitting sound of suppressed fire. Rounds chased Sonyea, throwing up showers of leaves from the forest floor, but none reached her. Robert ducked back behind the tree and flattened himself against it.

"You good?" he asked.

"I'm good. Tell me when you're ready and I'll fire."

"Go!"

Sonyea curled around the tree and sent five evenly spaced rounds into the forest. Robert pushed away from his tree, sprinting for a fat white oak. He tried to zigzag but was disappointed in his agility and speed. He'd trained for all kinds of things but this was not one of them.

He reached his target tree just as a line of fire raked up the side of it. Chunks of bark bit into his arm and neck. He flinched and slapped a hand to his neck. There was blood but it was just scratches.

"I'm good," he called. "You ready?"

When she confirmed that she was, Robert fired aggressively behind them. Shortly, Sonyea called to him that she was secure again. So it went, tree to tree, and with blind gunfire until they were able to conceal themselves behind a ridge and begin running. Robert did not like the feeling of that. He was certain that at any moment the shooter would cut them off. He may even have a partner and the two of them would box Robert and Sonyea in.

The pair had no radio with which to call for help. Their only hope was that their gunfire would draw reinforcements as it had earlier. It did. Their retreat came to a sudden stop when three men in ghillie suits burst from cover and began shouting orders at them. The pair skidded to a halt and threw their hands up.

"Identify yourselves!" one of the men barked.

"We're returning to the compound. I'm Robert Hardwick! We took fire and got turned around!" Robert was certain these were Arthur's men. He and Sonyea had left on horses and were returning on foot. They were lucky they weren't shot.

The man spoke into his radio. When he received instructions he ran to Robert, his weapon raised and at the ready. He patted Robert on the back.

"Go! Go!"

The man covered their retreat. The other two men in ghillie suits melted back into the shadows.

Robert and Sonyea fled through the woods. They'd come nearly a mile on the horses and it took them a good bit longer to get back on foot. Behind them they heard what they assumed to be the men in ghillie suits engaging the man or men who'd shot at them.

A bit further up the logging road they ran into Arthur and the doctor on a side-by-side ATV. They were still geared up from earlier. Each carried rifles in holders mounted on the ATV. Arthur was driving and stopped the machine.

"Are you two okay? Did you get hit?"

"Don't know about okay but not hit," Robert said. He was breathing hard as the adrenaline still surged through his body. His hands were shaking. Being shot at would do that to a person.

The doctor wasn't taking Robert's word for it. He was checking out Sonyea. She was still upset about losing the horse and the entire experience of coming under attack. He mistook her emotional state for an indication that she'd been injured.

She pushed him away. "I'm fine, I'm fine."

The doctor backed off.

The radio in a case on Arthur's vest chirped. "*Thermal shows one shooter. Has a shooting position in a tree stand.*"

Arthur plucked his radio from his vest and pushed the transmit button. "Engage the target."

There was a loud boom from the direction Robert and Sonyea had come from. It was louder than all the previous gunfire. To Robert it sounded like a single round from a long-range rifle. There was a single follow-up shot, then silence.

"*Target down,*" came the update.

"We're surrounded," Sonyea said.

"You may be right," Arthur said. "They can only tighten the noose if it's completely around our necks."

"Then we're not getting out of here," Robert said.

"Not now," Arthur replied.

Chapter Eighteen

The Hardwick Farm

Since her surgery Teresa Hardwick could not sleep for long periods of time. She became uncomfortable if she remained in one position too long. A series of naps taken throughout the day seemed to be working best for her. She hadn't been asleep that long when she heard the rattle of a pill bottle on her nightstand. She dispensed her own medications so there was no reason that anyone else would be touching the bottles. She opened her eyes.

At her bedside stood a scraggly-looking stranger. He was reading her pill bottle with a jagged smile breaking across his face. Terrified, Teresa snapped her eyes shut, hoping she could play possum until he was gone. It didn't work. He had caught the flicker of movement.

"I saw that, woman. I know you're awake. Don't be trying to fool me."

Teresa still did not open her eyes. She did not want to see the man again. Did not want to see him standing over her in her most sacred and personal space.

"Open your eyes," he demanded.

Teresa willed her eyes to open. They fluttered as she forced them. She found herself staring into the barrel of a revolver.

"I'm taking these pills and I'm going out the door. You stay in the bed. You move out of this bed and I'll give you some pain these pills won't even touch."

Teresa did not react, did not know *how* to react. The man backed away from her, exiting her bedroom door and shutting it behind him. She could hear some rustling at the knob, a few thumps, and then it was silent.

She immediately thought of Blake, wondering where he was and if the stranger had hurt him. Forgetting about her incision, she tried to quickly raise up and sharp pain wracked her body. The spasm was so intense it threw her backward on the bed. She felt a pulling deep inside her, a tearing pain that she could not fight her way through.

She ended up flat on the bed sucking in air through gritted teeth. She could do this, but she would have to take it easier. She could not force it. She rolled to her side and carefully raised herself onto her elbow. From there she pushed herself to a sitting position and paused. She breathed deeply. Carefully, she rose to a standing position.

You can do this, she told herself.

Despite the pain, she made it. A cold sweat broke out all over her body. Once on her feet she leaned toward the nightstand and picked up a copy of Truman Capote's *In Cold Blood* from a stack of books on her nightstand and flipped it open. It was a hollow book and inside was a Glock 19.

If the Hardwick family had an official handgun it was the Glock 19. If her husband was telling her the truth, they owned six of them. If he was like most gun lovers, he told her they owned six but they actually owned ten. She drew back the slide and confirmed there was one in the pipe. There were two spare mags in the hollow book and she went to stash them in her pocket, only then becoming aware that she was wearing the kind of frilly pajamas that women wore when they were sick or in the hospital. The only pockets were decorative. They would not hold the Glock or the magazines. Even the waistband was not substantial enough to tuck a pistol into.

Holding the magazines in one hand and the pistol in the other she moved to the door and twisted the knob. It turned easily in her hand. She pulled to crack it open and peer into the hallway. It would not budge. She tugged harder and could feel that the door moved slightly but there was not enough movement to even create a gap that she could look out.

She tugged even harder and immediately regretted it. The movement engaged the core muscles that had been sliced through during her surgical procedure. A gasp of pain escaped her and she released the knob to grip her abdomen. She took a step back from the door and tried to calm her breathing.

The pain and frustration made tears rise within her. That she did not know what was happening with her son and could not escape this room was terrifying. It was the worst torture imaginable, combined with the fact that she was physically impaired and in no condition to fight.

The only other way out of the room was the window. She had looked out this window thousands of times since they had lived in this home but she assessed the view differently this time. She was looking for an escape route but found none. The window was about sixteen feet off the ground. There was nothing she could climb down and nothing she could jump onto. She wasn't in any condition to do any of those things anyway.

Teresa took a moment to calm herself. She was trapped for now and panicking wouldn't help anything. She needed to focus on the things that she could actually control. The first thing she was going to do was find some clothes, preferably something with functional pockets.

She went to the closet and found a pair of oversized sweatpants. They were chosen for no other reason than that she hoped they would be loose around her incision. She put them on, then struggled with socks and tennis shoes. She applied more thick gauze over the incision, creating a padded barrier between the wound and her clothing. When that was done she slipped on a button-up shirt.

While she was in the closet dressing she recalled that her husband kept a shotgun in there. She winced at the thought of the recoil. She didn't know if she could fire it without doing permanent damage to herself.

Now fully clothed she put the spare magazines in the shirt pockets and returned to the door. She studied it, then she felt like an idiot. She wasn't trapped at all. The door opened inward. While he had obviously restrained the handle so that she could not swing the door open the conventional way, there were other options. The hinges were on her side. If she simply removed the pins she could pry the door out of the opening.

She went to her nightstand and pulled open the top drawer where she kept a small Phillips screwdriver she used for changing batteries in Blake's toys. She raked her fingers through the drawer, through spare batteries, spare shoelaces, old pairs of glasses, and small flashlights. She finally found the screwdriver when it jabbed her in the hand.

She returned to the door and slid the screwdriver into the bottom of the hinge and up against the tip of the hinge pin. Using her palm and trying to make as little noise as possible, she drove the screwdriver upward. It took several firm hits before the pin moved and began to slip upward. Each tap of her palm gained more ground and put her closer to escape. In just a few minutes she had the pin high enough that she was able to pull it free.

Soon, she had all the pins removed. Friction still held the door in place. She could easily pry the door out of the frame with the screwdriver. But what then?

Teresa knew that taking the door off the hinges was a step that could not be undone. Once the door was off its hinges and she was in the hallway she was committed to the fight. Unfortunately, the waistband of the sweatpants was too loose to hold the Glock. She started to bend over and set the gun at her feet while she worked on the door but the pain made it difficult. She chose to leave it on the nightstand for now. It would only be a few steps away.

Returning to the door, she jammed the tiny Phillips bit into the gap at the hinge side of the door. She pushed sideways against the screwdriver and the door shifted in the frame. The hinges went out of alignment, showing that her effort was working. She pushed harder and the halves of the hinges separated. The door dropped to the floor with a slight thud and she hissed in frustration. She used her fingers and gripped the half of the hinge that was screwed to the door. She used that as a handle to swing the door inward. As the door moved, the bolt withdrew from the strike. In seconds the door was standing completely free and unattached to the frame.

While this exhilarated her, it also presented her with a dilemma that she had not fully planned for. She could not lift the door because it required using all of the muscles compromised by her hysterectomy. Lifting with both arms required the core, and her core was damaged. She had no choice but to try to slide the door to the side and hope that it didn't make too much noise. She pushed on it, cringing at the wood-on-wood grating noise. When there was just enough opening for her to get through, she leaned the door against the wall and shuffled to the nightstand where she retrieved her Glock 19.

She held the gun with both hands. It was in front of her but her elbows were bent, the weapon drawn back against her body. From this position she could shoot quickly, but it was not extended so far as someone would easily be able to yank it from her hands. At the doorframe, she peered around the corner. The hallway light was on and there was no one in the hall. She could hear noise coming from the kitchen, shuffling and banging. There was the hushed murmur of conversation. The door to Blake's room was closed.

She ventured halfway around the corner and into the hallway, raising her gun ahead of her. She kept her trigger finger extended and outside of the trigger guard. She wanted that extra second to process what she was seeing in case one of the children or Leslie bolted out into the hallway. She shuffled forward, too scared to even breathe. Her heart was racing and her mind was not far behind it. Who was this man in her house and where was her child? Where was Leslie?

When she reached her son's door she paused and listened. She heard nothing. She leaned closer to the door and placed her ear against it. Inside she could hear the low murmur of voices. It sounded like children. She hoped that it was Dylan and Blake and that they were okay. She watched the end of the hallway, toward the kitchen. She placed her hand on the doorknob and twisted it slowly. It was not locked and she heard the mechanical sound of the lock's mechanism, the bolt retracting.

When she was certain the door would open freely, she switched her attention from the hallway to the door in front of her. She pushed and it began to swing open, creaking slightly, and the sound was immense in the quiet house. She looked back toward the kitchen again and saw nothing. She pulled her gun from that direction toward the room, holding it at the ready, and looked inside. Blake and Dylan sat terrified, paralyzed with fear. They'd seen the doorknob turning and did not know who was coming for them.

Teresa pushed the door closed behind her, turning the knob and then releasing it slowly after the door was pushed into place. She went to her son and hugged him, smoothing his hair with her hand. He hugged her back and it hurt, but the pain was a small price to feel those arms wrapped around her.

"Are you two okay?" Teresa asked.

"I'm scared," Blake said.

Teresa looked at Dylan and he nodded, wide-eyed. She'd never seen such a terrified child.

Dylan was staring at the gun in Teresa's hand. "Are you going to shoot my mommy?" he asked.

"Your mommy?" Teresa said, confused.

"His mommy is Mrs. Brown's daughter," Blake explained.

Teresa acknowledged this with the sound that indicated it was all making sense now. "Is your mom's boyfriend here with her?"

Dylan nodded. "Paul," he stated, as if the name explained everything.

Teresa assumed that whoever was in her house stealing her medication was a scumbag but this confirmed it. She'd heard Leslie's stories about her daughter and Paul, her piece-of-shit boyfriend. None of the stories were good.

"Boys, we have to get out of here and we may not have much time. I need you all to do exactly as I say, exactly *when* I say. I don't plan on shooting your mommy unless she tries to hurt me or one of you. Do you understand?"

Blake nodded in acknowledgment, and Dylan reluctantly nodded as well.

"There were noises," Blake said. "Like someone making a mess."

Teresa held a hand up to stop him. "None of that matters now. We need to go to the basement. We're going to the Ready Room. Dylan, you just have to trust us for now. Do you understand?"

The boys nodded again.

"I'm going to open this door and step into the hall," Teresa said. "I'm going to watch and make sure no one comes after us. I need you two to go to the end of the hall and climb through the heat duct in the wall."

Dylan raised his hand as if he had a question but Teresa waved him off. "We don't have time for questions now. Blake, do you remember how I showed you to go through the heat duct?"

"Yes, Mommy."

"So we go down the hall and through the heat duct. I will follow behind you and close it. That will put us in the laundry room. From the laundry room we take the steps into the basement. Blake, if you're to the Ready Room first you open the door. You and Dylan go inside and shut it behind you. If I'm not behind you, go on in there and don't come out. Everything you need is in there. You stay in until one of us comes to get you."

"You're coming too, aren't you?" Blake asked nervously.

"I plan on it. If the bad man slows me down, I may have to meet you in there later."

Teresa clapped her hands. "Okay. We go now."

She went to the door and eased it open, peering through the crack into the hallway. Seeing no one, she opened the door fully and stepped into the hall, waving behind her for Dylan and Blake to come along.

Blake shot out the door and swung to the right with Dylan behind him. They ran to the end of the hall and Dylan stared at the heat duct, not quite understanding what to do. Blake took over. The cold air return in the lower half of the wall was actually a dummy. There was no ductwork hooked to it. Blake flipped two levers and the louvered white door flipped down. He yanked the filter out of the way and set it to the side. Behind that filter was another filter installed in a matching dummy cold air return in the laundry room. Blake shoved his hand into the second filter and it flew out of the way, dropping the hinged door on the other side.

As they'd practiced before, he crawled through the door on his hands and knees. Once through, he gestured at Dylan to follow. Teresa alternated between watching the boys and the end of the hall. She was concerned that the white steel cover dropping in the laundry room had made more noise than she had anticipated. Once Dylan was through the opening Blake gestured for her to come along. She waved a hand at him urgently, prompting him to go ahead and go to the basement. She didn't want him waiting on her.

Keeping her eyes on the end of the hall, Teresa backed toward the opening. When she was there, she gingerly dropped to all fours and began backing through the door. It would have been easier to go through headfirst but she did not want to leave her back exposed. It was a good thing too. When she was halfway through the opening, Debbie came around the corner.

Debbie was walking loose-limbed, as if she was intoxicated. Maybe she had been into Teresa's pain pills. It took her a moment to register the open door and then anger flashed across her face. She assumed the kids had not listened to her. Then she noticed Teresa at the end of the hall, half her body protruding from the opening in the wall. For a moment Debbie seemed unable to process what was going on in front of her. Then she yelled, "Hey!"

Teresa raised the Glock 19 with one hand and fired two shots into the wall alongside Debbie. Drywall dust sprayed Debbie and she flinched, staggering back down the hall and jumping around the corner. Teresa backed through the opening, the effort wracking her body with pain.

Just as she retreated fully through the opening, the man she'd seen in her bedroom earlier came around the corner, the revolver in his hand. This time Teresa did not fire to warn. She aimed center mass and popped off two rounds. Her firing position was awkward and both rounds missed but sent Paul careening to the side. Teresa rolled away from the opening, then threw a hand on the washing machine to pull herself onto her feet, screaming from the effort.

She left the laundry room and headed toward the basement door. She gripped the handrail, concentrating on staying on her feet. She felt lightheaded from the pain, and sweat rolled from her body. Behind her she could hear yelling and loud footsteps as the intruders clambered through the house trying to find where she and the children had gone.

In the basement she could see the door to the Ready Room. Just as she'd instructed, Blake had closed it behind him. The door was not far away from her now, fully half of the basement being consumed by the structure. She heard footsteps getting closer. They were at the top of the stairs now.

She heard them starting down the basement steps. She spun, the effort again producing a cry of pain that forced its way from her. She fired by reflex, three shots hitting around the intruder's feet and forcing them back up the steps. She reached the door and punched in the four-digit combination. There was a whir of tiny motors within the electronic lock. When the light on the lock turned green, she heaved it open and lunged inside. Blake and Dylan sat waiting on her, terrified looks on their faces. Certain now that they were inside with her, she slammed the door, and it locked automatically behind her. For extra protection, she threw the heavy draw bolt.

They were sealed inside now. They were safe.

With the door locked behind her, Teresa stepped away from it as if people may come bursting through after her. They couldn't, but she was still in fight mode, prepared for anything. She hugged Dylan and Blake to her. They embraced her too tightly, causing her to grimace from the pain.

"Let's get away from the door," she said, hoping it would encourage them to release their hold on her.

The Ready Room was not some high tech, armored bunker. In fact, it was very low-tech. Robert had a background in construction and had built the room using common construction techniques to serve multiple purposes for the family. It took up roughly half of the basement. As the house was being constructed, Robert had a dividing wall of twelve-inch cinderblock laid across the middle of the floor. The cinderblocks were anchored into the concrete slab. When the block wall was laid, vertical and horizontal reinforcement was added and the twelve-inch blocks were concreted solid.

When the wall was just below the level of the first floor, light steel beams were added to support the ceiling. Corrugated steel decking was welded on top of the beams and a concrete slab was poured. The door into the Ready Room was a fairly standard commercial-grade exterior door. It was of solid steel construction but the front and back face of the door featured an additional layer of 3/8 inch steel plate. It was fairly common steel that was easy to get and the two layers sandwiched against the door would stop most bullets.

The door hung on heavy duty ball bearing hinges. The door hardware was commercial grade vandal-resistant hardware. Because the lock could theoretically be compromised if it were damaged enough, the inside of the Ready Room featured a large half-inch diameter draw bolt that would further secure the door to the block wall. There were also hooks that would allow rectangular steel tubes to be used to barricade the door.

The room could inevitably be breached if someone were persistent enough, but the room had another purpose that would help if the room was compromised. It also served as the family's primary gun safe. Robert also had a gun safe upstairs in the bedroom to keep a selection of weapons at hand, but he had always dreamed of having a gun room where you could display weapons under cool LED lighting. One entire wall of the bunker was set up in such a manner. A special commercial display system with weapon hooks displayed a small armory of weapons that Robert had collected over the years. A benchtop allowed him to clean and work on them. Cabinets underneath held ammunition, cleaning kits, and spare parts.

The back wall of the Ready Room held bunks, each with a rolled up mattress, a sleeping bag, and a pillow. When no one was sleeping on them, the bunks were also used for shelving and contained a variety of stored foods. Along another wall, wire rack shelving held more food and camping gear. There was a laundry sink connected to the gravity-fed water system. In the event that the water supply failed, there were also two blue barrels storing 110 gallons of drinkable water.

There were 12-volt batteries and a charge controller integrated into an outside solar panel. The batteries powered an inverter and LED lights in the ceiling. There was a variety of lanterns and flashlights, and several PVC pipes penetrating the outside wall provided ventilation. The intakes and outlets were offset to prevent someone from shooting through them. Each contained screening to keep out insects. The Ready Room was also designed to function as a tornado shelter for those rare occasions a tornado or microburst would pop up in the mountains.

They were startled by a sudden burst of pounding against the heavy door. It could have been a fist or even a foot. Someone was shouting at them but they could not make out what was being said. Teresa gathered the children around her again just as the loud report of a weapon could be heard. The idiot had fired against the door. Even through the layered steel door she could hear the ricochet of the round in the cinderblock room. She hoped they would be smart enough not to try that again. Deciding to revise that wish, she instead hoped that the round ricocheted through both of them and left them dead.

"Can they get in?" Dylan asked.

"No, Dylan. Were safe."

Teresa suddenly felt lightheaded and drained. It was the adrenaline leaving her. "Let's fold out some of these bunks. I need to sit down and rest a second. You two pick out where you want to sleep."

Dylan and Blake scrambled to get top bunks. Because Teresa was in pain, the boys set the boxes and buckets of food down to clear off their bunks. While they were doing that, Teresa chose the bunk that required the least work to set up. She rolled out the mattress, put the sleeping bag on it, and laid down. It was only when she was stretched out that she realized she was as weak as a kitten. Had the door burst open at that moment and someone came for them, she was not even sure she could get to her feet and defend herself.

"Blake, honey, can you go to the first-aid kit and get me an ibuprofen? I also need one of those red bottles of Gatorade off the shelf."

Blake monkeyed down from his bunk and went to the shelf labeled *medical supplies*. There were several first-aid kits there and Blake chose the one nearest him. After a little fumbling around he pulled out a paper packet of ibuprofen, took a Gatorade from the shelf, and took his mother the medicine and the drink.

"Are you okay, Mommy?"

Teresa tore open the paper pouch and took the ibuprofen. She washed it down with some Gatorade and then nodded, collapsing back onto the pillow. She was so tired that her stomach churned with nausea. "All that moving around just wore Mommy out. I'll be okay. I just need to rest for a minute. Make sure Dylan knows that we don't open that door for *any* reason. Do you understand?"

Blake nodded. "I'll tell him."

"Don't just tell him," Teresa said sharply. "If for some reason he tries, don't let him. If that door opens those people may hurt us."

"I know, I saw that woman. I know she's bad."

"How do we go to the bathroom?" Dylan asked from the top bunk.

"Show him, Blake," Teresa said. "Mommy's going to rest."

Blake went to the corner of the room where a shower curtain was hanging that walled off the corner for privacy. Blake got a camping toilet from the shelf and set it up. There were several boxes of chemical treatment bags and he installed one on the toilet. When those were gone there were heavy-duty trash compactor bags as backup. Teresa hoped they would not be there long enough for that.

She closed her eyes. She could hear nothing outside now. She didn't feel like it was particularly a safe moment to take a nap, but at this point it felt like the decision was beyond her control. While the children studied the chemical toilet, she faded into unconsciousness.

Chapter Nineteen

Arthur Bridges' Compound

There was a chirp from Arthur's radio pouch. "*I have a drone incoming,*" came the radio transmission.

Robert and Sonyea were standing on the porch with Arthur, the doctor, and Kevin Cole. Everyone was still on high alert. Arthur pulled the radio from its pouch.

"Knock it out of the sky," he said into the radio.

No sooner had he taken his thumb off the transmit button than a pair of shotgun blasts shook the compound.

"You get it?" Arthur asked.

"*That's affirmative. Should we retrieve it?*"

"Use caution. Check it with binoculars first. Try to make sure it doesn't have anything lethal strapped to it."

"*Roger that.*"

"It would be good to know if it's civilian or military," Kevin said. "That could tell us a little about who we might be dealing with."

"*It looks like there's a clear tube attached to it with a piece of paper inside,*" the guard reported over the radio. "*Should we retrieve it?*"

Arthur looked around to see what the others thought.

"If the purpose is to send us a message, it seems unlikely it would be booby-trapped," Kevin said. "That would defeat the purpose."

"Give us your location and we'll come to you," Arthur instructed the guard. "Don't do anything until we get there."

The group loaded up in Arthur's side-by-side and went to the crash site. Kevin insisted on examining the drone with binoculars before approaching it.

"That's a civilian drone. Looks like a ninety-nine dollar retail store version if you ask me. It's the kind you'd send out if you didn't expect it to come back," Kevin said.

Arthur approached the drone and examined it closely. Attached to its underside was a lightweight clear plastic tube that looked like the same kind of container realtors attached to their For Sale signs so they could leave flyers inside it. Inside was a sheet of white paper with a message written on it.

He bent down and unscrewed the red cap from the end of the clear tube, pulled out the rolled message, and studied it. The tube and the message were peppered with holes from the shotgun.

Arthur read aloud, "To the residents of the compound. Put down your weapons and exit empty-handed through the front gate and you will not be harmed. Otherwise, we take the compound and kill everyone inside."

"They don't mince words, do they?" Robert said.

"They sure don't," Arthur said.

"Did they give a timeframe for our decision?" Sonyea asked.

"The efficiency of this operation further convinces me that it's someone who's had their eye on your compound for a while," Kevin said. "This is someone who knows what you have and what your capabilities are. They seem to understand the skill level, and potentially the *threat* level, of the occupants. That has to indicate they have been gathering intelligence on your operation since before things collapsed."

"So what do we do?" Sonyea asked.

Arthur balled up the note and casually threw it to the side. "I ain't giving them shit."

"Agreed," Kevin said.

"Robert and Sonyea," Arthur said, "I know you two want out of here but I would strongly encourage you to wait this thing out and see what happens."

"I'm in agreement," Kevin said. "You got lucky twice. You might not be next time."

Arthur turned to the man who had shot the drone down. He had some degree of seniority among the men serving as guards but the organizational structure had never been shared with Robert. "Did your men retrieve the body of the shooter who ambushed Sonyea and Robert?"

"I sent an ATV down there but they're not back yet. They're proceeding cautiously in case there are other shooters or booby-traps," the man replied.

Arthur pulled his radio out. "Where you at with that trash pickup?" He held the radio at chest level, waiting for a response.

In a moment there was a voice, the whine of an ATV engine behind it. *"Got it. On my way back. Maybe five minutes."*

"Deliver it to my house," Arthur said. "I'll meet you there."

Kevin pointed at the drone. "You might want to totally destroy that thing just in case it has any electronic goodies in it. There could be a camera, microphone, or tracking device intended to gather intelligence about us."

"Good point," Arthur said. He turned to his senior man. "Take a hammer to it. Turn it into dust."

They loaded back into the ATV and returned to Arthur's house, where they found a man in another side-by-side waiting for them. In the bed of the vehicle was a green canvas tarp covering what everyone assumed to be the body. Arthur headed straight for it and went to draw back the tarp.

"Hold up," the doctor said. He turned to Sonyea. "Are you sure you want to see this?"

She frowned at him. "I don't hear you asking anyone else that question."

The doctor melted under her glare. "I apologize."

"Apology accepted. Go ahead, Arthur."

Arthur cast the doctor a disapproving glance then rolled the tarp off the dead man. Beneath it lay a man in a camo uniform and battle gear. He had a camo bandana tied around his head and his face was smudged with camo paint. There was a chest wound that had soaked the man's gear with drying blood.

Arthur examined the chest rig. "He's wearing plates. What did they get him with?"

"They used the .338 with AP rounds," the driver replied.

"We use special .338 Lapua armor-piercing rounds," Arthur said to Kevin. "The projectile is tungsten carbide."

"That's a devastating round," Kevin said.

"Yeah, don't roll him over," the driver cautioned, "or you'll see just how devastating."

"What does the body tell us?" Arthur asked the group.

"I see well-worn gear that looks like Crye Precision to me," Robert said. "The boots are desert tan though, which makes me think this guy may have been a security contractor in the Middle East."

"I agree," Kevin said. "This is all top-end gear and it's got a lot of use on it. Everything is frayed and battle-worn. Did you retrieve his weapon?"

The driver reached inside the cab of the side-by-side and removed a short-barreled rifle. He confirmed that the weapon was clear before handing it to Kevin, who checked it again for himself.

"H&K 416?" Robert asked.

"That's right," Kevin said. "Eleven-inch barrel and a suppressor. Looks like a government issue weapon."

"He's with the government?" Sonyea asked. "*That's* who's trying to get in here?" She was not comfortable with that thought.

"Probably not," Arthur said. "It just means that whoever is trying to get in has access to experienced men and the best gear."

"That's still concerning," the doctor said.

"Don't throw in the hat yet," Arthur said. "Whoever sent this man is not the only one with access to good men and good gear."

"What's the plan?" Robert asked.

"Don't have one," Arthur admitted. "But I will when we talk again."

Chapter Twenty

Damascus, VA

When Grace awoke on the floor of Leslie Brown's kitchen she was stiff and uncomfortable. There was nothing worse than overexerting your muscles then sleeping on a hard surface. Despite her physical conditioning, her body felt like it was full of broken glass when she sat up. Everything hurt.

She stood up, knowing that motion was the best remedy for the pain, despite the initial resistance. It was dark and the moon was up, shining pale light through the kitchen window. She turned from the window to wake Tom but found that her movement had already done the job. He was sitting up, leaned back against the wall.

"Not the best sleep I've ever had," he said.

"No kidding. I feel like a garbage bag of broken beer bottles."

Before they'd stretched out for their nap, they prepared their gear for the trip out of town. They each had headlights on in case they needed them. The only thing that remained to be packed up was the solar charger for Tom's track chair.

Tom took charge of that, disconnecting the alligator clips from the battery while Grace went outside and rolled up the solar panel. She placed it on the back of the track chair, securing it with bungee cords. The cable that connected the solar panel to the battery was rolled up and stashed in Tom's Go Bag.

Tom strapped himself into the track chair while Grace helped him with his Go Bag. Since they were leaving under cover of darkness they weren't as concerned about people noticing they were carrying weapons. Tom even went as far as to mount his AK pistols on the two swivel mounts he had fabricated for the track chair. The gimbal mounts would allow him to swivel the two pistols in almost any direction and shoot like he was the tail gunner on an aircraft. Grace put on her own Go Bag, then the single-point sling for her AR pistol.

Her familiarity with the street layout, combined with the moonlight, made them able to negotiate their way out of the town without resorting to headlamps or night vision. While they had a better idea about what had taken place in town, it was still empty and eerily quiet.

On their way out of town they didn't see a single light in any of the houses, didn't hear any whispering, nor saw any indications of life at all in the rest of the houses. Had the people been afraid for their life and fled? Were they just hunkered down like the backpackers in the park, waiting for someone to come in and rescue them?

The path they followed from Mrs. Brown's took them through an alley, down a little side street, and eventually connected them back with the bicycle path they had been on earlier. It was a rails-to-trails conversion, an old railroad bed in which the tracks had been pulled up to create a multiuse trail. People bicycled by the thousands on the trail in the summer. It was also used in lesser numbers by hikers and equestrians.

"I've never asked about the specs of your chair," Grace said, her voice barely above a whisper. "How fast and long can it go?"

"Up to four miles per hour. Like most battery-operated machines, operating at maximum speed drains the batteries a lot faster. If I throttle it back just a little I get maximum efficiency. At the most efficient pace and on flat terrain it has a range of about ten miles per hour when the batteries are fully charged."

"How much battery power do you have now?" Grace asked.

"It's between ninety-five and hundred percent. I was fully charged when we got off the chopper. The walk into town was slow and didn't discharge the batteries much. Then we got a couple hours of evening sun on the solar charger and that brought them back up. I've never done extended distances on this terrain so it's not an exact science."

"I've probably bicycled this route hundreds of times and I know it pretty well," Grace said. "The trail climbs gradually to the Taylor's Valley community. Beyond there you enter national forest. It's beautiful but the incline increases."

"If we completely discharge the batteries tonight, I may need a full day of sunlight to get them back. I'm not asking you to wait on me. I'm just making you aware of what may be required."

Grace didn't respond to that. A day ago she didn't know what lay ahead of her. Now she couldn't help but feel that there might be trouble waiting on her. She didn't want to jump to conclusions but her gut feeling was that there might be a fight at the end of this trail. If that was the case, she would feel much better going into that fight with Tom at her side. If Tom couldn't travel tomorrow she would have to continue on without him. If her family was in danger she couldn't sit idly by the trail for one more day not knowing what was happening with them.

Following the trail out of town was made easier by the fact that there was less tree cover and more of the moonlight reaching the ground. It made for easy travelling. Though the shapes of the various buildings around them meant nothing to Tom, Grace recognized several of the shops. They were places she had frequented and she wondered about the people that had run those shops.

There were a couple of backpacking outfitters, bicycle rental shops, and several shuttle services that would drop bicyclists off at the far end of the Creeper Trail so they could ride the gentle incline back to Damascus. Many of the people that worked at these businesses were people she knew by name.

Past the edge of town, the trail followed along the main highway for nearly a mile. They saw nothing unusual but they were vigilant due to the exposed terrain. They passed two darkened trailer parks that were just as desolate as the town itself. There were no moving cars and no one on foot. In a town of bicyclists it would have been normal to see people on two wheels but there were none of those either.

Despite the state of her town, Grace felt energized after the small rest. The more she walked, the more the endorphins began pumping, and the more invigorated she felt. Had she been on her own she would have taken off running. She could not have run the entire way but she would have alternated running and walking for as long as she could. In practical terms, she knew she could probably not reach her family's house under any circumstances tonight. It was too far and too dangerous to run that far in the dark.

For around three hours they navigated the wide trail by moonlight. A couple of times Grace hit her headlamp to make sure that they did not get too close to a steep bank that would drop them into the river. Her headlamp had a setting that made it project a red light instead of white. The red light would not damage their night sight and cause their eyes to have to readjust after they turned it off.

While they did not see any people along the way, there was a lot of trash at some of the trailside campsites. She poked through the trash once looking for answers but only came away with more questions.

After three hours, they reached the community of Taylor's Valley, a small cluster of houses with the trailside restaurant and several good spots to fish for trout. It was at Taylor's Valley they first saw signs of life. Across the creek and off in the distance they could see a bonfire. The murmur of voices told them that men sat the campfire in the dark, likely holding watch over their tiny community.

Grace and Tom chose to avoid contact, travelling on past the group. The hoped to do so without being noticed but that was unlikely. They were painfully aware that the sound of crunching gravel beneath Tom's tracks and the whir of the electric drive motors would probably travel in the darkness.

For a short distance, a paved road paralleled the trail. Grace led Tom in that direction, explaining that it might allow them to travel quieter. Though the sound of the electric motors still cut through the night, there would be less crunching gravel. When they paused again to listen, the conversation around the fire was gone.

"Shit," Tom whispered.

The men in the shadows of firelight were either listening quietly or were coming toward Tom and Grace.

"Keep going!" Grace hissed. "Follow the road."

Tom was hesitant to leave Grace but this was her show, her territory. He went on while she slipped her night vision monocular from her Go Bag and raised it to her eye. She powered it on and waited for it to fire up. She hit the button that turned on the infrared spotlight.

With the spotlight on she didn't have to rely on starlight alone. It gave her a pretty good picture for a distance of around two hundred feet. It was a piece of crap device, but it still gave her an advantage over those that didn't have crappy night vision.

She trained her night vision in the general direction of the campfire. She picked up a cluster of men on the other side of the creek but way closer than she was comfortable with. There were three huddled together, talking among themselves. They held long guns but they were not raised toward her. They appeared to be assessing the threat and just watching to see that it moved on. They showed no signs of aggression. Grace hoped that continued to be their attitude.

She was tempted to call out to the men and explain that they were just passing through but something told her not to. Best not to engage. Perhaps best not to let them know she was a young girl. Grace ran to catch up with Tom, then explained what she'd seen.

"Let's just keep walking and stay on guard," he said. "I'd keep that night vision up though. If the area is still populated, I don't want to walk up on someone. Getting startled when everyone is carrying guns could be a bad experience."

Grace did exactly that, constantly scanning with the night vision, and watching for threats. In another mile they left the last residence of the community behind and entered the forest again. Not long after that Tom's chair started to beep.

He cursed, then pushed a button to silence the warning.

"What's that?" Grace asked.

"Low battery warning. Twenty percent power remaining."

"What should we do?"

"Maybe somewhere in the next mile we find a place to hole up for the night. Find some place where I can get my chair off the trail. If there's any hidden campsites that catch a little sunlight that would be perfect. Then I could start the chair recharging as soon as the sun hits us in the morning."

"I think I know a place."

In less than fifteen minutes they entered an off-trail campsite.

"It's not as secluded as I'd like, but it's the most accessible and it has access to water," Grace said. "It's at least partially obscured from the trail. If I have to leave you here tomorrow to recharge your batteries, maybe we can throw some brush over the chair and make it less visible in case anyone goes by."

Utilizing gear from both of their Go Bags they were able to improvise a decent shelter. They used paracord to stretch an eight foot by ten foot backpacking tarp over a flat spot. Grace also had a folded square of Tyvek house wrap that she laid out beneath them.

The house wrap was waterproof and would keep them from absorbing moisture from the ground.

They each had bivy sacks in their Go Bags. Grace's was a bright orange commercial product. Tom's was an olive drab military version. While not as warm as a sleeping bag, they served as a sleeping shell that would hold in body heat and hopefully allow them to get some sleep.

"Make sure you rehydrate," Tom said as they each settled into their sleeping gear. "We didn't drink as much today as we probably should have."

"If you could see me, you would know that I'm making a face at you right now," she replied.

"Why?"

"I'm not a rookie. I've done this all my life. I have a water bottle beside me and I'm drinking from it every few minutes."

"I don't doubt you," Tom said. "I know you're capable. It's the buddy system though. In the military, checking your buddy's gear helps keep people alive. That's just the way I'm used to doing it."

"I'm sorry," she said. "I just get a little sensitive sometimes about guys telling me what to do."

"I'll try to be more aware of that when I say things to you," he said.

"You better," she said, finally laying down, her head on her pack. "I'd hate to have to kick your ass."

In the dark, neither of them could see that her comment had put a smile on their faces.

"I appreciate you coming back for me," Tom said.

"You'd have done the same for me," Grace said.

"That's the buddy system," Tom pointed out.

"Give me a break," Grace sighed. "I'm going to sleep."

Chapter Twenty-One

Arthur Bridges' Compound

The cabin Kevin built as his personal bug-out dwelling at the compound was a one-room log structure built from a kit. There was a storage loft, a wood stove, and a gravity-fed sink. The toilet was out back. Kevin hadn't had any time to settle in yet so his gear was still stacked around the room, along with the other gear he'd stored there since building the cabin.

Kevin was methodically laying gear out on his bed, as he always did when preparing for an operation. He did fewer of them anymore, but he still went through the same routine. Robert and Arthur watched. Feeling tired from her injuries and the exertion of the day, Sonyea had gone to bed already.

"Are you sure you want to do this?" Arthur asked.

"It's the only way to get good intel," Kevin replied.

"You know they probably have thermal, just like we do," Robert said. "If they do, you won't get far."

Kevin pulled a gallon-sized plastic jug from a tote. He smiled at Robert. "You'll see."

He disappeared into the bathroom and returned a few minute later in his underwear, his body smeared from head-to-toe with…something.

"What the hell is that?' Arthur asked.

"Thermal block," Kevin replied. "It will prevent me from registering on thermal."

"Really?" Robert asked.

"Really," Kevin replied. "Although it does hold in a lot of your body heat, so in hot conditions it's nearly impossible to use. It works like the IR-blocking paint they use on artillery."

Kevin slipped on a camo uniform and a pair of tall boots. He strapped on a battle belt full of gear and dropped a plate carrier covered in pouches over his head. He slid a handgun into the Safariland holster on the belt.

"You a .45 man, huh?" Arthur asked, noting the 1911-style pistol.

"Colt Delta Elite in 10mm." Kevin went on to pull an odd-looking rifle from a hard case.

Robert shook his head. "Just when you impress me with your pistol selection, you go and pull out that ugly rifle."

"The Tavor?" Kevin asked.

Robert nodded. "I think they're hideous."

"Yeah, but have you ever shot one?"

"Couldn't bring myself to do it," Robert chuckled.

"They'll make a believer out of you. That's an X95 with integral suppressor in 9mm. Handles like a Ferrari even in full-auto."

Robert nodded with new interest. "I might have to try one."

Kevin pulled a bump helmet from another case and secured flip down optics to it.

"What generation is that night vision?" Arthur asked. "I've never seen anything like it."

"This isn't available anywhere," Kevin said. "A defense contractor I did some work for gave me this set to try out. I'm right-eye dominant so the right eye is night vision, the left is thermal. The brain blends the images. You can hit a button to change either eye to thermal, to night vision, or just to clear."

"That's impressive," Arthur said.

When Kevin finished kitting up, he double-checked his gear.

"Make sure and coordinate with the perimeter security," Arthur said. "Don't want any mistaken identity when you return."

"Already done," Kevin said. "We established a re-entry point and protocol already. We're good."

"Then just be careful," Robert said. "These guys aren't playing around."

Kevin looked at him seriously. "Neither am I. The assault on this compound is personal for me. I do not like people screwing with me."

*

Kevin slipped out of the compound's perimeter. The guards on duty indicated where they thought snipers might be located. They were scanning with thermal but had reason to believe the snipers might be hiding beneath protective blankets. Inevitably something poked out of the blanket and got picked up by a scope if you waited long enough. That hadn't happened yet.

"If I have an opportunity to take one of those guys out, I'll do it," Kevin said. "However, my priority is recon. I can't collect intelligence if they're shooting at me."

The guard nodded and indicated he'd keep a weapon trained on the suspected sniper positions until Kevin was clear of them. After that, he was on his own.

Kevin hand-railed the main route into the compound. It was a remote gravel road and the only way into the compound on state-maintained roads. Kevin assumed that whoever was engaging them had a base established somewhere along that road. Along his path, he found several other men in concealed positions. This far back from the compound they were not taking measures against thermal detection and he spotted them easily. He gave them a wide berth and tried to not make any sound, which was difficult in the dense forest. He had to scan the ground with his night vision and chose each step carefully.

He didn't have to go but a quarter-mile before he found what he was looking for. On national forest property there were a lot of places to pull over and camp. At the first one he came to, there was an assortment of vehicles clustered together. He was pleased to find they were not military vehicles. They were pickups and Jeeps, along with several campers. There was an RV with a quiet generator going and lights on inside.

Kevin wanted to get closer but there were men gathered outside the RV. He couldn't tell if it was a meeting or just a social gathering. The blinds in the RV were open and he positioned himself to see inside. He raised the Tavor. It had a night vision-compatible holographic sight but there was also a flip-down 3x magnifier. He turned off the enhancements on his goggles, lowered the magnifier, and took in the scene inside the RV.

There were around a half-dozen men inside. Several had bottles of beer in their hands. It almost looked like a deer camp with everyone settled in for a night of drinking and telling lies. One overweight man wore a flannel shirt and a vest. Most were wearing hunting clothes in camouflage patterns. It was a confusing situation. No command structure was apparent from what Kevin was seeing. It didn't seem like a militarized group, although at least one of the men was wearing what looked like military camo.

Kevin pushed a button on his 3x magnifier and it began recording the scene to a memory card. When he'd managed to get every face on camera, Kevin shut things down. He could have easily opened fire through the window and done some damage but he wanted to talk with Arthur first. He needed to know if anyone recognized any of these men.

The fact that he didn't want to open fire on the RV did not mean he was totally intent on not drawing blood on this operation. On his return trip, he crossed paths with the second line of sentries, who were not taking any measures to hide themselves since they were situated some distance back from the compound.

Kevin removed the SOG Seal Team Elite from his battle belt. It was razor sharp. He took a position behind a wide tree and waited until the sentry wandered near him. He slapped a hand over the man's mouth and raked the blade across his throat. Kevin held on until the fight left him, then let the man sag to the ground.

A short distance from there, he did the same to another man and left him sprawled in the road. The last two human obstacles that Kevin was aware of were the two sniper positions that seemed to be concealed beneath thermal-blocking blankets. He worked his way into a position where he had a shot at both targets.

He fired a short burst from his Tavor into one of them, then immediately swung and did the same with the other suspected target. With the subsonic rounds, the only noise was the mechanical operation of the bolt moving rapidly within the weapon. A flurry of kicking dislodged the blanket from the first target and revealed the mortally wounded man beneath. Kevin flipped the selector switch to single-shot and finished him with a head shot. Warm blood spread beneath the man, visible as a growing redness in the thermal picture of Kevin's goggles.

He returned to the second target and found the man had crawled from beneath his blanket, trying to work his way into the bushes. Warm splashes of red behind him indicated he was hit. He put a round at the base of the man's skull and he pitched forward.

Kevin was certain that Arthur's perimeter team was watching him. Hopefully they understood what he was doing and didn't open fire on him. Kevin went to each body and examined the scene. He found a wallet on each man and took them, shoving them into a dump pouch on his belt.

One man was shooting a Ruger Precision Rifle with a thermal scope. The other had a Savage with the same scope. Kevin took both rifles and the spare magazines. No use letting good gear stay in the hands of men trying to kill you.

He slung the rifles over his back and made his way to his re-entry point. The perimeter security was expecting him.

"Good work over there," the guard said.

Kevin nodded. "You guys be safe," he said, then headed back toward his cabin.

The guard touched a button to trigger his microphone. "Rabbit back in the hat."

"Acknowledged," came the response.

*

Arthur and Robert were having a drink when Kevin showed up at Arthur's house. They'd been anxious to hear what he saw but wanted to give him time to wind down. Each man processed combat differently. They wanted to give him time to do it in his own way.

"Care for a drink?" Arthur asked.

"Sure," Kevin said.

"Gift from Robert," Arthur said, pouring two fingers of Four Roses Bourbon into a glass.

Kevin went to a nearby table and opened a laptop. While it booted, he spread out two ID cards on the table. Arthur joined Robert at the table and handed Kevin his drink.

"Capital Police Officer?" Robert said. "Where the hell did you get those?"

"Off the two snipers I killed tonight," Kevin replied.

Arthur and Robert regarded him seriously. With the laptop up and running, Kevin slipped a memory card into a reader and began playing a video.

"Either of you recognize any of these men?" he asked.

They stared at the video playing on the screen.

"I'll be damned," Arthur said. He pointed at the screen. "The man in the flannel shirt. That's Congressman Honaker."

"I've heard of him but I don't recognize him," Kevin said.

"I did some work at his house in Washington years ago," Arthur said. "We used to talk about preparedness and what was going to happen with the country. He knew I was fond of his home territory and dreamed of moving to his district one day."

"He must have pegged you as a survivalist," Kevin said. "Somehow he kept an eye on you over the years."

"Wouldn't he be eligible for better quarters in DC?" Arthur asked. "Don't they have accommodations for congress?"

"They do," Kevin said. "Depending on what the situation is, there are military bases and even private hotels set up to care for the needs of congressmen and their families. It would be like being in prison though. You would have to clear every move you made with the military. It would suck."

"So he built his own team to capture a better place," Robert said.

"Even lousy congressmen have access to intel on their states," Kevin said. "He probably has a good idea about your capabilities."

"So the question is whether he has any more team than what he brought with him," Arthur said. "If that's all he's got, then we might be able to take them."

"Hard to know," Kevin said. "We could possibly take out the men he brought with him as long as there's no real operators in the bunch. If he's got backup, air support, or access to heavy ordinance, we could be in trouble."

"What are you going to do?" Robert asked.

Arthur sighed. "For tonight, I'm going to have me another drink. Tomorrow, I think I'm going to get the congressman on the radio and have a powwow."

Chapter Twenty-Two

Jewell Ridge, VA

"It looks like you're riding the Tour de France with some bizarre team of alien clown space marines," Barb quipped.

Conor was kitting up for his ride and Barb, as usual, had something to say about it.

Instead of a normal bicycling helmet, Conor wore an OPS-Core FAST helmet, a type of combat helmet he'd gotten from a friend in the Special Operations community. On the front he wore a PVS-14 night vision device, certain that the bulbous device probably contributed to his alien appearance. The high-grade optic allowed him to easily ride his bike in the dark and navigate the mountain roads. Military troops regularly drove vehicles using this optic so he figured it would be simple enough on the slower speeds of a bicycle.

He didn't exactly have a uniform suitable for this particular mission. He had all manner of tactical and camouflage clothing but this was a different type of mission. He outfitted himself with a lightweight camouflage shirt with long sleeves. Over that he wore a plate carrier with soft plates and pouches for spare magazines, tall hiking socks, and a pair of desert tan boots. The part that sent his daughter into laughing fits was that he'd paired all of this with a snug pair of bicycling shorts.

"I need padding," he'd insisted while she laughed to the point of tears.

"Everyone has their weakness," Barb chuckled. "Your vulnerability is your delicate posterior."

Conor huffed in mock offense. "You try riding seventy miles without padding and let me know how you like it."

"No thank you."

Conor studied himself in his bedroom mirror. "Shame I'm riding at night. I feel like more people should have the privilege of taking all this in."

"The countryside will never be the same," Barb said. "I expect the trees will wilt as you pass and the crops will fail. Squirrels will intentionally jump to their deaths when they can't wipe the image from their tiny black eyes."

"You'll miss me when I'm gone," he said playfully. "You'll wish you'd been nicer when you're stuck home alone by yourself watching chick flicks and eating cookie dough."

"If I miss you I'll talk to a rock. The outcome is similar."

"Did you finish packing my food? I'd hate for you to get so distracted coming up with witticisms that you forget the one thing I asked you to do."

"It's packed. You'll miss no meals."

"Did you split it between the trailer and the backpack?"

"Yep. How long is your ride?"

"No way of knowing. This is all an experiment."

"There are safer ways to conduct experiments."

"It's not *just* an experiment. I told you I was checking on a girl for a friend."

"You are checking on a girl you don't know for a friend you barely know."

"It's how I am. I'm too old to change."

"Too stubborn to change is what you are," she said. "Just don't get personally involved. If you get there and the situation is not salvageable, turn around and come on home."

He grunted, refusing to commit himself to any particular course of action. "I love you."

She sighed. "You always say that when you want me to change the subject."

Conor widened his eyes as if she'd finally received a revelation. "Now that you understand that, please change it."

"You have a tendency to go overboard when things get personal."

Conor feigned offense. "I have no idea what you're talking about."

She waved her arms, encompassing their surroundings. "This shop in the backwoods? Our crazy life?" she said. "It's all because you went overboard."

"That was *indeed* personal," Conor said, serious now. "I did way less than I should have done. And just for the record, I think our life and this shop are delightful. I'd have it no other way."

*

132

As the sun dropped beneath the farthest ridge and darkness settled over the mountains, Conor set out on his journey. The early miles would be in familiar territory, through the nearby town he visited on a regular basis. Beyond that, the route would be less familiar.

He would follow a four-lane highway for about twenty miles, then take another twenty mile route across three steep mountains. He hoped that the motor would assist him on those climbs but he hadn't had a chance to experiment with it under those conditions. He did carry extra batteries and he had a solar charger for them in the trailer. The trailer was a bicycle-drawn child carrier that he'd picked up at a yard sale. He couldn't help himself. He was always picking up used bikes and bike accessories for projects.

Conor had loved bicycles his entire life. He came from an era when a kid's life centered around his bicycle. It was entertainment, transportation, and freedom all rolled into one. His family didn't have cable television in those days so he was outside all the time. To have been forced to spend the entire afternoon inside would have been torture. In fact, it was a common punishment for children. Commit a bad enough infraction and you may have to stay inside all evening. He still remembered how miserable that had been. He didn't understand how children did it now, how they enjoyed being trapped inside.

He loved the pensive nature of bicycling. There was something about the rhythm of riding a bike that freed the mind to travel in different directions than the body. Even riding at night in the green glow of the night vision was relaxing in a vaguely alien way. He thought about what Barb had said as he was preparing to leave. He did have a tendency to personalize things. He assumed it was an inherited trait, one that had come from his father.

His father had been a preoccupied and distant man. He'd been in prison in 1980, when Conor was just fifteen. He'd been an IRA bomber and the British came looking for him during a crackdown. One of his bombs had taken out a military barracks and there was a lot of anger directed toward him.

Conor's mother had been concerned about potential repercussions. She chose to move to the United States with her son and hope that they could disappear in the vast country. They settled in North Carolina where the terrain was similar enough to Ireland to keep the homesickness at bay. No one ever came after them and they lived a relatively normal life. Conor played football, graduated high school, and went on to graduate from the local community college as a machinist.

He used his skill both in his day job at a local manufacturing company and at night to supplement his income. He did welding for anyone that needed metal tacked together, some gunsmithing for folks who needed his more precision skills, fabricated parts for people who broke things for which parts were no longer available. All the while, his skills grew.

Despite his mother's concerns that he may have inherited some of his father's proclivities for living on the wrong side of the law, Conor kept himself occupied with his work and stayed out of trouble. Part of that was due to a girl who'd come into his life.

When he was at the community college he started dating a girl in the cosmetology program. Despite all the jokes that Conor had to listen to about the Irish, he found that women swooned over his accent. Khrystiana had been different. Conor could tell some of the women he met were only interested in the novelty of dating someone from a different country, who spoke with a different accent. While Khrystiana may have initially been attracted to him for those reasons, their connection was deeper. When he was twenty-two he bought a house and took her to look at it.

"I know it's not much, but if you marry me I'll do my best to make it a good home for you," he promised.

Khrystiana broke down in tears and accepted his proposal. They'd barely been married a year when their daughter Barbara was born. Conor's mother lived just long enough to meet her granddaughter. Before the baby was a year old she died of lung cancer. Conor had tried to contact his father to make him aware of both events but could not reach him.

He assumed his father was merely an insensitive bastard, but later learned he had already died in prison by that time. The guards, perhaps loyal to mates in the regiment, sought to make his punishment worse by beating him on a regular basis, one such beating rupturing his spleen. By the time anyone figured it out, it was too late and he died in a prison ambulance.

When Barb was three years old, Khrystiana picked her up from daycare one day. They were driving home, singing a song from Barb's favorite show, *The Wiggles,* when a drunk driver crossed the median and hit them head on. Conor's wife was killed instantly. Barb was almost killed but survived after weeks in the hospital.

In the manner of such things, the drunk driver walked away with no injuries. He was sentenced to twelve years in prison but was out in three due to good behavior and overcrowding. Conor found no justice in that. There were things he knew from childhood, bits of his father's craft that no one knew he was aware of. His father, a true believer, assumed there would be a day when Conor would fight for Ireland in his father's name. When his mother was not around, the father taught his young son the trade of the bomb maker.

When the man was released from prison, Conor kept an eye on him. He watched as the man found a place to live and eventually a job. One night while the man was working the night shift at a furniture factory, Conor stole the headrest from the driver's seat of his pickup truck. The man was not supposed to be driving but the judge gave him special permission so he could work and pay off the debts incurred by his imprisonment. Conor wired the headrest full of explosives with a proximity trigger and replaced it in the vehicle.

While the man drove home that night, he drove under a low railroad bridge he passed every night. This time, an RFID chip fastened to the underside of the bridge signaled the proximity trigger and detonated the headrest. When the truck rolled to a stop, the interior looked as if it had been spray painted with blood. As for the driver, everything from the ribs up had been vaporized by a shaped charge.

Although all eyes were on Conor as the likely bomber, there was no evidence linking him to the crime. His dad's history as a bomber was not even linked to him because his mother had adopted her maiden name when she and Conor immigrated to the United States. Whether it was the sophistication of the bombing or the grisly nature of the murder, word of the crime made its way through law enforcement circles and inevitably reached the ears of folks who were interested in people with Conor's skill set.

He got a visit at home one night, two men who made no threats and exerted no coercion. They stated that they assumed him to be the bomber responsible for killing the man who killed his wife. They neither wanted a confession nor an acknowledgement of any kind. They wanted to recruit him for a special apprenticeship program for machinists. If it worked out, they would set him up with his own shop.

He knew what they were asking. He also understood that sometimes opportunity only knocks once in your life and you should be ready to open the door to it. Perhaps there was even a little of his father in him after all, and he found himself intrigued by what the opportunity might offer. He took the night to think about it and called them to accept the next day.

*

From Jewell Ridge, Conor cycled through Richlands, Virginia, across Kents Ridge, and down the four-lane Route 19. At Elk Garden he took Route 80 across Hayter's Gap, following it all the way to the interstate at Meadowview, Virginia. This was the first point where he anticipated potential trouble. Because of the interstate, there were roadside convenience stores and truck stops. These were the kind of places that people were becoming stranded when the fuel supply dried up. These were the places that people were setting up encampments. He expected there might be clusters of dangerous, desperate people.

Near the interstate Conor stopped in the middle of a deserted section of road. He turned on the handheld GPS unit that was mounted to the handlebars of his bicycle. After he powered it up, it took several moments in the wooded valley for the unit to acquire satellites and pinpoint his location. Once everything aligned, he familiarized himself with his location and planned his next step. The GPS led him to the take Route 11, an old US Highway that paralleled the interstate.

At a particular point along Route 11, all that stood between him and the interstate was an enormous farm. There were no dwellings, only hundreds of acres of fields on both sides of the interstate. Conor chose that as his point to cross. It was a good choice. He saw nothing but cows.

Once on the other side of the interstate, his plan was to take a small secondary road that would lead him to Damascus, Virginia. He didn't make it far on that road before his night vision revealed a line of cars barricading it in the distance, and shadowy figures manned a roadblock. He quietly came to a stop and considered his options.

He had expected this type of roadblock. He'd heard chatter that communities along the interstate had been forced to do this to stop the hordes of trapped travelers from overrunning their communities. Conor was fairly certain that the men at the roadblock could not see him in the dark. They did not have his technological advantage.

He assumed that with his natural charm, given enough time, he could talk his way through the barricade. Should that fail, there was a strong possibility he could take the men by force. It was barely a couple hours until dawn and sentries at this time of night were often exhausted and less vigilant. All of those options presented complications, potential delays that he was not prepared for.

Instead, he chose to backtrack, consulting his GPS to find an alternative route. He found one and was beyond the barricade in a matter of thirty minutes without so much as an encounter. Sometimes avoidance was the best strategy. It saved time, ammo, and resulted in fewer holes in the hide.

As he neared Damascus, Conor's anxiety level increased slightly. Not only was it a proper town, but Kevin had warned him on the satellite phone that there was some sort of mob scene there. Those were the worst types of encounters for the low-key solo traveler. It was impossible to predict the reaction of the crowd. Typically, you couldn't outgun them or talk your way through them. There were too many variables.

It was likely that a group this size had sentries on duty. He fully expected to run into them. His biggest advantage was that most of the mob would be asleep at this time of night. That would reduce the number of people with whom he had to interact. If he had an encounter, his best option was to keep the situation quiet and resolve it with immediacy.

When he realized that The Creeper Trail ran dead center through the middle of town, Conor decided the best cover was to hide in plain sight. Rather than skulk about the streets and back alleys he opted to get on The Creeper Trail and follow it through town like he didn't have a care in the world. When this approach got him halfway through town with no significant encounters, he was pretty pleased with himself. He wondered if this most dreaded part of his journey would be a piece of cake after all. Then he spotted the sentries blocking the old railroad bridge near the town park. He shouldn't have counted his chickens so soon.

Conor paused on the trail. He considered his situation for a moment, then turned his bike around and backtracked until he was out of view of the sentries. He stopped and stashed all his visible tactical gear in the trailer that he pulled behind him. He took off his night vision and replaced it with a battery-operated headlamp like most of the backpackers wore.

Once everything was stowed in the trailer he covered the load with a backpacking tarp and pedaled back toward the sentries, looking a little less like an alien clown space marine this time. When Conor arrived at the roadblock, he simply looked like a bicycle tourist, of which the town saw thousands each summer. He approached the roadblock as if it were routine and expected under the current circumstances. He rode until the armed men raised their weapons and asked him to stop. Conor was completely casual, as if the men were fellow travelers stopping to exchange stories of the trail ahead.

"Hold up," one of the sentries said. He wore a bandana tied around his head.

Conor allowed his bike to coast to a stop. He threw a hand up in greeting. "Easy boys. What's with the firepower?"

Since Conor had not immigrated to the United States until his late teens he had retained his Irish accent and he turned it on now to full effect. He found that most Americans loved that particular accent. It disarmed and charmed them.

"Where do you think you're going?" the other sentry asked. He was wearing a long-sleeved paisley shirt that seemed inappropriate for hiking but Conor wasn't one to judge. The shirt was grubby and even across the distance Conor could tell that it smelled like a mildewed towel.

Conor shrugged and stretched his back as if it were sore from hours in the saddle, which it in fact was. "I'm riding across the United States. I'm taking in your fine country from sea to shining sea."

"I guess you missed that the shit hit the fan?" Bandana Man asked.

"No, I noticed. It's hard to miss, in fact. There's not much I can do about it. I can't get back to Ireland right now so I might as well finish my trip."

"Haven't you found circumstances to be a little dangerous for travel?" Paisley asked.

Conor nodded. "Indeed. That's why I'm riding at night."

"What about food? You've been able to get enough?" Bandana Man asked.

Conor laughed. "Apparently you two didn't grow up in Northern Ireland. This trip has, of the last week, reminded me a lot of my childhood. Riding about on a bicycle with too little to eat and the threat of violence everywhere you go."

Conor could tell that he was disarming them. He detected the easing of fingers on triggers. Barrels had drooped away from him. It was exactly what he wanted. He had them.

"That was all before my time," Paisley said.

Conor chuckled. "There was food but most people were too poor to buy it. There wasn't a lot of work so no one had money. Then there was *the troubles*, as we called them. Bombings every day, police violence, danger everywhere."

Bandana Man looked at his partner. "It does sound like today, doesn't it?"

Paisley nodded.

"Is there some reason I can't continue on?" Conor asked.

"We had some trouble with the town," Paisley said. "The roadblock is for our own safety."

"Ah, more *troubles*," Conor said. "Always troubles."

Paisley looked apologetic. "We'll have to check with the men in charge to see if we can let you through. I'm sorry but it will take a little time. We'll have to go wake someone up."

"I hate to hear that," Conor said. "I do indeed. I've been trying to make as much distance as I can each night and hole up during the day."

Conor had been talking with his hands the entire time so the two men were not concerned when his right hand moved briefly out of their sight, as if it were merely reaching to scratch an insect bite. When it came back around, there was a pistol in his hand. He placed a quick round in the forehead of Paisley, then shot Bandana Man right through his bandana before either man could wipe the surprise from his face. Both men dropped and kicked spastically. A .22 caliber headshot made pudding of the brain but it sometimes took the body a little while to realize there was no one in charge.

Conor stepped over them and placed a follow-up in each man's skull. The pistol was a custom job he'd made in his own shop. He'd taken a Ruger 22/45, a fairly standard pistol that shot .22 caliber rounds, and built an entirely custom top-end for the pistol. The action left no marks on the shell casing that could be traced back to a factory pistol. The barrel had no twist at all and didn't leave rifling marks. It also had an integral suppressor which reduced the report without adding additional length to the pistol.

Conor slipped the pistol back in his shorts and immediately regretted it. He cursed and yanked it back out, his flesh already branded. Even with just four shots, hot gases had heated the suppressor. Conor tossed it into the trailer and returned to his business. Not one to dawdle at the scene of trouble, he took the men's camping chairs and dumped them over the side of the bridge. That was followed by rolling the bodies over the rail and pitching the men's rifles in after them. This was not a scavenging mission and taking the extra weight with him would only slow him down.

"Should've chosen curtain number one boys," he said. "If you'd just let me continue on, none of this would have had to happen. I would have been nothing more to you than a story to tell in the morning."

With the path before him cleared, Conor remounted his bicycle and shoved off. He journeyed through the town using the headlamp, continuing to adopt the persona of a cross country bicyclist. When the houses became fewer and more spaced out, he stopped again in the center of the trail, put his tactical vest and gear back on, and replaced the goofy helmet that his daughter had laughed at, dropping his PVS-14 back in front of his eyes. All was right with the world again.

He whistled a song he knew from his childhood. He no longer knew the words but the tune would never leave him. He found it disturbing that there appeared to be no one else in the town. Despite it being the middle of the night there were no other sentries and no barking dogs. The town seemed abandoned.

In little more than an hour he passed through the Taylor's Valley community. In the distance he could see men gathered around a bonfire. He pedaled slowly and tried not to alarm them. They appeared to be normal men performing the role of protecting their community. As long as he stayed on his side of the river and they stayed on theirs, he saw no reason their paths should converge.

He rode another hour, noting that with each passing mile the grade began to climb. Were he just pedaling his bike under normal recreational circumstances he would bear down and pedal harder. These were not normal circumstances. He had the additional weight of his pack, the additional weight of the trailer and the gear inside it, and the weight of the pedal assist motor and the spare batteries, which weighed in at approximately eight pounds all together.

Between all of it, it was likely he was carrying an additional thirty pounds. There was also the fact that he was neither a triathlete nor a soldier. He was a middle-aged man who spent most of his time tinkering around in a machine shop, although admittedly he had a specialized skill set that made him a little more lethal than most men his age.

He was pleased with the results of his bike experiment. The assist motor had surpassed his expectations. He pedaled just because it made him feel better, even though he didn't have to. He made it thirty more minutes past Taylors Valley before the battery finally started to run out. He decided he'd gone far enough for the night. He would stop, rest up, and pick back up in the morning with a fresh battery.

Even if he pushed himself and traveled on to Grace's house it wasn't like he could just drop in for a social call at this time of night. Those types of calls were usually answered with a gun. He would get up in the morning after a good night's sleep. Tomorrow he would find his way to Grace's house and plant himself in a nice concealed position somewhere. He would monitor the house and see what happened. Should he see a happy family, a young girl, and a young man who looked like he just came back from the war, Conor would introduce himself. If he found anything other than that he would have to play it by ear.

Chapter Twenty-Three

Outside of Damascus, VA

Grace was startled awake by a hand on her shoulder. Her eyes shot open and she reached for her Glock.

"Easy. It's just me."

She breathed a little easier, felt her heart rate slowing down.

"I tried to be gentle," Tom said. "I guess there's no easy to way to wake a sleeping bear."

"When I wake up, the world comes crashing down on me," Grace said. "There's this surge of panic about everything going on and everything I have to do."

"I'll try to find a gentler way next time," Tom said. "Maybe I'll sing you a song."

"Only if you can sing."

Tom's face clouded. "It won't be tomorrow morning. You'll probably be waking up alone."

She sat up. "What's the matter?"

He gestured at his track chair.

"It's dead?"

He nodded. "Yeah, it was dead last night. I wanted to think that overnight some helpful little elves may come in and replace the battery but it didn't happen."

"That would've been nice."

"I've already got the solar charger going but there's not a lot of sun yet. I don't have a lot of experience charging it with the panel so I have no idea how long it will take."

Grace saw a mix of emotions on his face. There was disappointment and frustration. There was also fear, but she was certain it was not fear for himself. If was fear for her going on alone.

"I'm sorry," he said.

"No, I'm sorry. I feel bad about leaving you behind. I feel like we're supposed to be doing this together. Still, I feel like I have to get to my mom and brother."

Tom scooted closer and put an arm around her. "Don't worry about me. The thing we talked about, about focusing on your mission, that's where your head needs to be right now. I'll be okay.

Trust me when I say that I've been in way worse places under much worse conditions."

Tom could tell Grace was mentally pulling herself together, steeling herself for what she had to do. She returned his hug then stood, stretched, and assessed her physical condition. There was a little soreness in her legs and feet. Too much running with too much gear. She also felt a little dehydrated.

"I need to fill up my water," she said. Tom held up two quart Gatorade bottles full of water. "Already filtered your water for you."

Grace used old Gatorade bottles because they were lighter than Nalgene bottles. She usually carried a full one in her Go Bag and any empty one she could fill up if she needed to.

"I used your Sawyer filter."

"I appreciate that. How long have you been awake?"

Tom shrugged. "An hour I guess."

Grace looked around as if surprised by that. "I must've been tired," she said. "I'm usually more sensitive to noise and light."

"You blew through a lot of adrenaline and energy yesterday."

"If I'm that well-rested, I guess I don't have any excuse for not getting on the trail as soon as possible. She took the two water bottles from him, stowed them in her bag, then looked around to make sure she had all of her other gear. "I'm just taking my bivy sack," she said. "I'll leave the tarp and ground cloth with you."

"Thanks," Tom said.

When she was certain she had all the rest of her gear, Grace slung her pack over her back. She re-holstered the Glock 19 that had been in her bivy sack with her. Finally, she slung her AR pistol sling around her neck and an arm.

"I guess this is it for a little bit, Tom. I...like you." She wanted to say more, maybe even wanted to say she loved him, but it seemed too soon. Maybe it was just the circumstances and not even real. She didn't know.

She bent down and kissed him. Despite it feeling right, it was still an awkward gesture for her. She held her emotions tight to her, and rarely shared much of what she was feeling with people. That she was opening up to this man felt strange to her.

When she pulled away she noted the look on his face. He also seemed to be in unfamiliar territory. She broke the awkward moment by saying, "I'll see you later."

She double-timed it down the connector trail from their campsite, watching carefully for roots and snags, rejoining the Creeper Trail after about thirty feet. As long as she didn't encounter any obstacles, she could make good time on this flat, smooth trail. Grace often ran in the morning so it felt natural for her to be up and running before she was even fully awake.

She preferred to run on an empty stomach, wanting to train her body to fuel itself with fat stores rather than from the sugar in her bloodstream after a meal, although she didn't feel as light and carefree as when she ran in school. Normally, back in Oxford, she ran with minimal gear. Beneath her running shirt she wore an elastic belly band with a pouch for a compact .380 pistol. She also carried an iPod, her room key, a water bottle, and her debit card. Together it was enough to get her home in a pinch.

Now she carried her Go Bag which she estimated to be about eighteen pounds with the two full bottles of water. The spare ammo added significant weight. She also had her Glock with its paddle holster. While the paddle holster was a comfortable way to wear a pistol, it was not particularly a comfortable way to *run* wearing a pistol. If she ran all the way home, the paddle holster would definitely be leaving some marks. Her hiking boots were heavier than the lightweight Solomon Speedcross running shoes she wore back at home. Then there was the AR pistol. It required two hands to hold in order to keep it from bouncing.

She ran at a jogging pace for about thirty minutes before she took her first break. It was already humid when she woke up and she was now soaked in sweat. She drank as much as she could tolerate, understanding that she still had a hydration deficit from yesterday, besides what she had already sweated out this morning. She walked while she rehydrated to keep her muscles limber.

Ahead, she saw the trail sign indicating a side trail off of the Creeper Trail. It was a connector trail that led to the Appalachian Trail or the Iron Mountain Trail, depending on which way you went. She hadn't considered taking that trail but maybe it would be quicker. It would be rougher than the one she was on now but would eventually lead her to a campground. If she cut through the campground and got on the road there, she might get home sooner.

Grace tucked her water bottle in the pocket of her pack and turned off onto the spur trail. She accelerated to a steady jog, the slap of her feet on the trail matching the pounding of her heart in her chest. The steady rush of her breathing was almost mechanical. She established a routine of running for several minutes, then slowing to a walk to let her heartrate recover. When it slowed back to within range, she would start running again.

While she continued her physical training in Mississippi, it was not the same as running back there at home. The Mississippi heat and humidity were devastating, but the streets of Oxford were relatively flat. The trails of Damascus were anything but. Her family's home was several thousand feet above the elevation of the town. There was no way to get there but up. Any plateaus in the trail merely offered short respite from the climb. The only variation seem to be that the trail was sometimes a shallow incline and other times a steep incline, but it was always going in the same direction.

Up.

She had been running for nearly an hour when she approached a campground several miles out of town. In the summer the campground was sometimes the base camp for people that came to the area for mountain biking, hiking, or trout fishing. Grace assumed that under these circumstances the campground would be empty. Anyone staying there would have tried to get home when things got bad.

She was surprised when she ran up the trail that offered her a vista of the campground to find it was anything but empty. The place looked like a refugee camp. She nearly skidded to a halt. Were these more of the armed backpackers from town?

She retrieved the monocular from her pack, bracing it against the limb of a tree to get a steadier view and determine what was going on there. She saw a few RVs and travel trailers, but also tents and blue tarps strung up over taut ropes. Clothes hung from sagging clotheslines stretched from tree to tree. Could these be refugees from the town? Had these people been forced out of town when the sheriff was killed?

146

Uncertain who these people were, and not seeing anyone that she recognized, Grace chose to skirt the campground as discreetly as possible. She wasn't carrying much in the way of resources but she still didn't want it stolen. If she ran into these people, she had no idea if they would allow her to go on her way or if they were the kind of people who would take the things she carried on her back.

She stashed the monocular in the cargo pocket of her pants and flipped her AR pistol off safety. She had no idea what lay ahead of her but she wanted to be ready for it. Aware that the scuffing of her shoes on the trail might draw attention if she kept running, she decided she would need to proceed cautiously until she was well beyond the campground. She didn't know who might be out wandering around in the woods.

Even though she wasn't running any longer, the muscles of her legs were fatigued. The trail around the campground presented a steep climb with lots of rocks and roots. She topped a nearby ridge, nearly to the main road, and started down the other side. She finally felt safe enough to pick up her pace again. She clutched her weapon across her chest and began jogging. She made it about seventy-five yards down the trail before she heard a loud voice call to her.

"HEY!"

She froze in her tracks, her eyes scanning around her, but she saw nothing. Her heart raced.

"Get back to camp!" a voice boomed. "You'll scare away the game."

The realization hit her like a bucket of cold water. She spun and stared upward. There, in a tree high above her, was a hunter's tree stand, a man in camouflage standing on the platform glaring down at her.

When her eyes met his, she saw two things on his face. First, the realization that he did not recognize her from the campground. Second, that she carried a weapon.

The man threw his scoped bolt-action rifle to his shoulder and tried to find her in the magnified image of his scope. Using a simple red dot optic with no magnification, Grace had an advantage in acquiring her target. She threw her AR pistol up, backpedaling, and placing the red dot on the man's center mass. She felt for the safety, then remembered she'd already taken it off earlier.

She double-tapped the trigger just as her foot caught a rock and she fell backwards, her body jolting hard when she landed on the rock. Her head hit something—a rock, the ground, a log—she didn't know. The pistol fell from her hands, though still secured by the single-point sling, it didn't go far.

She struggled to get her hands on the grip of the weapon and get it back on the target. When she had the weapon back in her control and found the hunter in the optic, she was just in time to see the man pitch forward and drop. She was certain he was going to land on her and fought back a scream. He only made it a couple of feet before his safety harness caught him.

His fall was arrested so hard that blood sprayed from his mouth, falling on Grace like a cursed rain. He hung there, kicking weakly, and bleeding out. He was trying to talk, extending a hand to Grace, but she would be no help to this man.

She struggled to her feet, slightly dizzy, her adrenaline racing. She fought to get her thoughts under control. Would people come running up the trail after her or would they assume that the hunter just took a shot at a deer? She wasted no more time thinking, launching herself down the trail without even a glance back.

Chapter Twenty-Four

The Hardwick Farm

Paul sat in the living room of the Hardwicks' home staring at the pill bottle in his hand. He was sitting on their comfortable couch with his shoes propped on their coffee table. It was the same bottle he'd taken from Teresa Hardwick's nightstand. It had her name on it and said *No Refills*. Every so often he would shake it, disappointed at the insubstantial rattle that came from it. This was not enough pills to keep him and Debbie going. Hell, it wasn't enough pills to keep him going by himself.

He'd dumped out everything in the bathroom, raked out the medicine cabinet, and emptied every drawer into the floor. He'd dumped out everything in the hall closet, gone through every kitchen cabinet drawer. He could not find any more pain pills. Maybe they didn't have them. Or maybe they were behind that locked door with them in the basement. Then there was the whole issue of that room in the basement. How could he even snort a pill and relax with those folks down there? If he were to get high and nod off on the couch, he could wake up with his throat slit or a gun to his head.

At the same time, it would suck to leave this house. He'd never seen a place set up so nicely for the current situation. Most of the things in the house seemed to work. The house had something called *solar power* but he didn't have any idea how it all worked. He only knew you could watch DVD movies, drink cold beer, and microwave food. Even the bathrooms worked.

He had a lot to think about. He needed a plan and he wasn't a man used to making plans. There was a lot of food in the house, though he suspected much of it was locked up in the basement with those people. Maybe he could trade some of the food in the house for better drugs. He'd even considered the idea of letting some folks come live with them if they provided the dope. He would provide the power and a roof over their heads. He could provide food, they could provide the buzz. If Paul couldn't have a buzz most days, the rest of those things didn't matter to him. What good were the basics if you couldn't get high?

Even though he was a drug user, he didn't feel like you could trust most druggies. They weren't a demographic known for the trustworthiness. It wasn't like he was a silver-plated example of honor and integrity, but what would he do if he invited somebody to come live with them and they tried to take over the place? He'd always considered himself a lover and not a fighter, so it wasn't like he could just whip out some ninja skills and take them out. He just didn't know what to do.

Maybe the best plan was to bring in one of Debbie's friends. She had a woman friend who was a dealer and always seemed to have meth or pills. She was a hard woman but he felt like he might be able to control her a little better than he could control a man. She wouldn't likely try to take over this sweet house and run him out of the picture. Maybe she would take what he offered and be happy to hang out and enjoy the roof over their heads, the running water, and the flowing electricity.

"Hey, what do you think your friend Sharon is doing?"

Debbie shrugged. She'd been there beside him the whole time but lost in the murky soup of her own thoughts. "I don't know. It ain't like I can call her and ask her."

"We need some help around this joint. We need somebody that can bring in some dope in exchange for food. Somebody who can help keep an eye on things when we're passed out. I can't even go to sleep for worrying that crazy bitch in the basement is going try to kill me."

"I know where Sharon lives but I ain't sure she's home. She's got a trailer over on Devil's Branch," Debbie said. "Don't know if she's got anything either. If she's in as bad a shape as the rest of us, she might have used it up or traded whatever she had."

"Why don't you go check in on her?"

"You mean like riding to her house and seeing if she's there?"

Paul nodded like that was the dumbest thing ever said. "Yeah, that's what I mean, unless you've sprouted wings and can fly over. Tell her how sweet this deal is. See if she might be interested in coming and staying with us. Tell her we'll trade food for dope. If she brings the dope, we'll let her stay here with us. Make it sound good."

"What about when the dope runs out? What happens to her then?" Debbie asked.

Paul hadn't thought about that but he realized it would happen eventually. There was no way she had enough dope to keep them high forever. "Then we throw her ass out. Find somebody else."

"What if we can't find somebody else?"

"Dammit woman, how the hell do I know? I ain't got an answer for every damn thing. Just do what I told you. Go ask if she wants to come stay with us."

"I ain't sure I want to go," Debbie said.

"I ain't sure it was a question," Paul replied. "Get your ass up and go."

Debbie stood up, looking a little confused. "What do you want me to ride?"

Paul sighed like he was struggling to be patient. "I don't know. Do I have to figure everything out? Look around. See if you can find the keys to something."

"Can I just take the dirt bike?"

"I reckon, but you can't haul her back with it. She decides to come back with you I reckon I'll have to find the keys to something else and go back after her. You even know how to ride it?"

Debbie nodded "I reckon."

"Then take the dirt bike, I don't care. Just get out here. I'm tired of talking about it. Get going."

When he got this way there was no use arguing. He just got meaner and meaner and it always ended the same way. She needed to get gone before it got uglier. She went outside and climbed onto the dirt bike. It had been a couple years since she had ridden one but she remembered the basics.

She was pleased to find that it had electric start and she soon had the engine running. Standing in the driveway made her wonder about her mother. Had she crawled off somewhere and died like an old dog? The thought gave Debbie a brief flash of pain but it was her mother's own fault. She shouldn't have provoked Paul, it was as simple as that. Debbie had told her how he was. She should have just minded her own business.

Debbie conveniently allowed herself to forget that her mother was at their trailer on a mission of mercy, delivering food to them. You remembered what you wanted to remember though. You shaped your personal history in the way that allowed you to sleep at night.

Chapter Twenty-Five

Whitetop, VA

Grace felt like crap. Either from heat, dehydration, or lack of calories she was developing a pounding headache. She was also starting to feel nauseated. Everything was hurting her now. There was yesterday's pain and fresh new pain piling on top of it. Her dad always told her that pain was just weakness leaving the body. Right now weakness must be leaving her like water through a net. She would just have to work her way through it.

To distract herself from the suffering, she fell into a routine of running a hundred steps and them walking one hundred steps. At some point in that distracting routine she began to feel a little better and reduced it to seventy-five steps of walking, and then even to fifty steps of walking, while still keeping with one hundred steps of running.

She didn't realize the progress she'd made until she came upon the picnic area that marked her departure from this trail. Still running, she veered off the trail and cut through the jumble of picnic shelters, tables, and permanently-mounted barbecue grills. In better times this little area was mowed and the weeds regularly trimmed. With the rapid pace of summer growth, just a week or two without mowing made it look neglected and abandoned. In the past this area was a frequent fishing spot so she remained vigilant, but she saw no people. The last thing she wanted was a surprise as she got this close to home.

The road out of the picnic area was a wide and well-maintained gravel road. She jogged steadily up it, invigorated by her proximity to home. The rhythmic crunch of gravel beneath her feet even gave her a sense of nostalgia, reminding her of the many times she'd run on the same gravel road before going to college. When she reached the end of the park road, she turned left onto another gravel road. It wound through the steep mountains, occasionally passing houses with no residents visible. These houses had once held people, and likely still did, but no one made themselves known.

When she came to the next intersection her spirits soared and she began to run harder. Any time the family had been gone on an extended trip, turning onto this road was when they felt like they were home. She passed one neighbor's house, the yard growing higher than she'd ever seen it before. No one was out. In better times she'd have checked on these folks but now all she could think of was her own family. Her arms pumped harder. She was no longer jogging but flying at a dead run.

Around another bend in the road a dog started barking. She recognized it as the neighbor's dog. It recognized her too, and wagged its tail. The dog had seen this girl run by its house before. Grace called a greeting to the dog but kept running. In response to the barking, a young woman came onto the porch. Grace threw up a hand and waved. The girl did not wave back, perhaps not recognizing Grace as she was dressed now and with gear strapped all over her.

Grace hit a straight stretch and burned through it like it was a fifty yard dash. The finish line was her family's mailbox. She hung a right there, turning onto her own driveway.

Finally.

The gate on the road was closed. Grace stepped through it and fastened it back.

She was home. She was finally home. Grace's heart raced with the urgency and exhilaration of being back on her family's property for the first time in months.

The house was on top of a hill, hidden in the woods. The driveway was steep but Grace ran on in her exhilaration. She knew this road like the back of her hand, having walked it every day when the school bus dropped her off. She ran through a gauntlet of livestock fencing and past the small pond, past the old sheds that were there when her dad bought the place and then past the new ones that the two of them had built together. She ran past the woodshed where her father split and stacked firewood for the winter, pushing on until the land around her opened up into a large clearing. Their house sat in the middle of it, looking off toward hundreds of miles of mountain views.

When she caught sight of their home with its rough-sawn siding and stone chimneys, her heart told her to run through the back door and yell out that she was home. She imagined her family running to her and taking her in their arms. Despite the urging of her heart, she stopped dead in her tracks and stared at the house. Her brain was overriding her heart now.

She didn't have any concrete reason to think her home had been compromised but what if it had? What if she burst into her home and found strangers there? She moved off to the side of the road where she would be hidden by a tree and removed the monocular from her pocket. She examined the house. There were no strange cars there, a good sign.

She moved closer but more cautiously this time. She went tree to tree, cover to cover. The front of the house rose high from the steep hillside so the family mostly used the back door. Grace headed in that direction. There were immediate signs that something was wrong.

Trash was strewn on the back porch and out into the yard. She recognized packaging from MREs and freeze-dried food. That was trash her family knew better than to throw outside. Her dad always told them that throwing those items outside was just advertising that you had emergency preparations. It invited theft and compromised operational security. Her family knew to burn or bury those things.

She moved to a better vantage point, closer to the kitchen door. Through the glass of that door, she could see into the house, into the living room, and get a better idea of the conditions inside. Besides more trash, cabinet doors were open and the contents scattered around the kitchen. Drawers had been opened and the contents dumped onto the floor. The sight of her family's normally orderly house in such a state caused her physical pain.

Then she saw the man sitting on the couch staring at the pill bottle.

Her hand clenched the grip of her AR pistol. She started to raise it, knowing she could easily top him from the porch with a single bullet to the head. But what if there were more of them?

Her family had a safe room in the basement, but what if they hadn't made it down there before the house was overrun? What if they were being held at gunpoint right now? What if her shot triggered a shootout and got her family killed?

For the second time since making it back to her hometown, Grace had to use restraint when all she wanted was to use her gun to solve the problem. It made her ache at all levels. It felt like a hand squeezing her heart and wringing everything from it. She backed off the porch with tears in her eyes.

She had to get out of the driveway before she was spotted. The practical side of her understood that standing there anguishing over the circumstances would not change anything. The reality of the situation remained the same. She needed to observe the house from concealment and try to determine what was going on in there, which would best be accomplished from the barn if it was still safe.

She cut through an open field to the left of the house. The field held the family's shooting range and a small field where she and her father did training exercises that he came up with. There were stacks of tires to drag, cinderblocks to carry, sandbags to be shouldered. She ran across this field and cut up a hill, following a small farm road that led her to the back side of the barn.

When she reached the barn, Grace slipped the metal latch open as quietly as possible. She tugged on one of the heavy rolling doors and slid it open just far enough apart that she could get between them. Once inside she left the door cracked about a foot to allow light in. Her dad kept the floor cluttered with farm equipment, welding projects, and tools. It was a hazard to walk across the barn floor in the dark.

As she made her way across the floor, the light from open door diminished. She wasn't too concerned because she could see where she was going now. She aimed for the crack between the other two barn doors, those on the front that faced the house. When she got there she could keep an eye on the house and see what she was dealing with.

She was still about five feet from the thin strip of light that shone between the front barn doors. She was shuffling her feet now, barely able to see, and walking carefully just in case there were unseen obstacles on the floor. She began to relax as she got closer to the door, her mind moving to the next stage of this mission.

Two steps from her destination, a pale figure staggered from the rich blackness to her left, arms extended, moaning. For some irrational reason the first thought that came to Grace was *zombie*. Her second thought was that she needed to put a bullet in it, preferably in the head.

Her AR pistol was dangling free of her grasp. She had not anticipated needing it in the barn and was not holding it when the threat appeared. Her hands dropped in the dark, trying to find the grip, trying to fish the rifle up by the sling. Before she could even get a hand on it, the figure was upon her. It both embraced and sagged upon her. Grace thought she was being tackled as the figure fell upon her, knocking her backward. Her attacker moaned eerily as Grace fell. She hit the ground hard, the figure landing on top of her.

Grace rolled violently to the side, throwing the figure off her, and kicking it away. She jumped to her feet but still couldn't make out any detail. She ran for the open back door. When she reached it, she swung around and shouldered her rifle. She had an optic on but at this range she wouldn't need it. It was a point and shoot situation.

She aimed, found the trigger, and realized at the last moment she was staring into the damaged face of Mrs. Brown.

Grace averted the rifle in a safe direction just as she was preparing to pull the trigger. She recognized the figure in front of her as Mrs. Brown, but it was more by shape, hair, and clothing than by features. The woman was heavily bruised, her face puffy and swollen. Her eyes were black and swollen shut, her lips like thick sausages encrusted with blood.

Grace pushed the barn door open, allowing more light into the barn. Only then did the panic release its hold on her. She ran to Mrs. Brown and set her weapon down on the lid of a feed bin.

"Mrs. Brown, Mrs. Brown. You hear me? What happened to you?"

Ms. Brown tried to answer but her words were distorted. There was no doubt why. Her lips were so swollen they would not form words. When she opened them to try to speak, Grace saw jagged, broken teeth and a tongue bloody and swollen.

As Grace studied Mrs. Brown's injuries, she suddenly froze, as if an icicle had been shoved into her heart. If this was Mrs. Brown's condition, what had happened to her own family? Had whoever did this to her done something similar to her mom and brother?

Grace touched Mrs. Brown's shoulder. "Where's my family? Are they okay? Just nod yes or no." Grace's voice was becoming more demanding, more frantic. She was approaching panic. "Did the people in the house do this to you?"

Mrs. Brown's eyes were open and appeared to be slightly more focused now. She was still making sounds that Grace couldn't decipher. She patted Mrs. Brown on the shoulder, realizing she was wasting her time. The woman could have a concussion or brain injury.

"I'm going to the house. I'll be back for you in a minute. We'll get you some help."

Mrs. Brown went ballistic. She was clutching at Grace, her fingers clawing at Grace's forearms. She gestured wildly, making noises, attempts at words Grace could still not understand.

"Is it dangerous at the house? Nod for yes!" Grace asked.

Mrs. Brown nodded frantically. That stopped Grace in her tracks.

"Are my mom and Blake okay?"

Ms. Brown looked apologetic and shrugged, though the gesture made her wince with pain. She made another sound that Grace thought she might understand. It meant she didn't know. Grace's family may be alive or they may be dead.

Chapter Twenty-Six

The Hardwick Farm

When Teresa Hardwick woke up in the Ready Room she was incredibly sore. Healing muscles had been stretched, stitches on both the inside and outside of her body had been tugged and strained. She had felt like an invalid the last week, recovering from her surgery. Now she had a renewed sense of purpose. She knew what she had to do. Of the things she had to do, she had already accomplished the first task. She had gotten the children to a safe place.

Blake and Dylan were playing a board game in the floor. Several forms of entertainment were available in the Ready Room to keep people occupied. There were books, games, and even a small television with a DVD player that ran off the inverter.

"Mommy, you're awake!" Blake ran and hugged his mother.

Teresa winced. "Easy now. Mommy is still a little sore from her operation."

"I'm sorry." Blake released her and patted her on the back like she was a puppy. It brought a smile to her face.

"Are you okay, Dylan?" she asked.

Dylan nodded, but with the distant expression of a terrified and traumatized child. She didn't know what to do for him at this point. The only thing she could think of that would make a difference to him right now was to be reunited with his grandmother, the one person who seemed able to reach him.

That made Teresa wonder what had happened to Leslie. Surely her daughter and this daughter's boyfriend wouldn't have harmed her. Surely Debbie, regardless of what she'd sunk to in life, would not be party to harming her own mother.

Would she?

Teresa got up and used the camping toilet. When she slid back the curtain, she washed her hands and face in the gravity-fed sink. She didn't know how long she'd been asleep but she felt better than she had at any time since the surgery. She remembered there was a battery-operated digital clock on one of the shelves and took a peek, shocked to see it was 9 AM.

"Did I sleep all night?"

The boys nodded.

"I'm sorry. I didn't mean to sleep that long. What big boys you were to take care of yourselves."

"We fell asleep watching a movie," Dylan said.

"How long have you been up now?"

Blake looked at the clock. "Almost two hours."

"Let me get you boys something to eat. I'm sure you're starving. You didn't get dinner or breakfast."

Blake nodded enthusiastically.

"We had a few snacks," Dylan said.

"How about something easy this morning?" she said. "We've got cereal."

She went to a shelf and removed several varieties.

"Do you have milk?" Dylan asked.

"Yes, we have milk. It's instant so I have to mix it up, but it tastes just like plain old regular milk."

The boys decided cereal was fine. Each picked the type they wanted. She mixed up some instant milk in a pitcher, then made the boys their cereal. When she was done she put the remainder of the milk in a dorm fridge and plugged it into a receptacle on the wall that would run it off the main solar.

For herself she had a protein bar, certain that her body craved protein more than carbs with the healing she was doing. There was an electric kettle on the shelf and she plugged that into the wall, using it to make instant coffee. It wasn't the best coffee she'd ever had but it was close enough. The caffeine perked her up nicely.

While she ate, she thought. With the children safe, she felt like she needed to go and look for Leslie. She wasn't in top condition but she assumed that if she was armed she could probably take care of herself. She hoped she could. She had never been in a fight in her life, never physically harmed anyone. But that this man would violate her home and terrorize her family made her blood run cold.

It made her want revenge in a way she'd never experienced before.

When Teresa finished her breakfast, she took her coffee and stood in front of the wall of guns. Her husband often stood there just like that, a miser admiring his gold.

Like a lot of women, she enjoyed shooting but didn't share her husband's obsession. Although she enjoyed knowing how to use guns and how to protect herself, she didn't salivate over particular weapons the way he did. Right now she saw them purely as tools, and she was trying to pick the right tool for the job. Her biggest concern was that she was still sore from her stitches. Under normal circumstances, not involving her being slit open and sewn back shut, she would have opted for a shotgun. She liked that her aim didn't have to be precise, the sound was terrifying, and buckshot loads could be devastating.

She was certain that shooting a shotgun in her current condition would be very painful. The push against her shoulder would cause her to tense her abdominal muscles. Things might pull and tear. She was concerned that choosing a weapon that was painful to shoot might even cause her to hesitate. Hesitating might cause her to die, and that was not in the plans.

Shooting her Glock had not been painful. With a handgun, her arms absorbed most of the recoil. Perhaps her best option would be to choose another handgun to go along with her Glock. She didn't recognize a lot of what was on display. So many of the handguns looked similar to her.

Most were shiny black automatics with slides. There were a few revolvers and even a few automatics that weren't black. Still, most of them looked the same to her. Then her eyes fell on the chunky silver revolver. It was a distinctive handgun that she recognized. She'd shot that gun before and it brought a smile to her face.

It was a Taurus Judge, a revolver that shot .45 Long Colt ammunition as well as .410 shotgun shells. Before Robert had bought the gun he showed her a video on the internet, an advertisement for the weapon. It showed a woman confronted in a parking garage by men whose heads were watermelons. The woman fired on the men and vaporized the watermelons. That commercial intrigued her. Apparently it had intrigued Robert also because it wasn't long before he showed up at home with a shiny new Judge.

There were also a variety of defensive loads available for the weapon. Some of them were just novelties but Robert enjoyed picking them up to experiment with. The two of them would try them out on various targets on the property, including watermelons. One of Robert's favorite commercial loads for the weapon was a .410 shotgun shell that held a small stack of washers, then a ball bearing, then more washers stacked on top of it. When you shot the round it sliced and diced everything in front of it.

She picked up the Judge and hefted it in her hand. It felt lethal. It felt substantial. In fact it felt so substantial that she thought it might be equally effective as a bludgeon.

She had several changes of clothes in the Ready Room but she didn't think she'd find anything as comfortable as the sweatpants she was wearing. Comfort was still critical. Besides guns, the display system also held several tactical vests. Robert shot in his almost daily and he had spent a ridiculous amount of money on both the vest and outfitting it. He also had several less-expensive vests that Teresa and Grace used when they trained in one. They had a ton of pockets and attachments for adding more pockets, pouches, and holsters, empty at the moment. Robert stored them that way so he could set them up for whatever particular training they were doing on a given day.

Teresa took one of the vests down and slipped it on over her T-shirt. Beneath where she'd found the Judge she found a holster for the weapon. The holster wasn't made for the vest and it took her a moment to find a good way to attach it. She ended up mounting it in a cross draw position.

She also mounted a collapsible nylon pouch to the vest. Robert called it a dump pouch and used it for empty magazines, water bottles, and whatever else he needed a place to stash. She chose five boxes of the washer and ball bearing loads for the Judge. It wasn't like that was a massive arsenal. Each box only held five rounds. She dumped the shotgun shells into the dump pouch.

"Are you going somewhere?" Blake asked. He was standing behind her, eyes wide with concern.

"I'm going to start a movie for you and Dylan. Then I'm gonna go out and have a little look around. I want to see if I can find Mrs. Brown. She may need our help."

Blake lunged at her and wrapped his arms around her. Teresa flinched, anticipating the pain of his embrace. When the initial panic was gone she lowered her hands to his back and squeezed him.

"It's okay, baby. Mommy will be all right."

"What if he's waiting on the other side of the door? What if he's out there with a gun and shoots you? What are Dylan and I going to do if he kills you?" Blake looked up at her expectantly.

"Honey, I'm going to tell you a secret. We never told you about this before because you were too little. You're a big boy now so I think I can trust you with this."

"Told me what?"

"There's another way out of here. We never told you before because we didn't want you playing around in there."

"In where?"

Teresa released the painful embrace and limped toward the wall. Along the outside wall was a stack of cardboard boxes. The printing on the boxes indicated that they were cases of MREs. "Help me move these boxes," Teresa said.

Dylan was looking at a book and not paying any attention to their conversation, but when they started moving boxes he became interested. He came over and helped Blake move the stack. When the boxes were moved, a metal hatchway was exposed. It was a square around 3' x 3', with a hinged steel door in the middle. The door was held closed by a steel bar that was dropped into notches. There was also a padlock on a hasp.

The purpose of the padlock had been to keep the children, namely Blake, from leaving through this hatch if he were to somehow find it. The combination was written down on the wall and Teresa entered it into the padlock. In a moment she yanked the shackle open and put the padlock on a nearby box. She pulled the steel bar out of the way and swung the door open. It creaked loudly, revealing a dark passage.

Both boys crouched and stared into the blackness.

"Where does it go, Mommy?"

"When we built this house, your daddy bought a whole truckload of big drainpipes. This entire part of the house was above ground then. We knew that when they finished the house they would scrape dirt up against the house to make the yard flat. Before they did that your daddy put this hole in the wall and put this door on it. Then he put all the pipes leading away from the house and made an escape tunnel."

"Where does it go?" Blake asked.

"It comes up in an old storage building behind the house. When you follow this tunnel to the end, it turns straight up. All you have to do is stand up and push up on the piece of plywood above your head. It's not nailed down and will slide out of the way. Then you'll come up in the shed and you can leave."

"It looks scary in there," Dylan said. "It's dark and there's probably things alive in there. Snakes and rats and praying mantises with their creepy little arms."

"You're not going through there," Teresa said. "I am. I'm going to go check on your grandmother. You and Blake are going to stay here and watch a movie."

Dylan nodded eagerly. "I'd like that a lot better."

"I'm still scared, Mommy." Blake swallowed hard. "What if something happens to you?"

"It'll be okay. When I leave I want you to lock this hatch behind me. I don't know which way I'm coming back yet but if I come back through the tunnel I'll knock on the door and then I'll talk to you so you know it's me. Okay?"

Blake nodded but did not look reassured. "Are you leaving now?"

"I need a few minutes to finish getting my stuff together first, then I'll go."

Blake nodded seriously. "Okay. Can we watch *The Goonies*?"

Teresa laughed. "Of course."

Chapter Twenty-Seven

Whitetop, VA

When Conor woke up in his hammock, he initially thought he'd experienced his best sleep in years. Then he moved.

His calves, thighs, and lower back felt like they had rusted together overnight, making it difficult to even get out of the hammock. Attempts to swing his legs over the side eventually tipped it too far and he was dumped out onto the ground. Since the hammock was only hung about eighteen inches off the ground to begin with, the fall wasn't too bad. In fact, he had to admit it was probably the only way he would have made it out of there.

"You've become a crusty old man," he said to himself. "How did that happen?"

In his world, consciousness wasn't fully attained until he had sucked down at least two cups of coffee. Conor dug into his trailer and pulled out a little folding aluminum stove that burned quarter-sized hexane tabs. He filled a one quart camping pot from the river, not bothering to filter it since he was going to boil it anyway. He did give it a brief visual inspection to check for any floating wildlife.

While the water heated he took down his hammock, shaking any leaves and bugs out of it. He rolled it up, stuffed it in its sack, and tucked it away in the trailer. He'd slept under a lightweight sleeping bag that night, which he packed up also. Were he just camping in the woods he wouldn't go to much effort with his grooming, but since he expected he'd be meeting company today, he brushed his teeth and combed his hair.

It didn't work any miracles. He didn't look a whole lot better afterward than he looked before, but it made him feel better to have at least made the effort. Conor noticed that his water was at a gentle boil. He poured it into his metal mug and added a packet of instant coffee. Generally, he hated the instant stuff but this was the Starbucks instant and it was halfway decent. Any port in a storm.

Conor disconnected the old battery from his bicycle, stashed it in the trailer, and replaced it with a new one. The six-pound battery was supposed to give him assistive effort for a range of around twenty miles. He'd see if that held true today. The topo lines on the GPS made today's route look like a roller coaster ride. Constant ups and downs, twists and turns.

Conor became impatient waiting for his coffee to cool. He decided to pour it into a water bottle and let it cool on the ride. He tucked the hot bottle into the holder on the frame of his bike. As he was doing this, his satellite phone rang.

"Hello?"

"Hope I'm not disturbing your beauty sleep." It was Kevin Cole, calling from the Bridges compound.

"No, I slept like a baby but I'm awake now. I getting ready to pedal out into a beautiful morning," Conor replied.

"Pedal?" Kevin asked incredulously. *"You're on a bike?"*

"It's an experiment, and it would take too long to get into right now. To what do I owe the pleasure of hearing your voice so early in the blessed a.m.?"

"Status update, mostly."

"I traveled all night and got past Damascus. I spent the night camping in the forest. Had to stop and take a power nap. Now I'm getting ready to get back on the road. Once my coffee cools, that is."

"Coffee? You always did travel in style."

"You're not turning me around are you? Have Robert and the lady made contact with their families?"

"No. I wish I was, but our travelers have run into a little trouble getting to their reunion. There's a lot of hostile activity around us right now and their attempts to leave have not ended well."

"Everyone's safe, I hope?"

"No one's been hurt, but that's just been luck. It's not safe for them to make another attempt. I don't want to go into details right now but they'll be delayed at least for a few days, maybe longer. They wanted you to pass a message on to their families when you reach them. Let them know about the delay and that they're safe."

"I can do that," Conor agreed.

"How has your trip been so far? Any issues?"

"Nothing that ruffled me feathers. Just a scenic tour of the countryside so far."

"That's good to hear. When your journey has run its course, can you call back with a status update?"

"I plan on it."

"Good. Safe travels, my friend."

"Same to you, buddy."

Conor clicked off his phone and stashed it. With his gear all packed up and strapped in, he pushed his bike toward the trail. Walking limbered his muscles a little, but the first mile would be rough. It would be like breaking loose old rusty fittings, which was what his joints were apparently becoming.

The world was green and the light illuminated it in all shades of the color. The beautiful morning made him reflective. It made him think of family, both living and dead. He missed them all. The world hadn't got noisy yet and it was easy to float among his thoughts. It was times like these when he recalled his life and the things he'd done, the people who had once been part of his life, but weren't any longer.

So many miles, so many years had passed between him and that boy from Ireland. He still loved bikes and perhaps he was still the same in a lot of other ways too, but the world was certainly a different place. He wondered about the state of things and whether the world would ever get back to normal again. He thought about his own daughter and hoped he'd prepared her to be okay with whatever the world brought her way.

He thought about his wife and wondered what she'd be doing today if she were still alive. Would she have laughed at his outfit when he left the house, then kissed him on the cheek for luck? He thought of his mom and the many times he'd needed her support since she left him. Then, in the odd way that the mind sometimes worked, he wondered if aliens were real because that was one of the things he desperately wanted to know before he died. It was weird how the mind worked. He laughed at himself because it made him feel better.

At the trail he looked in both directions and saw no one. He mounted his bike and began pedaling. He couldn't help but let out sounds that reflected the soreness escaping his body. He tried not to curse, the morning being so peaceful and beautiful that it would seem an atrocity. Yet there were more than a few grunts and groans, but they would diminish as he moved on.

Ahead of him was about seven miles of riding, he estimated. He was looking for an old abandoned railroad station called Green Cove. Once there, he could get off the steep trail and take up a gravel road for a short bit. He had a physical address for where he was going and if the GPS was accurate, which it wasn't always with rural locations, he should be there by midday. He could stash his bike in a thicket and start the next phase of his mission.

Chapter Twenty-Eight

Konnarock, VA

It took Debbie nearly twenty-five minutes to motorcycle to her friend Sharon's trailer. Sharon's living conditions were very much like Paul and Debbie's. Both lived in decrepit trailers with peeling paint and leaking roofs, the yards decorated with garbage, cast-off furniture, and cheap cars that sat where they died. Despite the fact that their homes looked nearly identical, Debbie always thought that Sharon's place looked trashy. She didn't see her own place that way. It was home. She didn't seem to notice that it was the same filthy pigsty that she criticized her friend for living in.

There was a group gathered in the yard playing some kind of drinking game on a folding coffee table. They were rough-looking people with stained clothes and bad skin. None looked like they showered frequently, even in the best of times. Again, this was a case of Debbie noticing things about others that she did not seem to notice about herself. The game ground to a halt when they heard Debbie coming. They watched her with a wary curiosity.

Debbie killed the engine. A rusting Mazda pickup truck, the bed full of bagged aluminum cans, sat nearby with the door open, Hank Williams, Jr. blaring from the stereo. Debbie recognized some of the people, but there were others she didn't know. Some were people she knew but didn't like. She had every reason to assume the feeling was mutual.

There was one man that held a grudge because she wouldn't go out with him. There were at least two more that had threatened Paul for owing them money for drugs they'd fronted him. She and Paul had been able to avoid those men for most of the summer but there was no avoiding them now. If Paul was there, they'd have come at him already. She wasn't completely sure they wouldn't give her the beating they intended for Paul just to send a warning.

There were two women seated around the table. She knew both of them, recognizing them as women who would do anything a man wanted if he would keep them high. Yet again Debbie found it easier to overlook her own shortcomings. She made her way uneasily to the table. All eyes were on her but no one said a word.

169

There were no greetings, no gestures of acknowledgement. She felt tense and uneasy.

"Sharon here?" she asked, her voice conveying her nervousness.

None of the men answered, only stared at her. It was apparent their goal was to make her uncomfortable. They were succeeding.

Debbie glanced at one of the women. The woman didn't say anything but cut her eyes toward the trailer. Debbie didn't acknowledge the clue but left the table. The steps to the trailer were a wobbly pile of cinderblocks. They swayed beneath her feet as she climbed. She imagined these would be a challenge to someone in an impaired state of mind.

She banged on the screen door with her fist. There was no answer. She glanced back at the table and found the group still watching her. Anxious to escape their gaze she pulled open the screen door and went on inside uninvited.

"Sharon?" she called. "Sharon?"

No one answered but she heard noises coming from the bedroom. Debbie looked around. The living room had rebel flags for curtains and little light made it inside. It had the same layout as her own trailer, like most singlewides did. Between the living room and the kitchen was a bar covered with two-liter soda bottles. What looked like the aftermath of a children's birthday party was actually a collection of "shake and bake" meth labs. It was a hillbilly tweaker's version of a home office.

She went through the kitchen and started down a dark hallway. It wasn't more than a couple of steps and then she was at the closed door. She dropped her hand to the plastic knob, then decided she better knock again. She tapped on the door.

"Sharon!" she hissed.

She thought she could hear mumbling inside, low voices. Somebody was definitely in there. Debbie reached down and rattled the knob. It was locked. She was standing there with her hand on the knob, trying to decide her next move when the door was jerked violently open.

She was startled and jumped back. There was a hulking shadow in front of her. A foul smell curled her nose. It was body odor, mildew, and some sort of chemical smell.

"What the hell you want?" a voice boomed.

She recognized that voice as belonging to Johnny, another man Paul owed money to. Of all the people she could have run into, he was the worst. He was big, dumb, and mean. There was more than one rumor of him killing men who owed him money. Debbie had no doubt they were true.

Debbie hated Paul for sending her off to do stuff like this. If he was the one always coming up with these ideas, then he needed to be the one carrying them out. It was always her though, like she was his gopher. One day she was going to find a new man and leave him in the dust. He'd be sorry then.

"Is Sharon in there?" She tried but couldn't see past the large man.

Johnny threw the door the rest of the way open and stepped aside. The tiny bedroom was a jumble of trash, dirty clothes, and sheets. Light the color of urine seeped in through the dingy windows. She could make out Sharon sitting in the bed melting a pill in a bent spoon.

"Can I talk to you second?" Debbie asked.

Sharon shrugged as if it made not one bit of difference to her. Debbie stepped into the room, having to brush against Johnny to get past him. He made no effort to give an inch, purposely wanting to make her uncomfortable. Just like the men outside, his only goal seemed to be to instill fear in her. Once past him she went to sit down on the bed.

"Whoa, whoa! Don't shake the bed!" Sharon said, her voice an almost musical slurring.

Debbie sat down gingerly, taking care to make certain that Sharon didn't spill any of her precious chemicals.

"What the fuck do you want, girlfriend? What are you doing here?" Sharon asked. She wasn't angry. She just seemed strung-out. "You after dope? I ain't sure I'm selling anymore dope. I might need every bit I got."

"I saw those pop bottles in the living room," Debbie said. "I know you're making the stuff. I don't know what you're worried about. You can always make more."

"I still have to have ingredients. Can't make it if I can't get the ingredients," Sharon replied. "I only make that stuff to trade for pain pills anyway. Meth makes me jittery. Don't need it, don't want it."

"Heck, I'll do about anything I can lay my hands on," Debbie said. She was relaxing and trying to be conversational.

"I always knew that about you," Johnny said. "Your favorite drug is *other people's drugs*."

Debbie had almost forgotten he was in the room. She cut him an angry look.

"So why you here?" Sharon asked. "Never did say."

Debbie turned on her sweetest, friendliest girlfriend demeanor. She needed to sell this. Paul would be pissed if she didn't. "Paul and I got this sweet deal going on. We found a good place to live and we want to see if you might want to come stay with us."

The whole time she was saying this, Debbie was aware of how lame it sounded. There was no way to say it and the obvious meaning not be clear. She might as well have said they were out of drugs and wanted her to come over and bring her drugs. Paul had said as much. It sounded reasonable when they were talking about it in the living room of the Hardwicks' house. Now it just sounded stupid. She was embarrassed she'd even said it but it was too late. It was out there.

Johnny laughed. "Look who's all caring and shit now. Looking to be your best friend and take care of you. Just as long as you bring your drugs with you."

Sharon nodded, an amused look on her face.

"Who's been taking care of you, girl?" Johnny asked.

"You have," Sharon said.

"Who's been feeding you?" he asked.

"You have."

"Who's been running around finding your pain pills? Who's been going out and digging up the stuff you need to cook your meth?"

"You have," Sharon replied.

Johnny turned on Debbie. "So ain't nobody here needs your charity. Ain't nobody buying what you're selling. I know that piece of crap boyfriend of yours put you up to this, so you go back and tell him the next time he has some stupid idea like this he better think twice about it."

Ignoring Johnny, Debbie turned her back to him and leaned closer to Sharon. "This place has solar power. The lights are working and the water is running. They have air-conditioning, movies, and cold beer in the fridge."

"Where is this?" Johnny asked, obviously listening in.

"None of your business," Debbie said, a frustrated lilt in her voice that made her sound like a fourth-grader.

"Where she goes, I go. If you're taking her, you're taking me. Simple as that," Johnny said. He squared off to her and stuck his chest out. If he was trying to intimidate her, it was working. She was wishing she was anywhere but here.

Debbie turned her back on Johnny again. She lowered her voice. "Look, this offer is just for you. I can't invite him. But if you want to come, the offer is open."

"Where the hell are you even talking about? I ain't never heard of any place like that around here. How they got the lights on?"

Debbie leaned closer, trying to keep her voice even lower. "My mom is housesitting. It's for the Hardwicks. My mom says the man is a writer and has a lot of money. He's got all kinds of crazy stuff." She went on to describe the location and Sharon nodded, understanding now where it was that they were talking about.

"I'll think about it," Sharon said.

Sharon sucked the drug into the syringe and began working to raise a vein on her arm. Debbie called the woman's name, trying to reengage her, but only received a cold, impassive stare. Sharon looked like a coyote that had already eaten her fill and was observing while the other coyotes did the same. Debbie felt a deep chill when it dawned upon her that she had no friends here. There was no one here who cared if she lived or died. In fact, there were probably more who would prefer her dead. Perhaps even a few who would like to do the honors.

Realizing she'd overplayed her hand, Debbie stood to go. She wanted to be anywhere but there. "Well, honey, I'll just be going. Forget I said anything. You all take care of yourselves and stay safe."

Debbie got to the door and Johnny stood there in front of her, his body filling the opening. She was about a foot and a half shorter than him and he stared down at her. She was too terrified to ask him to move, afraid she could not control her voice. After staring at her for a while, something seemed to click in Johnny's head and he decided to let her pass. Debbie rushed past him before he could change his mind. She had been in some bad situations before because of the company she kept but she suddenly felt more endangered than she'd ever felt in her life. Coming here had been a bad idea. She should have turned around and zipped off when she saw the crowd outside. This had been a dumb move.

It was all she could do not to run as she stepped through the kitchen, the living room, and out the front door. She walked carefully down the shaky block steps to the table of people in the yard still sitting there. They studied her as she came out. She found the gesture to be both menacing and invasive and quickly walked to the dirt bike.

Each step closer to the bike eased her anxiety. She thought she was home free until she heard the voice from behind her.

"Hey, why don't you come back here and play with us?" Apparently seeing her flee had triggered their predatory instinct. They tell you when confronted by a bear to never turn your back and run. That was exactly what she'd just done.

She froze for a moment, then resumed walking even faster. It was one of the men that Paul owed money to. She had an idea that if she went back there she would be the one losing, perhaps in more ways than one.

Two of the men began walking toward her. She jumped on the dirt bike and hit the starter button. The starter whirred but the bike didn't start. A wave of anxiety nearly crushed her. She couldn't breathe. Then she remembered to turn the ignition on. She tried the starter again and the bike roared to life.

The men were nearly to her when she popped the clutch to speed off. She did it too fast, and the bike stalled.

"Shit!"

She repeated the process as fast as she could, the bike starting right up. The men were nearly upon her. They were all smiles. Inviting. Welcoming.

She hit the throttle and eased out on the clutch this time. The bike started rolling and she looked back over her shoulder. The two men had stopped and were standing in the road watching her. One of them waved.

Relieved, she turned back to the road ahead of her, screaming when she saw Johnny standing in the middle of the road with the shotgun raised. She accelerated and leaned the bike, determined to speed around him. She was not fast enough.

Johnny reversed the shotgun and swung it like a bat. The stock caught Debbie in the side of the head, the impact knocking her from the motorcycle. She rolled in the dirt and came to a stop, her arms flailing around her. Coated in dust, she looked like a piece of chicken fried steak about to be lowered into the frying pan.

She tried to sit up and keep running but nothing worked right. She couldn't stand, she couldn't crawl. She fell over and the world spun. The last sight she ever saw was Johnny standing over her with the shotgun, a grin cracking his face. She closed her eyes.

Johnny turned to the people in the yard. "Boys, I think we got us a new place to live."

Chapter Twenty-Nine

The Hardwick Farm

Teresa did not proceed down the escape tunnel until she heard Blake latch the hatch behind her. Only then did she click on her headlamp and start crawling down the drain pipe. It was not roomy by any means but neither was it cramped. She could crawl on her hands and knees without feeling claustrophobic.

That it was of a comfortable size did not exactly mean it was a painless process. The corrugated surface of the drainpipe was bruising her knees, and the pain from her incision was like a hot poker twisting around her insides. She was also deathly terrified of snakes and concerned that some may have found their way inside, but she hadn't found any so far. Robert had assured her that there was no way snakes could get into the drainpipe but snakes always found a way to get where they wanted to go. Still, the drainpipe did appear to be fairly well sealed. There was no standing water and she couldn't see any leaking dirt anywhere.

Hoping that Robert was correct in his assurances, she crawled forward, fully aware that a black snake in a black drainpipe would probably be invisible until she was right on it. After crawling for what she thought may have been around one hundred feet she reached the end of the drainpipe. Here the pipe came to a dead end and turned ninety-degrees straight up.

Teresa shifted her feet beneath her and stood slowly. It was a painful process. Her back and abdominal muscles started to cramp. She was not quite standing erect when her upraised hands hit a piece of plywood that covered the top of the pipe. She pressed on it and it didn't budge. She felt a moment of panic, wondering if perhaps someone had parked the lawnmower on top of it. Maybe somebody had forgotten and accidentally nailed the boards down?

She pounded on it with the palms of her hands. She felt it budge and let out a sigh of relief. With her cramping muscles, going back through the tunnel would be an even more painful ordeal. She pushed up as hard as she could, slid the plywood out of the way, and popped her head out of the drainpipe. Her headlamp revealed the inside of the storage building, just as she'd been assured. She was standing inside a 4x4 square in the floor where a piece of plywood had been just a moment ago.

She could see where compacted dirt and grime had glued the square of plywood in place, which had caused the initial difficulty with breaking the plywood loose. When she stood straight up, the floor was level with her chest. Under normal circumstances she would have moved to one corner of the square opening and boosted herself out. In her current condition that was not as easy as it sounded.

Indeed, getting herself out of the hole required several minutes of pushing, pulling, and kicking. There was also a fair amount of groaning and praying. When she was finally out, Teresa lay back on the nasty floor of the storage building. She needed a moment to let the muscle spasms subside and the pain ease.

Lying on that dirty floor was something she never would have done in everyday life, but they were far, far away from everyday life anymore. If there was any doubt of that, all she had to do was look down at her outfit she wore and the weapons she carried. When she was able to stand, she slid the plywood back in place. She did not want anyone discovering this access tunnel, nor did she want to accidentally back into the hole in the dark building. She wasn't sure she could get herself out again if that happened.

At the far end of the building was a pair of French doors, not as glamorous as it sounded. It was simply a pair of windowless white steel doors that opened out to create an opening large enough to drive a lawnmower in. Teresa unlocked the handle on one of the doors and cracked it open.

She had a view of the house now. She could see the driveway and the parking area, the backyard, and part of the side yard. When she studied the house and the back porch she saw a figure in a rocking chair. It took a moment for her to realize it was Paul, sitting there in a rocking chair, drinking a cold beer from *her* refrigerator.

Teresa was immediately furious. The *nerve*. Invading her home, stealing her medication, and now drinking what may have been the last cold beer in thirty miles.

Teresa had enjoyed long-range shooting with her husband. She particularly enjoyed shooting his Remington 700 in 6.5 Creedmor. What she wouldn't give to have that rifle in her hands at that moment. Whatever pain the recoil caused her would be worth it. At this distance, with that scoped rifle, she could have chosen which retina to put the bullet through. Either one would do.

With the weapons she carried, she did not have many options. The Glock would hit at that distance but she hadn't trained for it. There was no assurance of a hit and it would give away her position. She contemplated it though. She was considering her next option when she heard what sounded like a scream come from the direction of the barn. It died as quickly as it started and she wondered for a moment if she'd imagined it.

She thought of Mrs. Brown. Did he have her tied up down there? He seemed like the type. Was she dying? Injured?

Though the thought of Mrs. Brown injured and in pain disturbed Teresa, she was pleased that the sound made Paul move from the porch. He stood there for a moment with his head cocked, his posture clearly demonstrating how upset he was that someone had disturbed him when he was enjoying one of the last cold beers in thirty miles.

He tipped the bottle up and drained it. To her horror, he shattered the empty against the foundation of the house. Teresa was enraged. It was almost enough to make her charge from her hiding place and drop him on the spot. She had to remind herself that she was not combat-ready. She needed to choose her battles carefully because she may only have one shot.

After Paul lit a cigarette, he reached into his waistband and retrieved the same revolver he'd threatened Teresa with earlier. He scanned his surroundings again then trudged off toward the barn.

When he was no longer close enough to see her, Teresa slipped out the door of the shed and carefully closed it back. She paused, letting Paul put more distance between the two of them. She could not move as effectively as she'd like, still very sore and limping. The climb through the drainpipe made her realize that she may have the spirit for the fight but her body was lagging behind. Still, she had to know where he was going, where the scream came from. She did her best to pursue Paul, moving from one concealed position to the next.

Chapter Thirty

The Hardwick Farm

Grace had no idea she'd screamed at the sight of Mrs. Brown coming toward her in the dark. She was focused on what she should do with the older lady. The woman was in no condition for Grace to drag her into a fight. She decided all she could do at the moment was make Mrs. Brown comfortable while she went and checked on her family. She stood up and extended a hand to Mrs. Brown.

"Come on. Let's find you a comfortable place to sit and I'll be back for you in a few minutes."

Grace extended her hands to Mrs. Brown with the intention of helping her to her feet but the older lady didn't respond. She mumbled something that Grace couldn't understand. She pointed to the arm she cradled and made a sound that Grace interpreted as *broken*. Grace realized that Mrs. Brown's injuries must be even more serious than they appeared. She went around behind the older lady and slipped her hands beneath Mrs. Brown's armpits.

"This is going to hurt but I've got to get you on your feet. I can't leave you on the floor. I need you to help me."

Mrs. Brown nodded.

Grace counted out loud. "One, two, three."

She lifted gently but powerfully. Mrs. Brown stiffened and groaned in pain but Grace did not stop. When she had the woman most of the way up, Mrs. Brown got her legs beneath her and stood on her own. Once Grace was sure that Mrs. Brown wasn't going to collapse, she turned her in the direction of the open door, looking for a place to let her sit down. She caught a movement from the corner of her eye and looked up to find Paul standing in the door, his revolver trained on them.

Grace froze. Mrs. Brown emitted a whimper. Grace looked for her AR pistol but it was not within reach. He'd kill her before she could get it. If she were to go for a weapon at all, it would have to be the Glock 19 on her waist. While she considered how to pull it off, Paul fired a round through the metal siding of the barn not three feet from where Grace stood.

"Don't even think about it," he said. "I want you to take your pistol between two fingers and toss it to me. If you try anything, I'll put a bullet through that old lady." Mrs. Brown stiffened in fear in Grace's arms, making her wonder if Paul was responsible for her injuries.

Grace did as she was told, tugging the Glock 19 free from its holster and tossing it in his direction.

"Who are you?" she asked. "What are you doing at my family's house?"

"This is my house now. You two are trespassing. I suggest you get your asses out of here before I kill you."

Grace looked at him defiantly. "This is my family's house and I want to know what you've done to them."

A grin broke Paul's face. He gestured toward the house with his gun. "Those people up there are your family?"

She glowered. "You better not have hurt them."

"I ain't done nothing with them yet because I can't get them out of there. They're hunkered down in the basement like rats in a hole."

Grace grinned. "The Ready Room. You'll never get in there."

"Maybe I don't have to," Paul said. "Maybe they'll come out on their own...if they hear you screaming outside."

"I won't help you," she said.

"Oh, I think you might, even if you don't want to. You scream loud enough and they'll open the door. Trust me, I can do things that will make you sing like a scalded dog."

A chill ran down Grace's spine as she fully caught the implication of his words. He was correct. If her mother heard her being tortured, she would come out. It occurred to Grace that she had to do everything within her power to get away from this man. She could not let herself be used as a weapon against her family. She couldn't live with that.

Boom!

The gunfire startled them all. Mrs. Brown jerked against Grace and started to fall down. Grace let her go, knowing she'd be safer on the ground. Paul flinched at the sound, then spun in the direction it came from. He must have spotted the shooter and thought another shot was coming because he lunged into the barn. He leaned back out and fired two rounds toward the woods. It all happened in a matter of seconds.

Grace acted purely out of reflex, drawing her Glock and pointing it at Paul. He caught her movement and ducked just as another shot came through the door and splintered a post by his head. Grace moved, trying to line up a shot but it was too late. He was gone, having slipped out the door.

She started to fire through the thin steel siding to where she thought he was, but she hesitated, uncertain where the other shooter was. She did not want to hit a friendly. Just then, Paul raced back in front of the door and Grace snapped off two rounds at him but only caught dirt. Outside, there were two more booms, shots fired by someone else in Paul's direction, although neither connected.

Grace moved to the open barn door looking for another shot, but she couldn't see Paul. He had disappeared completely now. He had to be in the woods. She could catch him if she went after him. She wanted to pursue him, but was afraid to run out the door for fear of friendly fire. It would suck to be mowed down by her own family after coming this far.

She called out the opening, "It's me! It's Grace. Who is that? Who's shooting?"

A voice replied. A voice Grace had longed to hear for nearly a week now. "It's me! It's your mother, baby."

Then it hit Grace that her mother was possibly still in danger from Paul. Grace stuck her head out the door, looking around, trying to locate her mother. She spotted her coming from behind some brush. While Grace wanted to run and hug her, it was more important to remain focused on safety. Grace kept her mother covered until she reached the barn door. Her mother hugged her briefly then released her.

"We have to get back to the house," Teresa said. The kids are locked in the Ready Room. We have to try to beat him there."

"Kids?" Grace asked. "More than Blake?"

"There's no time," Teresa said. "We have to go." She took off running.

"Mom!" Grace called after her, "You help Mrs. Brown. I'm in better shape to fight than you are. You don't need to be running."

Grace took off, easily passing her mother. Grace didn't look back, didn't want to invite debate from her mother, who was clearly not ready to give up this fight.

Chapter Thirty-One

The Hardwick Farm

Paul crashed through the woods between the Hardwicks' house and the barn. He was shaken but he was also angry. He'd pissed on himself when someone fired at him. He came close to getting his dumb ass killed this time. He hadn't expected that shot. He thought everyone was locked in that room in the basement but there must be more people here than he'd thought.

Like that girl in the barn. The daughter. Where the hell had she come from?

When he reached the yard below the house he clambered out of the weeds and ran for the far corner of the house, trying to put the house between him and anyone coming up from the barn. The way the house was cut into the hillside, it appeared to only be one story from the back but was very tall on the front. Paul cut along the foundation, planning to circle the house and go in the back door. He wasn't used to this kind of exertion and staggered, his legs tired from plowing through the underbrush. For him, a hard day was walking through Wal-Mart to buy beer.

He passed what appeared to be plumbing coming out of the foundation wall. He didn't know anything about construction so he paid no attention to the large curved fittings until he got close to them. When he passed beneath them, he heard sound coming from one of the pipes. The realization hit him that these pipes might go to that room. He stopped dead and backed up.

He angled his head to the pipe and listened. There was conversation. No, not conversation. Dialogue. And a soundtrack. Someone inside was watching a movie.

Paul craned his neck to see if he could see through the pipes but he could not. He tried to shove his hand inside one only to have it shredded by what felt like balled up barbed wire blocking the inside. He cursed out loud. Then it occurred to him that if he could hear what was going on in the room then they could probably hear him too. Maybe he could use that to his advantage.

Paul leaned close to the pipe. "Hey, can you hear me?"

He listened. There was no reply but the volume of the movie was turned down. Somebody had heard him.

"Hey, Dylan? Can you hear me?"

Paul listened again but there was no response. He suspected that Dylan heard him but was just not answering. He was probably sitting in there laughing at Paul. This infuriated him.

"You little bastard! Answer me!"

There was no response. He had to calm down or he was going to blow this. Paul sagged against the house and rested his head in his palms. He was angry and embarrassed. His damp pants clung to him, the smell rising from them overpowering his already pungent body odor. He couldn't believe he'd peed on himself like a two-year-old. Somebody had to pay for this.

"Dylan, look, I'm sorry I yelled at you. I'm just scared. Your mommy is hurt bad and I'm trying to take care of her. Do you hear me?"

When there was no response, rage swelled in Paul. He balled his fist and wanted to pound it against the basement wall. He wanted to scream threats at the child. He choked it down and struggled to keep his voice calm.

"Dylan, can you hear me? Your mom needs you. She's hurt really badly. I'm not sure I can take care of her by myself. If you don't come out and help me, she's probably going to die."

Paul shook his head. It was a lost cause. The kid would never come out for him. He'd burned that bridge a long time ago. He would remember this though. If he ever got a hold of that kid he would make him pay. He couldn't afford to linger at the basement any longer. He had to get back in the house before somebody beat him there. He started to walk off when he heard the tiny voice through the vent.

"Mommy's hurt?"

Paul scurried back to the vent and pressed his ear against it, his eyes wide with excitement. Inside, he could hear heated debate. He didn't know who all was in there now, but he heard a warning voice, someone trying to tell Dylan to not answer. Paul needed to overpower that voice. He needed to make Dylan feel the urgency of the situation. He needed to make Dylan feel that his mother would die and it would be his fault if he didn't come out right now.

"Dylan, I need you. Your mommy is bleeding. Bad people hurt her. I need your help. You *have* to come out here." Paul felt like he had this fish hooked. He was reeling him in and he didn't want to lose him. He had to play this just right.

The argument inside became more intense. Paul pressed his mouth toward the vent. "Dylan, I'm coming in the house. I'm coming to that door and I want you to open it. I won't hurt you. You come out and help me take care your mother. If you don't, she's going to die. Don't let anyone stop you."

Paul smiled. The kid would listen. He had no guts at all. He was a simpering little baby and he knew who was in charge. It was Paul. Now Paul had to get in the house and get to that door in the basement. He needed to be there when Dylan opened it so the kid wouldn't change his mind.

He ran to the corner of the house, huffing and puffing, and turned left up the steep bank that would take him to the backyard. When he reached the corner, he was a left turn away from the back porch. The back door would be right there. He swung around the corner, all his attention focused on getting to that back door.

Paul didn't realize how much time he'd blown talking into the vent. When he came around the corner, there was already someone standing at the back door. When he finally noticed, he tried to bring himself to a stop, to run, but his momentum was not cooperating. His feet slid out from under him and he went down. He yelled in frustration but the fall probably saved his life. There was a loud *boom* and a shot whistled over his head. He scrambled to his feet and ran back toward the corner.

Boom! Boom! Boom!

Semi-auto fire rained all around him, punching up divots of dirt. Then a round caught him, piercing the flesh of his bicep. He cried out but didn't stop. Then he was around the corner and still running. His legs were going too fast for the steep bank and he wiped out again, rolling all the way to the bottom.

At the bottom of the yard were large rocks that been pushed aside during the excavation. Some were as big as cars. They formed the boundary of the yard now. He took shelter behind one, aiming the revolver over top of the rock and toward the corner of the house. He saw the girl's head bob around the corner and he fired in that direction. It was a long shot and his aim was lousy. She got the point though, yanking her head back.

Paul slid his sleeve up and examined his arm. It hurt like crazy, burning like someone had stabbed a burning stick through it. The shot had taken a chunk out of his arm but it didn't appear that the bullet was still in there. He was bleeding like a stuck pig. He wrapped his shirt around the wound and tried to tie it off.

He heard yelling up there now, other voices, and he ducked. Paul couldn't believe those women had beaten him into the house. He would stay here for now. He had a secure position and he wasn't ready to leave. He had to admit he was at a disadvantage now but he was not giving up. The reward was too high.

How could anybody abandon this house? It was his best chance of surviving whatever mess the country was in now. No, it wasn't his, but that was a minor detail. The owners wouldn't give up without a fight, but that was okay.

As he thought of renewing the fight, he realized he hadn't even thought to check his gun. He hadn't counted how many rounds he'd fired. He didn't know how many rounds most guns carried but he understood you couldn't just shove another magazine into a revolver and he didn't have any more cartridges for it.

It took him a moment to figure out how to open the cylinder. When he finally accomplished this he found that there were no unfired rounds remaining. He slapped himself in the head and started to throw the gun into the weeds. Had he gotten into another gun battle with these folks, he'd probably have been killed. It would have been just his luck to take an empty gun into a gunfight.

This changed everything. He couldn't stay and fight. He would have to get out of there and get better weaponry, or at least more ammo. Finding some backup would be nice too. That made him wonder about Debbie again and what the hell she was doing out there. She should have been back already. Was she just goofing off somewhere? She'd probably gotten high and forgot all about him.

Paul tried to plan the easiest route of escape. He didn't want to get shot while he headed for safety. That would be his dumb luck. He scanned the yard for threats. As his eyes passed over the storage building in the backyard, he saw the door move.

He froze. Was someone coming after him? If they were, he was screwed. He had nothing. He would have to throw his gun at them and run away in his urine-soaked pants with blood running down his arm. Then the door swung open fully and Dylan stepped out of the building.

"I'll be damned," Paul breathed. "I did it. I talked him out of there." This wasn't as good as the kid opening that secret vault to Paul but it was the next best thing.

Paul had to assume Dylan was coming to him because of what he'd whispered through the vent. Dylan was trying to find him because he thought his mother was hurt and that Paul needed his help. Paul didn't want to expose himself to potential gunfire but he needed the kid to come to him.

"Dylan!" Paul hissed.

The boy didn't hear him

"*Dylan*!" he called a little louder.

This time the boy heard him and it startled him. He turned in Paul's direction and Paul raised a hand to wave at him. He could see indecision in the boy's expression, that he was unsure of whether to approach the man or not.

"Come on, Dylan, we need to get to your mother. We have to get back to her or she might die. Come on!"

That statement appeared to have some effect on the child and he reluctantly moved toward Paul. Paul kept urging the boy until he was at the edge of the yard, almost within his grasp. Paul's fingers curled as if he wanted to lunge at the boy and snatch him away.

When Dylan stepped into the weeds and came toward him, Paul knew he had him. He tried to curb his anger. It was to his benefit to continue to allow the boy to believe his mother was injured. The kid needed to believe Paul was only trying to rescue her. He would be more cooperative that way. Paul wouldn't end up having to carry him kicking and screaming.

When the boy was within reach, Paul grabbed him. He tried to mask his excitement at finally nabbing the boy as concern. Dylan looked at Paul's hand on his forearm, terrified, as if it were a snake latched onto him.

Paul got a grip on his anger and released the boy, patting him on the back. The gesture did not seem to calm Dylan at all. Since

Paul had never buddied up to him that way, the boy found the gesture unsettling.

"Sorry, Dylan. I'm just a little nervous about your mother. We have to get to her now. There's no time. Let's go."

With no trail to follow, Paul moved in a general direction away from the house. He wanted to put as much distance between him and the house as possible. If they knew he had Dylan, they'd come after him and he had nothing to fight back with but an empty gun.

"How the hell did you get out of there anyway?" Paul asked. "How did you get into that storage building?"

Dylan looked at Paul apprehensively. He was scared to lie to the man but felt an obligation to preserve the family's secret. Especially since it was his loose lips that had led Paul to the Hardwicks' home in the first place. He hadn't wanted to give away their secret back at Paul's trailer in the first place but he hoped that doing it would make his mother like him. He hoped it would make her come home.

"I got out of that room when nobody was looking. I ran out to the house. I was in the front yard and I heard shooting. I got scared so I ran and hid in the building."

Paul nodded. It sounded reasonable to him and he had no reason not to believe the kid.

As they got away from the house, the woods opened up more. The trees were taller and there was less underbrush, but it was still slow going. Shortly, Paul saw a gap in the woods below him and realized it was the driveway coming into the family's home.

"Let's go that way," Paul said. "These woods are killing me. I'm starting to feel like a mountain goat."

Paul cut down through the woods, turning occasionally to make sure that Dylan was still with him. The boy was his ace in the hole. If he could get the boy somewhere and stash him for safekeeping, he could use him for leverage. They'd probably give him food, weapons, whatever he wanted. Debbie's mother would do anything to get the boy back. He was lucky she was still alive. He hadn't been certain up until he saw her in the barn. He was certain she'd crawled off and died like a sick cat.

They slid down the bank and onto the surface of the driveway. Paul had never been so excited to see a gravel road in his life. His lifestyle wasn't one that required a lot of walking, and he'd done more today than he'd done in years.

"Where's my mama?" the boy asked.

"I ain't got time for your damn questions," Paul snapped. Catching himself, he realized he needed to take a different tone if he expected this boy to be cooperative.

He looked back behind him and saw the boy pouting as he shuffled along, kicking at rocks. Paul stopped in the road and waited for the boy to catch up with him. He tried to adopt a friendlier manner, but it wasn't his thing. He wasn't a nice, kind person. He tried to remember situations where he'd seen people be nice before. Maybe he could fake it.

"You mother got shot, Dylan. Those people up at the house hurt her. They've fooled you into thinking they're nice but they're really not. I managed to drag her off and keep her alive but she's hurt real bad. I can't remember exactly how far it is so we'll just have to keep walking until we get there. Okay?"

The boy appeared satisfied with that and walked alongside Paul for a while. Then the physical proximity seemed to make the boy uncomfortable. He slowed down and allowed some distance to build between them. Paul was okay with that. He hated kids.

Chapter Thirty-Two

The Hardwick Farm

Teresa had just gotten to the house as Grace was firing at Paul.

"I'm going after him!" Grace yelled.

"Leave him! You help Mrs. Brown into the house. I'm going to check on the kids."

Grace was hesitant to leave an armed attacker alive on their property. It went against everything she knew. She had him on the run and she should have finished it. Giving him time would only allow him to strategize and come back when it was advantageous to him. Still, she did as her mother asked.

She peeled off the corner of the house and ran back. Mrs. Brown was still struggling to make it across the yard. She'd started strong but was losing steam. She was limping and holding her broken arm.

"Keep going!" Grace said, trying to watch all directions at once, not knowing if the man was coming back to reignite the fight.

She realized that Mrs. Brown needed assistance or she'd never make it inside. Grace ran across the yard to meet her and wrapped an arm around her. She allowed her AR pistol to dangle from its sling and drew her Glock, scanning the perimeter of the property and the corners of the house. She might not make a shot that long but she could make a man duck and cover.

It took the two of them forever to get across the remainder of the yard and up the steps into the house. Once inside Grace locked the door behind her and led a stumbling Mrs. Brown to the living room. She laid the older woman on the couch where she slumped down. Grace couldn't tell if she was even conscious at this point.

"Where are you, Mom?" Grace called to her mother.

"In the hallway!"

"Coming to you." Grace ran to the hallway and met her mother there.

"There was a woman here—Mrs. Brown's daughter—but I can't find her," Theresa said in a rush.

"She may have left," Grace said.

190

"Or she may be hiding. Let's check the basement."

Grace got ahead of her mother and beat her to the laundry room. She eased down the steps with her Glock raised. "If anybody's down here come out with your hands up. If I find you, I'll kill you."

Grace didn't hear any reaction to her warning so she headed down. The basement was fully illuminated. Paul and Debbie had left the solar lights on, not having a grasp of conserving power when it came from batteries. The room contained a lot of boxes and storage containers but there were few places to hide. Just to be sure, Grace thoroughly checked the perimeter of the room.

While Grace was clearing the room, Teresa went to the vault door and punched in a code. By the time the door was unlocked, Grace was finished and at her mother's side. There was a whir of electric motors as the vault door unlocked. Teresa turned the latch. "It's Mom, Blake," she said. "Don't shoot."

"Okay," came a shaky reply from the interior of the Ready Room.

When the door was open, Teresa hurried inside, Grace on her heels. Blake was standing in the center of the room, a 20 gauge shotgun in his hands. Teresa took the gun from him and threw her arms around him. Grace joined the hug and everyone used the moment to recharge a little of what they'd exhausted over the day.

"I thought you said there were two kids?" Grace said.

Teresa pulled free of the hug and scanned the room. The cots were empty and the curtain around the porta potty was drawn back. "There were. Where's Dylan?"

"He went out the tunnel," Blake replied.

Teresa face clouded. She tried to crouch to her son's level but the movement caused her tremendous pain. She winced and stood back up right, clutching at her guts. She swooned, the pain causing a wave of dizziness. She'd seriously overdone it today.

Grace stepped forward and took her mother by the arm, steadying her.

"Why? *Why* did he go out the tunnel?" Teresa asked.

"The bad man, Paul, who was with his mother. He whispered to us through there." Blake pointed to the PVC vents that extended through the foundation wall. "He told Dylan that his mommy was hurt bad and she was going to die if he didn't come out and help him."

Teresa closed her eyes, fighting back cursing. She shouldn't have left the children. This was her fault. They weren't old enough. They didn't have the judgment.

"I'm sorry, Mommy. I tried to make him stay but he wouldn't listen."

Teresa stroked her son's head. "It's not your fault, sweetie. You're not responsible for Dylan."

"So what do we do?" Grace asked.

Teresa sighed. "We get Mrs. Brown down here to stay with Blake and we go after Dylan."

Anger flashed across Grace's face. "You're not in any shape to do that. You're probably about ready to collapse right now. You're a liability out there in this condition, Mom."

"I'm not letting you go alone," Teresa argued.

Grace fumed but knew her mother would do as she pleased. She couldn't make her mother stay behind any more than Blake could make Dylan stay.

"Okay. We'll go together but I'm not waiting on you. If you can't keep up I'm going to leave you behind and you can come back here. Are we clear?"

Teresa gave her daughter a hard look but didn't answer.

After reminding Blake not to leave the room they bolted up the steps. They found Mrs. Brown conscious but extremely weak. Grace was becoming more concerned that the woman may have internal injuries. Without advanced medicine, they had no way of knowing. Even if they knew the extent of her injuries, they couldn't deal with anything severe anyway.

It was a struggle to get the older woman back down the steps and into the Ready Room. Once there, Teresa made a quick and dirty splint for Mrs. Brown's arm with a section of foam mattress and duct tape. It wasn't perfect but it would keep until they could do something better.

Once they had her settled into a bunk, they gave Blake instructions to get her some water and food. They also reminded him that under no circumstances was he to leave the room. Even if Dylan came back and asked to be let inside, he was not to open the door. It could be a trap. He was only to open the door for Grace, Teresa, or his dad.

Before they left the Ready Room, Grace convinced her mother to trade the Taurus Judge for something that would be a more effective across open distances. She decided to give her the AR pistol she was carrying herself. It was light, had minimal recoil, and was able to hit at a hundred yards shots with the current optic. At that distance, the grouping on the targets was not tight when fired from the shoulder, but they would all fit within the torso of an average-sized man. That was all they needed.

Grace picked up a couple of fresh magazines for her Glock 19. She took down an AR-10 from her dad's armory. It was basically a 7.62 caliber version of the AR-15. She snagged one of the tactical vests from a rack and shoved the magazine pouches full of fresh mags for the weapon.

Their gear assembled, the women were out of the room and moving. They climbed the steps, immediately on guard in case there were people hiding in the house that they weren't aware of. When they didn't encounter anyone, they exited and locked the house behind them. Teresa remembered to take her house keys so she could get back in. She didn't relish the thought of going back through the escape tunnel again.

Chapter Thirty-Three

Arthur Bridges' Compound

Arthur sat at the controls of his ham radio equipment scanning frequencies, trying to see if he could pick up any chatter that would let him know what frequency the congressman's men might be using. After nearly thirty minutes of testing, he came across a strong signal he thought could possibly be the folks down the road.

Arthur saw no reason to bother with call signs at this point. "This is Arthur Bridges wishing to contact Congressman Honaker. Do I have his party?"

There was a pause in the radio chatter, then, "*Stand by.*"

Robert was standing at the window watching Sonyea. The horse that had run from them had returned and she was outside checking him over. Kevin was sitting on a couch reading a gun magazine.

"*This is Congressman Honaker,*" came a voice. "*Am I to understand I have Arthur Bridges on the line?*"

Arthur adjusted a dial on one of the units in front of him. "Long time, no see, Congressman."

"*You can cut the friendly bullshit. I've got four dead men this morning thanks to you. Four families that I have to console.*"

"Those deaths are on you," Arthur replied. "The lives of your men are no more important than the lives of my men. If someone had to die, I'd rather it be your men than mine."

"*No one had to die,*" the congressman said. "*My men had instructions to only fire warning shots when necessary.*"

"That's bad advice on your part," Arthur said. "There are no warning shots in the theater of war."

"*So this is war? You think you're up for that? You should take my advice. You should drop everything and leave.*"

"That's not happening."

"*Oh, it's happening, all right. The only variable is how many bodies we have to bury when the smoke settles.*"

"I used to think you were a decent man," Arthur said. "I thought we had a connection. All those conversations between two country boys stuck in the big city."

"Times have changed. The country is going to get a lot worse before it gets better. We need a place to weather the storm. I've had my eye on your place for some time. It's perfectly suited to my plans."

"Do your plans include me personally putting a bullet in your gut?"

"Look, Arthur, we're only the scouting party. I have more men coming. A lot more men. These men have families with them. Be reasonable."

"Then there's nothing else to talk about," Arthur said.

"We're in no hurry. We'll just wait until the next group arrives and then we'll take you by force. You have no idea of the resources we have at our disposal."

"You better bring all of it," Arthur said. "You're going to need it."

Arthur ended the communication. He sat back in his chair. Robert and Kevin stared at him.

"That went well, didn't it?" Arthur said.

Chapter Thirty-Four

The Hardwick Farm

Conor was pleased that his GPS took him right to the Hardwicks' gate. Of a generation that had grown up traveling with maps, the device still seemed miraculous to him. He unlatched the gate, walked his bike through, and parked it deep in the weeds. Once he was certain it was out of view, Conor drew his sheath knife and cut some small branches to lay over top of it.

He dragged his gear out of the trailer and kitted up. He had been in stealth mode earlier, aiming for speed and concealment. While he didn't know exactly what lay ahead of him, he felt it safe to assume that he was in battle mode now. He slid on a pair of camouflage pants over his bike shorts. It did occur to him that the bicycling shorts might have a disarming effect on his opponents. Were they distracted by his outfit, it might buy him an additional second to draw his weapon. His bike shorts could save his life. Despite that, he decided that the benefit of camouflage might be greater. Plus the camouflage fatigue pants certainly had more storage capacity than his bicycle shorts, which barely had capacity for him.

He slipped on his gun belt. It had a Safariland holster for his Springfield Operator 1911 and pouches that held magazines for his weapons. The belt also contained his IFAK, or individual first-aid kit. There was a larger sheath knife permanently affixed to the battle belt and a smaller pouch that held a multitool.

Conor took the opportunity to change shirts. His other was sweaty from riding the bike. This one would soon be sweaty too in this humidity, but for now it would be clean and fresh. Over top of the clean T-shirt, he slipped on a plate carrier. Sleeves in the front and back held armored plates that would stop most rounds. The sides of the plate carrier held soft armor with Kevlar that were not as strong but would hopefully be strong enough. The armor was good Level IV stuff, given to him by a grateful client.

Molle webbing on the front of the plate carrier held an assortment of pouches. There was more ammo for his rifle and his .45. There were also pouches with smoke grenades and other goodies. The smoke grenades were designed for paintball games but as far as Conor was concerned smoke was smoke. If it worked, who cared what the original purpose was? Broken down into two pieces in the bicycle trailer was an AR-9, a 9mm version of the AR-15. The weapon had a Primary Arms optic on it. Conor deftly assembled it, slapped in a magazine, and charged the weapon.

Once he was completely geared up he spread a piece of camo fabric over the gear he left behind and placed foliage on it. He slung a pack on his back, which held his emergency gear. If he came back from his mission and all his gear was gone, he would at least have what he needed to get home.

Conor had no intention of walking straight up the road. There could be traps or sentries. He moved about fifty feet off the shoulder of the family's driveway and began paralleling it up the mountain. The terrain was dense but Conor felt strong from his days on the bicycle. Instead of pedaling bike pedals he was just pedaling dirt now. The adrenaline was kicking in too, and doing its job.

He hadn't gone far when he heard the sound of an approaching engine. So rare was vehicle traffic he wasn't certain that was what he was hearing at first. When he was sure, he paused to listen. It sounded as if the vehicle slowed at the entrance, then he heard the screech of the gate swinging open. It was definitely coming up the driveway.

Conor crouched in the weeds. Soon, an old dump truck came into view, grinding its way up the hillside. A tag on the front said *Farm Use*. It was a Chevy Apache from the 1960s, so eaten with rust that the body appeared to be partially made of brown lace.

The cab was packed with people. More were in the bed, hanging over the sides and front. Conor could see a few weapons. If this was the group that had taken over the Hardwicks' home, they were ragged but armed. He slipped a pair of binoculars out of his pocket and observed them closely as they passed. They looked like a scraggly band. Not soldiers. They didn't even look like backpackers, more like an army recruited from the lobby of a methadone clinic. At least that was encouraging. If he had to fight, he'd rather fight the untrained than the trained.

After the truck passed Conor picked up his pace. He had no idea if there were more of these people at the house or if this was a group that just happened to be showing up when he did. He wasn't in any condition to run up this mountain but he did pick up his pace as best he could. Around the next bend, he found the truck stopped in the road and the doors flung open. He wondered if it broke down or overheated climbing the hill. It wouldn't be surprising from a truck that old.

As quietly as he could in the dry undergrowth, he worked his way into a position where he could see the front of the truck and try to determine what was happening. When he did, he found an odd sort of standoff taking place. Two men from the cab of the truck were standing in front of it speaking with another man in the company of a small boy.

Conor whipped out his binoculars again and studied the scene. The little bit of intelligence that he had on the family told him that they had a small boy, though the man with the boy didn't fit the description of any of the family. Conor was told he would find Robert Hardwick's wife, a young boy, hopefully a young woman, and possibly a physically-challenged man. This guy looked more like the people in the truck.

He had to know why this boy seemed to be leaving the property with this man. He tucked the binoculars away and began to work his way forward.

It didn't take long before profanity and arguing reached his ears. Two things became immediately apparent. One, the man with the boy knew the men in the truck, and two, they did not like each other.

*

"We appreciate the invitation to come stay with you. Your girlfriend was really gracious," said the man who had been driving the truck. It was Sharon's boyfriend, Johnny.

"That invitation wasn't supposed to be for you," the man with the boy spat.

"That's not the impression I got from your girlfriend," Johnny said. "She said a *real* man would be a welcome sight."

Where's Debbie?" Paul demanded. "If you've done something to her—"

"What?" the other man from the truck cut in. "What you gonna do?"

"Have you seen my mommy?" the little boy asked Johnny. "We're trying to find her."

"You're not going to find her," Johnny told the boy. "Paul sent her to me and I'm keeping her."

The boy looked at Paul. "You said she was hurt. You said the people at the house hurt her."

"Shut up, Dylan," Paul said.

"Don't believe everything you hear, kid," Johnny said. "Especially if it comes from the likes of him."

Conor was still confused as to the identity of this boy. Could this boy's mother be Mrs. Hardwick? Was she being held prisoner by this other group? Either way, the manner in which the boy was being treated infuriated Conor.

"I want to know if my mommy is hurt," the boy demanded.

"Yeah, is she *hurt*, Paul?" the big man mocked.

Paul didn't like being made fun of. Since he couldn't hit Johnny, he did the only other thing he could do. He lashed out and backhanded Dylan, dropping him to the gravel. The boy started crying and curled up on the ground. It was all Conor could do to not shoot the man where he stood. He couldn't tolerate seeing kids mistreated.

To distract himself, Conor tried to process what he was seeing on a tactical level rather than a human one. So the kid didn't belong there at the house; the guy walking with the kid didn't belong at the house; none of the folks in the truck belonged there either. He still didn't know if the family was in control of their house or if they'd been compromised.

The other man from the truck noticed something and pointed to Paul's pants. "Look at that," he jeered. "He pissed on himself."

Johnny laughed. "That what happened? You peed on yourself like a little baby?"

Anger flared within Paul. "No. I spilled my coffee when the shooting broke out."

The two men nodded at Paul but their amused expressions indicated they did not believe him.

Paul mumbled to himself, trying to regain face. "I ain't got to stand here and take this."

"Not when you got a diapey needs changing," Johnny taunted.

Paul started walking off, trying to cut around the two men. Johnny stuck out a hand out. It was nearly as broad as Paul's chest. He stopped the smaller man. "You forgot your kid."

Paul shrugged, agitated. "He's Debbie's kid. He ain't nothing to me. You can be his daddy if you want. He's your problem now."

Johnny shook his head. "I ain't got no way to take care of a kid."

Paul shrugged. "Then kill him. I don't care."

"You'd let us just kill your girlfriend's kid? Just like that?" Johnny asked.

"Ain't no skin off my ass," Paul said.

Johnny whipped out a pistol and stuck it in Paul's face. "I don't like you. I've never liked you. Tell me one reason I shouldn't blow your head off right now."

A look of panic crossed Paul's face. Johnny was more than capable of doing what he threatened to do. In his panic, Paul looked at the kid, hoping he might have something to offer, but instead he found Dylan grinning at him, obviously pleased to see Paul being the one terrified for a change. Paul's mind raced. He was a cornered rat looking for a place to scurry.

"This house up there, it's something special. It works even when the power is off but you'll never figure it out without me. I know how to make it all work—the power, the water, everything. If you kill me you'll never figure it out."

Johnny glared at Paul through the sights of his pistol. His finger was on the trigger. He was as likely to pull it as not, knowing there would be no consequences. "If a dumb ass like you figured it out, I can figure it out too."

"No, no!" Paul said adamantly. "It's more complicated than that. The old lady taking care of the house was Debbie's mother. She showed me how it all worked. It's complicated. There's lots of switches and gauges and stuff. Things you have to check every day or it will quit working."

Paul was just making up stuff now but he was desperate. He'd seen that Johnny was leaning toward killing him now. He had to swing the pendulum back the other way.

"But—" Dylan interjected.

"*Shut up!*" Paul screamed, cutting him off.

Johnny didn't drop his gun but Paul could feel the tension easing just a hair. "I guess we could go up there and check it out before I make up my mind. No harm there."

"No. It's not that easy. There's people up there. They control the house now. They have guns. You can take the house but it won't be so easy as that."

"We have guns too," Johnny said, waving his around as if to prove the point.

"They have more guns. Better guns," Paul said.

Johnny tucked his gun back in his waistband. "So what do you propose?"

"We can use the kid," Paul said, gesturing at Dylan.

Johnny laughed as he tucked the gun back in his waistband. "You really are a lousy person."

Chapter Thirty-Five

The Hardwick Farm

Grace began running as soon as she was out of the house. As much as she'd run the last two days, this pace felt like second nature to her. She glanced back over her shoulder and saw her mother struggling already. She was trying to run but couldn't. It was painful to watch.

Grace was torn. Should she take off without her mother and reach Dylan sooner, or stay with her mother?

She slowed. Her mother was moving along at a fast walk, tears rolling down her face from the pain. Grace admired her mother's determination. She had never realized her strength before.

"I'm sorry," Teresa said. "I tried, but I can't run like that."

"It's okay, Mom."

"I know you could go faster without me."

Grace didn't respond. They both knew the answer to that already. At least traveling on the gravel road was relatively easy. Assuming the man who took Dylan stuck to the woods, the women would make better time. Yet who knew if they were even going in the right direction? Grace began to think the entire effort might be futile. They may never recover Dylan.

They were about two hundred yards from the house when they heard a diesel engine approaching. When you lived in the country and heard your family coming home day after day, you learned to distinguish between the sounds of their engines. Grace and Teresa immediately knew this was not one of their vehicles.

"What should we do?" Teresa asked.

Grace wasn't sure she had the answer for that. There was no time for a complicated plan. "You go over there behind that woodshed," Grace said, pointing to the wooden structure filled with firewood.

"What are you going to do?"

Grace hesitated. "I'm going to ask whoever it is what they're doing here."

Teresa didn't like the sound of that plan but the engine was getting closer with each approaching second. There wasn't time for extended debate. With worry clouding her face, Teresa loped off painfully toward the woodshed and situated herself behind one corner. She got down on her knees and laid the barrel of the AR pistol across a chunk of firewood. From that position, from that distance, she could take out the driver if she needed to.

While Grace may have seemed confident, maybe even overconfident, to her mother, she was actually terrified. The engine sounded like the growl of an approaching monster. She had no idea who or what was coming or what it would bring. When the sound of crunching gravel reached her ears, she knew the vehicle was nearly upon them. She stood in the center of the road and spread her feet defiantly. She prepared her rifle, holding it across her body. She flicked the safety off and double checked the chamber, confirming the glint of brass. She made sure she had her next mag ready.

When the truck crept into sight, she realized it was someone's old *Farm Use* dump truck. Lots of her neighbors had them. They were typically dump trucks that were no longer safe for construction, or even for highway use. There were people riding on the hood of the vehicle.

With the difficulty of obtaining fuel, people had been resorting to all types of transportation. When you did see a vehicle on the road, it often looked like something from a Third World country, with people clinging to every surface of the vehicle. She couldn't tell how many people were in the truck but it was more than she felt comfortable with. Not quite a dozen but maybe close to that.

Her palms began to sweat. She had to force herself to control her breathing. She tried to distract herself from her growing anxiety by coming up with a plan. If this turned into a fight she was going to have to take out the driver first and then try to find cover. That would be her plan.

As the vehicle drew nearer, she recognized both of the people on the hood. One was Paul, the man that she and her mother had been trying to track and kill. The other person riding on the hood was Mrs. Brown's grandson, Dylan. He was sitting on Paul's lap, the man holding tightly onto him.

She raised her rifle to get a better look at what was going on. The AR-10 had a Vortex 1x4 optic. It was set to 2x power. When Grace had the truck in her field of view, she could see Paul had a grin on his face and a revolver pressed to the side of the child's head.

The sight of that nearly stopped her breathing. There was something so wrong about it. She centered the crosshairs of her scope on the middle of Paul's face. Under ideal circumstances she could have made this shot. Ideal circumstances involved shooting at a stationary target though. Paul was not a stationary target. The truck was constantly bouncing and jostling. One moment Grace had a kill shot, the next her crosshairs were landing on Dylan's face.

She could not take that kind of chance. If she missed and caused Dylan's death she was not sure she could live with the consequences. Grace reluctantly lowered the barrel of her rifle, not wanting to provoke someone into taking a shot at her. She still wanted to be ready though. She could raise the rifle and take action in a split second if shooting started. Yet there was still the matter of Dylan right there in the middle of things. She didn't know what to do.

The truck jolted to a stop thirty feet from where she stood. The driver killed the rattling engine and set the parking brake. All fell silent except for the ticking of the cooling engine. There were three men in the cab. None were brandishing firearms but it was a safe bet they all had them.

Over top of the cab, there were people standing in the truck bed. Not all were men. There were a few rough-looking women in there with them. Most of these were brandishing weapons, either pointing them into the air or levelling them across the cab in her direction. She'd never had so many guns pointed at her in her life. If this was a standoff it was likely to be her last. The odds were against her. She took several deep breaths trying to calm herself.

The man on the hood stared at Grace with a maniacal grin. She decided it would be up to her to break the silence.

"We've not been introduced," Grace said. "My name is Grace."

Paul sneered. "I told you once to get off my property," he said. "Since you're not gone I guess I'm going to have to make you leave."

"How do you intend to do that?"

Paul tapped the barrel of his revolver a little too hard against Dylan's head. The boy frowned. He tried to move his head away but Paul wouldn't let him.

"I'm taking that to mean that you kill Dylan if we don't hand our home over to you?"

Paul grinned. "Guess you're smarter than you look. That's exactly what I mean."

Grace took another deep breath and tried to let it out without telegraphing her nervousness. There was a lot on the line here and she was in over her head. She had no experience that even remotely prepared her for something like this. She would have to go with her gut.

"That kid means nothing to me. He's not family. My family is safe. Do want you want," Grace said. She didn't mean it but she was trying to disarm Paul. She didn't want him to think they'd roll over for him just because of Dylan.

The man driving the truck stuck his head out the window and yelled, startling Grace. "You said you could do this. Get on with it!"

"I told you I'd handle this!" Paul shouted back.

The driver threw his door open and slid out of the cab. The truck lurched slightly backward when he took his foot off the brake. The parking brake caught it but jolted everyone in the vehicle. The driver walked around his open door and snatched Dylan by the arm, yanking him violently off the hood of the truck. Dylan cried out and tears rolled down his already stained cheeks.

The driver spun on Grace. He was a big man, wearing a sleeveless t-shirt, his arms lined with crude jail tattoos. There was something in his eyes that warned Grace he was more a threat than Paul. Paul was a loose cannon and might do anything, but Grace didn't feel like he was eager to kill. This man gave off the vibe that he'd killed before and liked it.

"Let's test this theory," he spat. He whipped out a hunting knife and laid it against Dylan's ear. "Maybe he's not family but can you watch him get sliced up?"

Grace didn't answer. She didn't want to see Dylan harmed but she also couldn't just drop her gun and surrender. She'd screwed this up royally. She'd gambled on meeting them in the road and confronting them. She'd gambled on telling them that their hostage meant nothing to her. Now Dylan was going to get hurt and she wasn't sure she could do anything about it. Her brain scrambled for a possible solution.

Boom!

A shot rang out and a round caught the truck driver in the neck, just below his ear. Blood sprayed everywhere. The geyser of blood drenched Dylan but the knife dropped away from his ear. The driver threw his hands to his throat in a futile attempt to stem the loss of his blood supply.

Grace was paralyzed by what was happening but something hit the ground in front of her and broke the spell. She staggered backward, startled and unsure of what it was. It sounded like a rock, then there was a hissing sound. Thick smoke poured from the object. There was another thud to her side, then more smoke.

Grace snapped out of it and raised her rifle. She intended to drop Paul but he was not there. He'd disappeared in the cloud of smoke. Grace spotted Dylan crouched down by the front of the truck, his head and chest soaked in blood. His hands were held out in front of him. He appeared to be staring at them in shock.

She ran for the child and swept him into her arms. He was too big for her to carry for any distance but she managed to get him to the nearest cover, a steep embankment at the shoulder of the road. She shoved him over the edge and then dropped down beside him, pressing his head down into the weeds.

She raised her rifle and turned back to watch for a target. Teresa opened fire at some point, shooting into the truck after she saw Grace pull Dylan out of the line of fire. The people in the truck were firing back at Teresa, making little effort to protect themselves. Grace managed to drop one from behind with a head shot before the attackers ducked below the level of the truck bed, naively assuming the steel dump bed would protect them. Grace began punching holes at random intervals in the steel skin. It was no match for the 7.62 caliber rounds. Blood sprayed and people screamed.

Amidst the chaos a hand snaked from behind Grace and covered her mouth. Another hand grabbed her rifle barrel. She went ballistic, trying to bite the hand while going for her Glock.

The man held her tighter. "Easy now. I'm a friend. Your dad sent me." The voice belonged to an older man with an Irish accent.

Grace didn't believe him. She didn't believe anything anyone said anymore. She struggled to break loose, to put a bullet in the man. She would *not* be taken.

"Stop it! Listen. They call me The Mick but my real name is Conor. A man named Kevin called me from a compound where he is staying with your dad, Robert. Your dad asked me to check on his family because he was delayed. I'm here as a favor."

The man released her and Grace rolled over defiantly. She met his eyes and searched for the truth. Her face was red from exertion, her expression fiery. She was still considering going for her Glock. She hesitated. The man knew about the compound and about Kevin. Still, she trusted no one. Especially not strangers showing up at her home.

"Your name is Grace. You came here with a man named Tom. Your brother is Blake and your mother is Teresa. You can kill me if you want but I'm telling the truth."

Grace tried to make herself relax. Despite her distrust of everyone, this man seemed to be telling the truth. Another burst of gunfire drew everyone's attention back up to the road. Two people had jumped from the bed of the truck and were firing at Teresa. Conor threw up his AR-9 and dropped each of them proficiently with a single shot.

"Stay here until I call you up," he said, starting up the bank.

Grace grabbed him by the ankle "No! My mom will shoot you."

Conor hesitated. "Good point."

"Mom!" Grace yelled. She waited a moment. "Mom!"

"I'm here!"

Grace breathed a sigh of relief, concerned for a second that her mother might have been shot in the exchange.

"We're coming up. There's a man with us. He's on our side. Don't shoot."

Grace, Dylan, and Conor climbed back up to the road. Teresa edged out from behind the shed, her AR pistol on Conor, uncertain what the appearance of the stranger meant.

"Who are you?" she asked. "What are you doing here?"

"He's a friend of the people who dropped Tom and I off in town," Grace said. "Dad sent him."

"Tom?" Teresa asked, confused. "Who's Tom?"

Grace realized she hadn't even had an opportunity to tell her mother about Tom. In fact, her mother knew nothing of what she'd gone through over the last week. "Tom's a good friend. He came here with me. He's in a battery-operated track chair and the battery ran down on the trail last night. I had to come on without him."

Dylan finally broke his paralysis and ran to Teresa. She wrapped the small boy in a hug. She tried to shield his eyes from the death around him but it was probably too late at this point. He was drenched in blood and terrified.

Conor checked the bodies, circling the truck to make sure he had everyone accounted for. "I've got six dead, two wounded!" he called out.

Boom! Boom!

The sound of a pistol shot startled everyone and weapons flew up.

"My bad," Conor said. "Eight dead. No wounded."

Conor reappeared at the front of the truck. "It looks like some of them got away."

"What about Paul?" Grace asked.

"The one who was holding the kid on the hood?" Conor asked.

Grace nodded.

"I don't see him. He must've turned tail in the confusion and ran."

"Mom," Grace said, "you and Dylan go to the house. I'm going after Paul. No way I'm leaving him out there to come back another day. We only fight this coward once."

"I'm not so sure about that," Teresa said. "I don't like the idea of you going after him alone."

"What if it's Blake he takes prisoner next time?" Grace spat.

"She won't be going alone," Conor said. "And she's right. I wouldn't leave that weasel alive. He'll come back another day with more men."

Teresa conceded, though it was unclear if she did so out of agreement or because she was too exhausted to argue. She put her arm around Dylan and they began walking toward the house.

"Stay in the Ready Room until we get back," Grace called after them.

"Okay."

"The Ready Room?" Conor asked.

"It's our combination gun safe and bunker," Grace replied.

"Excellent," Conor said, nodding in approval.

Chapter Thirty-Six

The Hardwick Farm

Grace and Conor double-timed it down the driveway in pursuit of Paul. Conor pointed out occasional droplets of blood splattered in the dusty road.

"Somebody's hit, but not bad."

They ran to the bottom of the driveway and exited the gate. They turned left and ran up the road, heading back the way both of them had come in earlier. They accepted that it was always possible Paul was hiding in the bushes along the way or had taken to a trail in the woods, but a lazy man would usually choose the road. It was the easiest traveling and it was familiar.

"How did you even get here?" Grace asked. "Did you come in on a helicopter too?"

"I don't live too far away. A hundred miles or so," Conor puffed.

Running in the heat was exhausting business and neither had much breath for conversation. Still, there were things that Grace wanted to know.

"Why did my dad feel like he needed to send you? I thought he was driving up here right behind me in a couple of days."

"The compound he's staying at with my friend Kevin came under attack. They're safe but they can't get out."

That worried Grace. Arthur's compound had seemed more secure than any place she'd been lately. She couldn't imagine there being any attack, short of a heavy assault, that they couldn't repel. That alone told her something. Maybe the attack was not just a band of locals.

They had run about three-quarters of a mile when Grace and Conor rounded a bend to find Paul and the two women sitting on an abandoned vehicle stopped dead in the road. They were all sprawled out on the vehicle, trying to catch their breath. When they saw Grace and Conor, they scrambled into motion, taking cover behind the car.

One of the women had a bolt-action hunting rifle and she popped off a round in their direction. She hadn't even aimed. The round was nowhere close to hitting them, but running into gunfire was generally a losing proposition. Conor threw a hand up and latched onto Grace's shoulder. He steered her toward the ditch and dived into the weeds after her. It was not ideal cover but it was all they had. At fifty yards, it might not be enough.

There was another shot from the rifle, this one whizzing over their heads. Knowing that the shooter would immediately have to cycle the bolt before firing another round, Grace rolled into a shooting position with her AR-10. She aligned her scope on the driver's side door and popped off a couple of rounds, knowing the round should punch straight through to the other side. That would give Paul and his buddies something to think about.

There was a flash from beneath the car and a round whizzed by Grace's head. Their aim was improving with each shot. It made Grace wish they'd been able to choose a better hiding spot. She popped several rounds off at the pavement near the car, hoping to send the ricochets splattering beneath it. It must have worked because it provoked an immediate response.

Another woman threw herself across the hood and began blasting away with a semi-automatic shotgun. Buckshot sprayed the weeds around the ditch.

Grace ducked, trying to make herself as small as she could. When there was a lapse in the fire, she raised up and found a target. She creased the hood with a 7.62 round and caught the shooter in the lower half of her face. There was a spray of blood and she dropped away, the shotgun clattering across the hood.

"One down," Grace said. "We got this."

Their elation at evening the odds was short-lived. Unexpectedly, Paul came up with the first intelligent and strategic move he'd ever had in his entire life. He lunged inside the abandoned vehicle, popped the shifter into neutral, and released the emergency brake. The wheels turned, then began to pick up speed. The car gained momentum as it coasted down the incline toward them.

Conor raised up on his knees and dumped rounds on the car. The passengers aimed out the side windows and returned fire. Conor was forced back to the ground, the shotgun loads having such a spread at this distance that the shooter needed no skill to take the two of them out. The rolling car was closing the distance now, gaining speed.

Forty feet.

Thirty feet.

Twenty feet.

"We got to get outta here!" Conor yelled.

Conor raised his rifle above his head and began shooting blindly in the direction of the car. He was holding the AR-9 by the pistol grip, doing a spray and pray. The car bore down on them. Conor leapt to his feet and wrapped his hand around the drag handle on Grace's load-bearing vest. He twisted and swung with all his might, sending her careening out of the path of the vehicle.

The tumble disoriented her. She rose to her knees in time to see the vehicle plow into Conor and she screamed. The car came to a stop over the same ditch she had been laying in moments ago, the bumper digging into the embankment. Grace raised her Glock 19 and ran to the car, fully prepared to put rounds in everyone in the vehicle.

It was empty.

Whoever was in the car had abandoned ship. She was trying to figure out where they'd gone when she felt a hand latch on to her ankle. She immediately recoiled in fear and jumped back, aiming the pistol downward. What she saw paralyzed her with horror.

Conor's hand extended from beneath the vehicle, his fingers grasping for her. Grace called his name but he did not answer.

"Are you okay!"

There was no response. It was a stupid question. How could he be okay?

Grace fell to her knees and began reaching beneath the vehicle. She felt his body, it was compressed beneath the weight of the car. She understood now that he couldn't answer her because he could not breathe. He was being crushed to death beneath the car.

Grace was in a panic. This man had come to save her life and she could not let him die. She reached into the car and popped the trunk, then ran to the back and dug around for the jack. She found a raincoat, windshield washer fluid, and a can of tire sealant. She was still shuffling through the contents of the car when she felt the cold steel of a gun barrel at the base of her neck. She immediately froze, paralyzed with fear.

"Yesterday we didn't even know each other," Paul whispered. "Today we just can't keep from running into each other."

"You have to let me help him," Grace pleaded. "He's going to die."

The gun barrel did not move. "I'm okay with that. If the car kills him, then I don't have to."

"Kill her," said a female voice. "She killed Millie. Kill her *now*."

Grace assumed that Millie must have been the woman she shot across the car hood. It had been self-defense, but she wasn't going argue her case now.

"Shut up!" Paul told the other woman. "She could be useful. This puts me in the same position I was in before with the kid. Now I have someone I can take back for leverage. Without a hostage, they're never going to give me the house."

"You'll never get me back there," Grace said. "I'll die before I put my mother and brother in that position."

"Turn around. Slowly."

Grace did as she was told and turned to face Paul. He had a hunting rifle in his hands. She could see that the safety was off, the barrel pointed right into her face.

"If I can't get you back there as a hostage, you're no good to me at all. I might as well just kill you right now."

Grace didn't want to provoke or encourage the man in any way. She just stared him in the eye. She considered her options, fully aware that every second she wasted was a second Conor was pinned beneath that car. He could even be dead already.

She wondered if she could go for the rifle barrel and divert it to the side. She still had her Glock. If she could get that rifle barrel off her, maybe she could draw the pistol and drop him.

"I'm waiting on your decision."

Grace opened her mouth to render her final verdict. Then her ears caught the familiar whir of electric motors. She couldn't stop herself from searching for the source. When Paul turned to see what she was looking at, Tom fired the first round from his AK pistol. He held it to his shoulder, sighting through the optic, and managing to put a round into Paul's upper back. The round hit the slight man like a sledgehammer blow. He spun and staggered away from Grace, dropping the rifle. With a margin of distance now between Grace and Paul, Tom burned off more rounds, shredding Paul. The man staggered and fell in a heap.

The woman with Paul went for the dropped rifle. Grace had her Glock out by the time the woman's fingers wrapped around the stock and double-tapped the woman at nearly point-blank range. She was dead before she could scream.

Grace located the jack and ran around to the side of the vehicle. She dropped to her knees at the front of the driver's door and felt for the dimple in the frame that the scissor jack would fit into. She slid the jack in place, twisting the screw with her finger until the jack tightened and began raising.

She was locking the handle into position when Tom appeared beside her. He'd unstrapped from his track chair and joined her by the vehicle. He didn't know what was going on but sensed Grace's urgency. When he got closer, he saw the arm sticking out from beneath the vehicle and sprang into action.

"Let me do it!" he yelled. He took the jack handle, inserted it into the jack, and began cranking furiously. Grace lay down on her stomach and tried to see what was going on beneath the car. Between the shadows and the tall roadside weeds she couldn't see much. She took Conor's hand and squeezed it but he did not squeeze back.

"Go faster!" Grace urged, desperation in her voice.

Life on the farm gave Tom plenty of upper body strength and he threw everything he had into it. When the jack first started taking the weight of the car, it sank into the ground instead of lifting the car.

Grace groaned. All his effort was gaining them nothing.

Then the car began to raise.

"This is shaky," Tom warned. "It could turn over at any moment."

Grace backed away from the vehicle with Conor's hand in both of hers. She tugged as hard as she could. Between his weight and the pressure of the car, she could feel no movement. The car inched upward as Tom desperately worked the jack handle. Sweat poured from them. Grace tugged furiously at the limp arm. She was not going to let him die. Suddenly, she felt the first movement.

"He moved!" she yelled.

She got off her knees and sat down on her butt, digging her heels into the ground, tugging with all she was worth. Her sweaty hands kept slipping off his arm and her frustration grew. She let go of Conor's hand and scooted closer to the vehicle, reached beneath it, and caught a strap of his vest. She braced a foot against the tire and a hand against the side of the vehicle. She tried tugging that way, levering herself off the vehicle.

When she still made no progress, Tom flipped over onto his stomach and looked beneath the car. "I think he's hung," he said.

Tom shot an arm beneath the car. He fought to untangle a piece of webbing from Conor's vest. It was snagged on a heat shield beneath the exhaust. When he had it free, he rolled away from the car.

"Pull!"

Grace tugged on the vest. Tom got his hands on Conor's arm and pulled too. His body began to slide toward them. Grace scooted back and Tom did the same, adjusting their grips. They pulled again and in seconds Conor was free.

Grace threw herself across the man, pressing an ear to his lips. "He's breathing."

"Let's get this gear off him," Tom said.

Grace and Tom undid the buckles of the man's gear. Tom dragged the heavy plate carrier off his chest. Grace listened again at his lips. His breathing was shallow. She put her mouth to his and gave him a couple of assistive breaths.

"His color is better," Tom said. "Keep going."

Grace continued to help Conor breathe. He'd been breathing on his own when she pulled him out, but now his efforts were stronger. In a couple of minutes, Conor was twisting his head and moving his arms. Grace moved off him and patted him on the upper arm.

"It's okay. It's okay. Just relax."

Conor's eyes flickered open and he focused on Grace. "Are you okay?" he whispered.

She smiled, tearing up slightly. "Yes. Thanks to you."

"Thanks for saving my life," he said.

"Thanks for saving *mine*."

She put her hand on top of Tom's. "And thank *you* for saving both of us."

"That was too close, Grace. If I'd been a minute later..." Tom couldn't finish the thought.

She nodded, her expression reflecting that she fully understood just how close it had been. "I wasn't sure how long it would take to charge your track chair with that charger. I wasn't expecting you to show up when you did."

"When it hit twenty percent power, I got on the trail. I got off at the first road crossing and started looking for vehicles. I figured most of the cars had run out of gas but might still have functional batteries. Every car I came to I stole the battery and switched out. That's how I got here."

"I'm glad you did," Grace said.

Conor sat up and rubbed his face, trying to shrug off his near suffocation. Grace introduced the two men.

"You had a close call," Tom said.

"I was kind of addled when the car hit me," Conor admitted, "but I thought I would still be able to crawl out from under it. If I hadn't had on all that gear I probably could have. The weight of the car was pushing my gear against my body armor and my chest was being squeezed between the front and back plates. It didn't leave much room for breathing. I thought I was dead."

Tom maneuvered himself back into his track chair and strapped in. He mounted his AK pistols back on the gimbal mounts. Grace stood and helped Conor to his feet. Everyone geared back up. They retrieved the weapons that had belonged to Paul and the two women. There was very little ammo and no other gear. At Conor's insistence, they dragged the dead bodies off the road into the weeds.

"No use advertising what happened here," he said.

Chapter Thirty-Seven

The Hardwick Farm

Grace and the two men made their way back to the Hardwick farm. They found everyone in the Ready Room anxiously awaiting their return. Grace made the introductions. The job of the reunion was overshadowed by the glaring absences. The Hardwicks were still missing Robert. Tom was still missing his mother.

Teresa hugged Tom and gave him a kiss on the cheek. "Thank you for helping my daughter get home to me. I don't know that I could ever repay you for that."

Tom looked embarrassed at the attention. "We helped each other. You raised a very capable daughter. She can take care of herself."

"Did you see Debbie?" Mrs. Brown asked. Her voice was still difficult to understand, garbled from her damaged mouth. Grace's mom had given Mrs. Brown one of her own prescription pain pills and it at least allowed her to tolerate the pain.

Grace's brow furrowed. "I've never met your daughter so I don't know what she looks like. There were two women with Paul when we found them, but I don't know if one of them was your daughter not."

"What happened to them?" Mrs. Brown asked.

Grace hesitated. "I...killed them. In self-defense."

Mrs. Brown's hand flew to her mouth, the sudden movement causing her to wince in pain. She was in full panic for a moment, the automatic reaction of a mother. Then the panic subsided and a peace settled over her. "If you killed her, I'm sure she deserved it. I hate to say that and I know it sounds awful, but it's true."

Dylan got up from the video game he was playing with Blake and came to his grandmother's side. "I don't think she was with Paul. I didn't see her in the truck, Granny."

Mrs. Brown nodded. "Thank you, sweetie. You go play with Blake, okay?"

Conor leaned closer and lowered his voice. "I heard the man driving the truck say something about keeping someone prisoner. It sounded to me as if she were being held captive back at wherever these folks came from."

Mrs. Brown nodded somberly. "I think I know where that is. Debbie only had one friend she still hung out with. Do you have a way you could take me over there later to check?"

"I don't think you're in any condition to travel," Theresa said. "You have broken bones. You could have internal injuries. You need to lie down."

"I need to tend to family business," Mrs. Brown said. "Will you take me or do I walk?"

"Probably a four wheeler would be best," Teresa conceded, certain that Mrs. Brown wouldn't have even been able to walk to the property line.

"You have two of them?" Conor said. "I'd like to go along."

"We do," Teresa said.

"What are you going to do?" Grace asked.

Ms. Brown shook her head sadly. She said nothing else and the tears running down her cheek discouraged more questions.

Conor kept watch outside while Grace and Teresa tended to Mrs. Brown. They suspected she had two broken ribs. They wrapped her chest in gauze and then with duct tape. Since the fracture in her arm did not appear to be displaced, they applied an elastic bandage. She had dozens of cuts, scrapes, and bruises. Those would heal faster than the wounds on the inside.

While they treated Mrs. Brown, Grace recounted her adventure home. She'd arrived home to such chaos that it wasn't until she started recounting her journey that she realized she hadn't told her mother about Zoe. When she told the story of losing her best friend, her mother and Mrs. Brown both broke down into tears. The ladies had known Zoe also, and their hearts broke.

"I have to find some way to let her parents know," Grace said.

Teresa nodded. "We'll find a way, when we can."

When the tears stopped flowing, she continued the story with her arrival at Arthur's compound and how happy she was to see her dad. She told the story of how they ended up hitching a ride home on a chopper and what they found upon their arrival in town.

"Those poor hikers," Teresa said. "I wish there was something we could do for them."

"There's too many," Grace said. "They would overwhelm any resource we offered. Their group is the size of an army. If they become aware of any resource, I don't know that anyone could stop them from taking it. They would overwhelm us with sheer numbers."

*

Teresa, Tom, and the two children remained at the Hardwick compound while Grace and Conor escorted Mrs. Brown to the trailer where they believed the group had come from. Grace and Mrs. Brown rode together in a side-by-side ATV, Conor following behind them. They parked the machines in the driveway by the trailer. To Grace, it looked like any number of similar trailers that were scattered throughout the region.

"Stay out here with Mrs. Brown," Conor instructed. "I'm checking the trailer."

Grace got out and stood by the ATV with her weapon at the ready, safety off. Mrs. Brown sat rigidly on the bench seat, holding tightly to the grab handle even though the machine was not moving. Grace wasn't sure if the handle provided emotional support or just kept Mrs. Brown upright.

Not one for subtlety, Conor didn't knock. He twisted the handle and found it locked. He stepped back and booted the door off its frame, ducked to the side, and waited for any response before advancing. His rifle raised, he disappeared into the dark interior of the trailer for several tense moments. He came out a few moments looking only slightly more relaxed. He came down the steps of the trailer and over to the ATV.

"I got one dead female in there," he said. "From the description, it doesn't sound like your daughter. Looks like she overdosed. Still has the spike in her arm."

Mrs. Brown's lips pulled tight but she remained silent.

A desperate pounding suddenly reached their ears and everyone came on guard instantly, Conor swinging and raising his rifle. Grace threw hers up and stepped around the back of the ATV.

219

"There's someone in that shed," Conor said. "Cover me."

Conor made his way cautiously to an outbuilding. When he got there, he found it padlocked. While he could break the lock with a little effort, the chain was threaded through a cheesy hasp fastened to the shed with rusty drywall screws. A scrap of galvanized water pipe propped against the building gave him all the leverage he needed to pry the chain and the handle free of the door. It clattered to the ground and Conor backpedaled, raising his rifle and leveling it at the door. A woman pushed it open and staggered out. Conor had his rifle trained on her.

"Stop right there!" Conor barked. "Are you armed? Do you have a weapon?"

The woman was sobbing hysterically, her fingertips raw and bloody from trying to claw her way out. She held them in front of her, showing that they were empty. "I don't have anything. They were holding me prisoner."

The woman blinked and squinted, her eyes unaccustomed to the bright light. As they adjusted, she looked from face-to-face and then spotted Mrs. Brown in the side-by-side.

"Mama!"

The young woman staggered toward the ATV her arms outstretched. Mrs. Brown climbed from the side-by-side, her movements slow and stiff. She received her daughter's embrace, but was slow to return it. Finally, she conceded, wrapping her arms around her daughter and holding her tight. Debbie had shown no reaction to her mother's battered face. No guilt. No concern.

Debbie was babbling hysterically, a mixture of words and sobs. Mrs. Brown nodded sympathetically, stroking her daughter's hair. Conor and Grace moved in, standing around without comment, watching the reunion. Conor watched their surroundings, wanting to make sure that they didn't have any unexpected guests.

"Did you come to get me?" Debbie asked.

Mrs. Brown hugged her daughter tightly. Debbie continued to moan and cry.

"I thought I was going to die, Mommy. I thought they were going to kill me. Then I thought they were just going to leave me in that shed to die. It was horrible."

"It's okay, baby," Mrs. Brown replied. She stroked her daughter's back, consoling her as she'd done when Debbie was smaller. She remembered the bike wrecks and the skinned knees, the hurt feelings.

"I'm so glad you came for me. I don't know how you figured out where I was, but I'm so glad you came. I'm going to do better from now on. I promise. It was all Paul's fault. He was a bad influence on me."

As she held her daughter, Mrs. Brown replayed all the broken promises she'd heard over the years. She recalled the disappointment on Dylan's face time after time when Debbie said she was coming to visit and never did. She recalled all the birthday presents that Debbie had promised and never delivered.

Worst of all, there was single thought she would never in her life be able to banish from her head. It was what she saw as she was laying on the ground being beaten and kicked by Paul. It was the memory of her daughter sitting on the motorcycle and doing nothing. She hadn't even asked him to stop. It was as bad as if she had been kicking and punching too. There was no forgiveness in her for such a thing. What if it were her precious Dylan receiving the beating next time while Debbie watched?

Mrs. Brown trailed a hand from her daughter's back and down to her own side. She moved it to her back pocket and touched the warm wooden grip of her revolver. She paused there, then wrapped her hand fully around the grip. She began sliding it free of her pocket. She would move it between them, fire it upward through her daughter's diaphragm, and it would all be over.

But she couldn't do it.

Mrs. Brown closed her eyes and allowed the revolver to drop back into her pocket. She took several deep breaths and let them out slowly, hardening her resolve for what she had to say. "You're not coming back with us."

Debbie instantly turned off the tears and released her mother. "Excuse me?"

Mrs. Brown didn't respond. She could only look at her daughter and think about how close she'd just come to killing her.

Debbie pushed herself back slightly, opening a gap between them. She looked her mother in the face. She gathered a baggy short sleeve in her hand and wiped her eyes. "What you mean? What are you talking about?"

Mrs. Brown looked at her daughter sadly. "It's just what I said, sweetie," she said. "I'm not taking you back into our lives again. I'm not going to leave you in that shed to die but I don't want you in our lives either."

Debbie erupted. "What the hell am I supposed to do? You can't just leave your own daughter out here in the middle of nowhere with nothing. I'll starve."

"I can't trust you. I could never trust you again."

Debbie pushed her mother away from her. "You're not taking my child. I want him back. If you won't take me, you can't have him."

"That's not happening," Mrs. Brown stated firmly. "You can't take care of him. You can't even take care of yourself. I don't want you coming around again. I'm going to tell Dylan you're dead."

"You can't do that!" Debbie screamed. "You'll break his heart. He needs his mother."

"Unfortunately, he won't even shed a tear," Mrs. Brown replied. "That should tell you something. It should tell you what kind of mother you were."

Debbie yelled and screamed. What little of it was decipherable was the same thing Mrs. Brown had heard before. Empty promises, assurances that she had changed, and demands that Mrs. Brown do as she wished.

When these tactics failed, Debbie became aggressive. She stepped toward her mother and got in her face. Grace drew her Glock and aimed it at Debbie.

"It's over," Grace said flatly. "We're going now."

Debbie started in on Grace, hoping the same arguments that had failed on her mother might work on her. Grace hooked her arm around Mrs. Brown's and guided the lady back toward the ATV.

Conor had his rifle up also, just in case Debbie tried something stupid. He covered Debbie while Mrs. Brown and Grace got in the side-by-side and started it up. Debbie was ranting again and screaming at her mother. Mrs. Brown continued to gaze upon her daughter with the same disappointed expression. When the ATV drove off, Mrs. Brown never looked back.

With the other women gone, Debbie looked at Conor expectantly. "Could you stay with me? I need help. Or I could even go back to your place. I could help out around the house. I could do anything you needed. Anything."

Conor lowered his rifle. "Sorry. I live with my daughter and she's a hard-ass. She wouldn't tolerate the likes of you."

He mounted his own ATV and started it up. He backed down the driveway, not taking his eyes off Debbie. He didn't trust that she might not have a weapon hidden somewhere that she could pull out and start blasting at him.

When he reached the bottom edge of the driveway, he sped away. He caught up with other women and fell in behind them. As a father, he couldn't imagine the resolve it took to do what Mrs. Brown had just done. He couldn't imagine having to make that decision.

Chapter Thirty-Eight

The Hardwick Farm

Grace and Teresa cooked a large dinner that evening. Everyone was tired and hungry from all that had been going on. Conor and Tom kept watch outside while dinner was being prepared. Besides conducting a security assessment on the property, Conor, ever the machinist, insisted on studying Tom's track chair. He was able to offer some useful insight as to what were weak points in the design and what might give Tom trouble in the future. He also gave his suggestions as to how he could make those repairs if he didn't have access to factory replacement parts.

When dinner was ready, everyone filled their plates and ate where they could find a seat. The kids ate in Blake's room. Mrs. Brown had retired to the guest room and collapsed into sleep. The remainder of the group stayed in the kitchen. While everyone was eating, Conor pulled his satellite phone from his vest and dialed a number. Everyone stared at him expectantly.

"Hey, Kev. The Mad Mick here. Can I speak to your buddy Robert?"

While Kevin was getting Robert, Conor shoved a forkful of macaroni and cheese in his mouth. Teresa's eyes got wide and she looked at Grace eagerly, excited about the prospect of speaking with her husband.

"Hey, Robert. Yes, the Mick here. Mission accomplished, buddy. I've got your family here and everyone's okay." Conor said it matter-of-factly, as if he were telling a customer his tires had been installed and the car was ready for pick-up.

The room was quiet and they listened for Robert's faint voice over the tiny speaker.

"Well, no, I can't say it was all peaches and cream, but we made it work. There were a few hitches." He listened a moment then responded, "No, I can't. I expect I'll be heading out tonight. I've got a daughter of my own and you know how that goes. Yeah, you're welcome. Glad I could do it. Would you like to speak your wife?"

Conor handed the phone across the table to Teresa without waiting for an answer. Teresa took it with tears welling in her eyes.

The past few days had been the longest she and her husband had ever gone without speaking since they were married. Teresa offered Robert the same assurances that Conor had, not going into any detail that would unduly worry the man.

"When can we expect you and Sonyea?" she asked.

After a long pause, Robert replied, *"I don't know. The area around the compound is not secure. It's not safe for us travel."*

"Don't you bullshit me, Robert Hardwick," Teresa snapped. "Don't talk to me like I'm a teenager. I want to know what's going on. Tell me what you know."

The group around the table got up and wandered off, uncomfortable watching the way the conversation had turned. It had gone from happy reunion to very personal.

"There's another group that has their eye on this place. They're led by a congressman. They may have been watching this compound for some time, since before the collapse. It looks like their plan was to take this compound and all the resources as their own. Sonyea and I tried to leave twice and both times came under fire. We weren't injured but it was darn close. The safest thing for us to do now is sit tight. The compound is secure. There are a lot of men here, everyone's armed, and we're safe. I'm sorry I can't be there for you right now. You all just be careful and be safe. I'll contact you as soon as I can, or even better, I'll show up and deliver my message in person."

"Don't you worry about us, Robert. Don't you apologize. You just stay safe and get here when you can do it in one piece." Teresa was breaking down now, tears running down her face.

"I love you," Robert said.

"I love you too," Teresa replied.

She hung up, knowing from their years together that Robert wouldn't end the call until she did. She took the phone through the empty living room and onto the porch where she found the rest of the group sitting, well out of earshot.

"I'm sorry about that," Teresa said. "I lost it for a second." She looked at Grace. "Your father is not coming home anytime soon. They're trapped and it's not safe for him to leave."

Teresa started to tear up again but took a couple of deep breaths. She fanned a hand in front of her face, trying to dry the tears.

"Yeah, that's the impression I got from Conor," Grace said. "Things are safe as long as he stays put. That's okay. I'd rather Dad be safe there than in danger on the road."

"I think you'll be fine, Mrs. Hardwick," Conor said. "I've seen that daughter of yours in action. She's a crackerjack. And you've got Tom here. He's an impressive young man. You've got a good place and good people. As long as you can keep a low profile I think you'll be alright."

Teresa nodded, but it was clear she was struggling to hold the tears back.

Conor stood. "I'd best be leaving. I've got a long ride home and a daughter of my own waiting on me."

"How old is your daughter?" Grace asked.

"She's twenty-five," Conor said. "She's a crackerjack too."

"What's her name?"

"Barbara," Conor replied. "I call her Barb. You two would be thick as thieves."

"I hope I get to meet her one day," Grace said. She stood and hugged Conor. "I appreciate everything you've done. We wouldn't have done it without you."

Conor smiled. "Don't be so sure of that. I think you can do about anything you set your mind to."

Grace smiled back and took his arm. She and Tom followed Conor back into the house. He stopped off in the kitchen and picked up the bike battery he'd been charging in the wall outlet. Outside, he checked the air in the tires and sprayed lube on the chain. He double-checked the electrical connections and confirmed that everything was in good shape for the trip home.

He started to kit up in his bicycle shorts but decided he would wait until he was at the bottom of the hill and away from the Hardwicks. Right now they all had a good impression of him and he didn't want to blow it. He didn't want them laughing at the sight of him the way his own daughter had. He'd been too busy with all that had taken place over the course of the day to think much about his daughter. Now that this mission of his was winding down, he missed her terribly.

"Do you mind fetching me a piece of paper from the kitchen, dear girl?" he asked Grace as he finalized his packing.

She ran inside and returned with a notepad and a felt tip pen. She handed them to Conor, who scribbled on the pad and handed it back to her.

"Memorize that piece of paper and then store it in your Go Bag. That's the physical address of my property. If you need to bug out for *any* reason, either before your dad gets home or after, you all would be welcome at my place. I've never extended that offer to anybody. I don't really have a lot of friends. But I'd be proud to have you as my guests."

Grace and Tom were touched by the gesture. They both travelled among preparedness circles with their parents and knew that such invitations were not extended often or lightly.

"I'm honored by your offer," Tom said solemnly.

Conor nodded. "If it starts going that way, cache all the supplies you can to keep people from looting them. You know how to do that, right?"

Grace nodded. "We have watertight tanks stored in the ground just in case."

"That's good. Carry what you can, cache what you can't, and come to that address."

Grace hugged Conor again. The man shook Tom's hand and mounted his bike. They waved as he pedaled off, humming a loud melody into the gloaming.

Chapter Thirty-Nine

Russell County, Virginia

Being anxious to get home did not keep Conor from enjoying his ride. When he made the trip to Damascus, his mind was occupied with what lay ahead of him, and he didn't think much about the journey itself. This time his mind was free to wander. With his night vision and his electric bike, he rode in a green bubble. The world was quiet and he felt as safe as one could in this world. Still, it was a dangerous place, as each day seemed to constantly remind him.

The Hardwicks had been able to point him toward a different route that allowed him to bypass the town of Damascus on his way home. After several small roads, he picked back up with the same route he'd travelled before. The last big barrier between him and home was the Clinch Mountain range. He had to follow Route 80 and cross through Hayter's Gap. It was a winding, narrow road that seemed as if it had been designed by a man who dropped a string from a ladder and drew the route from the way the string landed.

Before he crossed the mountain, Conor coasted along a foggy river valley. The smell of wood smoke in the air told him that people still lived here. The smell mixed with the pungent smell of river banks and damp wood. He even got chased once by a persistent dog that probably woke the entire valley. Conor appreciated that dog, a reminder of normal times.

When he reached the base of Clinch Mountain, he climbed onto the pedals and began pushing. Within a quarter-mile he was tiring and had to kick in the motorized assist. He had a long ascent ahead of him.

The climb was uneventful but at the top of the mountain, at Hayter's Gap, the world opened up before him. Even in darkness there was a sense of the rich landscape that lay ahead of him. Without streetlights and communication towers, the countryside lay like a dark and convoluted fabric, like a barely visible sweater tossed on the floor in a dark bedroom.

It was the countryside of a hundred years ago. Of two hundred. Of two thousand. Conor sat there atop his bike for some time watching the stars and the sliver of moon.

After the long, slow ascent, Conor began the hair-raising descent. It was a narrow road with no shoulder and no guardrail. He tried to keep his speed down, concerned about hitting any road debris while driving by night vision.

And that was exactly what happened to him.

He was in a curve, leaning slightly, when the front tire hit a piece of gravel just slightly smaller than a baseball. The wheel skipped hard to the right and Conor was slammed to the ground before he even had time to process what was happening. The bike slid hard to the shoulder and struck an exposed rock face.

When he finally stopped skidding, Conor told himself he was lucky. Had he skidded toward the other shoulder he'd have been launched into the air, since there was no guardrail. At least on this side there'd been something to arrest his slide. He lay there for a moment assessing the damage.

His head had hit the ground but the military bump helmet had prevented any damage. He was hardheaded after all. He had on gloves also, which protected his hands. A long sleeve camo shirt covered his elbows but offered no protection. His sleeves were shredded and he could feel the burn of raw skin on his arms.

He carefully moved his arms and shoulders, aware that it was usually the collarbone that snapped in a bike wreck. Fortunately for him, it happened so fast that he hadn't had time to try to catch himself. That had likely saved his collarbone. He pushed free of the bike and rolled onto his back. He laid there a moment longer, assessing the damage, before determining that he was probably okay.

He got to his feet and went to his bike, standing it up to take a look at it. His heart sank. The back wheel had caught most of the impact against the rock face. There was a large flat section on the wheel now. There was no way it would roll well enough to ride.

Conor bit his tongue to keep from yelling out into the night. If anyone was awake there was no use alerting them to his presence. It seemed like remote, empty country but who knew? He stood the bike up and assessed it again. It would be slow going like this. He suspected he only had thirty miles remaining so he would just try to make a go of it and see what he could do.

He thought of just throwing the bike over the hillside and carrying his gear but he didn't want to give up the electric bike. It had proven itself on this trip. He would try to get the bike home if he could.

The walk down the mountain was a couple of miles. With each revolution of the wheel, there was thud as the flat section hit the ground. Still, he kept pushing. The mountain itself was uninhabited, but when he reached the bottom and the road flattened out he could see the shape of a few odd farmhouses scattered on the countryside. After several more miles, he had to admit he was not going to end his journey under cover of darkness. The sun would be up soon and he would have to figure out what he was going to do.

Had he been in a more populated area he would holed up for safety and slept for a couple of hours. He was definitely exhausted. This seemed like remote country, and since he had not encountered any other people, he decided to press on.

As the sun began to lighten the sky, Conor removed his night vision device. The world was not fully bright yet but it was at that in between stage where night vision was no longer providing him any advantage. He stashed it in his pack. The device was irreplaceable in these conditions and he wanted it immediately on his person in case he had to run.

Conor was starting to ache a little bit now. The wreck had banged him up more than he'd first thought. His knee was getting sore and he could feel his back stiffening. On a long grade, he passed by a pile of logs. It appeared to be a stack of culled logs from a timber operation. As he walked past the pile he couldn't help but stop and take a break, dropping the kickstand on his bike and leaving it in the center of the road.

"Mister, you need to keep moving!" came a voice from the log pile.

Conor nearly crapped himself. He'd not seen anyone. Whoever this was completely had the jump on him. If they wanted him, they had him.

Conor turned up his accent again, trying for the same approach he'd used on the bridge in Damascus. He was just a poor

Irish traveler, biking the United States when the whole country went to hell. "I'm just passing through. Not looking for any trouble."

"I don't intend to cause you any trouble if you get up and keep moving. If you stay, I ain't making any promises."

"Very well then," Conor said, standing and regarding his sad bike and the trailer he pulled behind it. "I just needed a break. I was making decent time until I wiped out on the mountain. Prior to that I was running a more conventional wheel profile. You know, the old-fashioned round kind."

A figure stood up from the recesses of the log pile. He was wearing a dirty piece of burlap around him like a poncho and even in daylight it would have hidden him well. He carried a hunting rifle with a scope and was pointing it directly at Conor.

"My dad rides a bike," the figure said.

"He must be a good man," Conor said, regarding the figure and understanding that it was a boy. "A man who appreciates the world from two wheels is of superior character, in my humble opinion."

"He is a good man," the boy said, still aiming the weapon at Conor.

"Look, son, can you lower the rifle? I'm not here to hurt anyone. I'm just passing through."

"I'll lower the weapon but if you try anything I'll kill you," the boy said. "I've killed a man before."

"I truly hate to hear that, son. I'm sorry the world put you in that position. Either way, they call me The Mad Mick and I'll not break the peace. You have my word on that," Conor said. "I have a daughter to get home to and I'd rather not do it full of lead."

"The Mad Mick?" the boy asked. "Where did you pick up a name like that?"

Conor smiled. "If I told you, I'd have to kill you."

The boy raised the rifle back up, unfamiliar with the expression.

Conor raised his hands in a soothing gesture. "Easy there, it's an old expression."

The boy lowered the rifle just a hair. "I'd go easy with expressions like that in this day and age."

Conor nodded. "Good advice. Truth is I'm pretty much dead in the water right now. The long ride ahead of me has turned into a long push. That dad of yours wouldn't have a spare wheel lying about anywhere would he?"

"Probably," the boy replied.

As the ambient light increased, Conor could see clearly now that the boy was a teenager. Young enough to think like a child but old enough to pull the trigger when he had to. It hurt Conor to think the boy had been forced to kill already. It reminded him of the violent world of his own childhood. He understood that it would probably not be the last time this boy had to kill, though. That was the world as they knew it. The world they inherited.

"I could trade you for the wheel," Conor said.

"Don't need a trade. My dad has a pile of old bikes," the boy said. "If I get you a wheel, how about you just put it on and get out of here, okay? Strangers make me nervous."

Conor nodded. "I promise."

The boy pulled a walkie-talkie from a pouch. "Mom, you around?"

It took a moment, but a reply came. *"Everything okay, Pete?"*

"There's a man passing by on the road. He needs a bike wheel. I think we should give him one to get him on the road."

"You didn't tell him that your father wasn't home, did you?" Ellen asked.

Pete looked at Conor, who'd clearly heard the comment. "No, but I think he knows now."

"I'll be there in a minute," Ellen said. *"Don't let your guard down. It could be a trick."*

Pete raised his rifle back up, levelling it on the man. He tucked the radio in his pocket. "I'm sorry," he said. "My mom is pretty serious about security."

Conor nodded. "As she should be. The world is a dangerous place."

"She'll be here in a second."

Conor gestured at one of the logs. "Can I sit back down?"

"Suit yourself."

Conor sat down. "Where's your dad?"

232

The question made the boy immediately uncomfortable. "I'm not supposed to talk about that."

"I already know he's gone," Conor said. "I heard your mother say so on the radio."

"He's on a work trip," Pete said. "He's not made it back home yet but he's on his way."

Conor nodded without comment. If the man was far away from home, it was unlikely he'd make it back. There was too much violence already. Unless he was prepared for that, he'd die in a ditch on the side of the road like so many others.

The roar of an approaching engine caught Conor's attention. To his credit, the boy did not take his eyes from the older man. A side-by-side UTV skidded to a stop and a woman sprang out with an M4.

"Who are you?" she demanded.

She meant business. She was the kind of woman that shot people. Conor gestured at the bike, at the damaged wheel. "My name is Conor. I was travelling by bike and had a wreck on top of the mountain there."

She backed away from the UTV. "I brought a parts bike with me. Take what you need, then get out of here."

Conor stood. "I appreciate it."

He went to the back of the UTV and found a rusty bike from someone's scrapyard. It was exactly what he needed. The tire was even aired up so he'd not have to switch his tube and tire onto the new wheel.

"I'll just be a moment."

Under the woman's watchful eye, and under the red dot of her weapon's optic, he deftly changed the wheel with his bike tool kit. He had to add a few pounds of air with his pump but was soon satisfied that he was roadworthy again. He tossed his bent-up wheel into the ditch.

"I appreciate your kindness," Conor said. "I hope your dad makes it back, son."

Pete nodded.

Conor mounted his bike but paused before pedaling off. He reached for a pocket on his vest, which triggered a volley of shouts from the mother. Conor paused.

"I'm reaching for a paper and pen."

"Go slowly," she warned.

Conor removed a pad of paper from his pocket and scribbled a note on it. He dropped it to the ground beside him and replaced his writing supplies in his pocket. "You two have a nice day and be careful," he said before pedaling off.

When Conor had topped the hill and left their sight, Pete went and picked the note up. His mother came to his side and read over his shoulder.

"The Mad Mick?" she asked, reading from the paper.

"He said that was his name."

"And an address?"

"It's *his* address, mom," Pete said. "It says: *If I can return the favor, let me know. Please be careful. Protect your family.*"

"He seemed like a nice man," Pete said.

"Any man can seem nice until he kills you," Ellen warned. "Don't ever trust a stranger."

Pete thought about the man with his odd accent. He hoped the man made it home safely. His thoughts returned to his own missing father and he hoped for his safety, too. The world had never seemed so menacing and unsafe to him. Even as a young man, even as little more than a child, Pete knew that this world would get worse before it got better.

Would it ever get better? Perhaps lawlessness and violence, once spilled upon the land, was a genie that could never be fit back in the bottle.

About the Author

Franklin Horton lives and writes in the mountains of southwestern Virginia. In his spare time he pursues outdoor adventures with his family. His first published novel, _The Borrowed World_, was published in May of 2015 and became an Amazon bestseller. Since that time he's continued the series with _Ashes of the Unspeakable_ , _Legion of Despair_ and _No Time For Mourning_. In 2016 he also released _Locker Nine_, a novel taking place within the same fictional world as _The Borrowed World Series_.

To find out more about Franklin Horton and his books, please visit:

Website: www.franklinhorton.com
Facebook page : facebook.com/theborrowedworld
Twitter: @jfranklinhorton
Amazon: amazon.com/Franklin-Horton/e/B00JTXX6BE